Shadows on the sand

A young woman is found strangled on a lonely stretch of the north coast of Norfolk in the summer of 1950.

Mike Tench, recently promoted to Detective Chief Inspector, sets out to investigate. Who was she? What was she doing in such a desolate spot with darkness coming down? Was she the victim of a random killer, or was there someone, somewhere who had reason to want her dead?

But the case of Phoebe Marriott is, to say the least, unusual. As the list of possible suspects grows by the hour – a drunken fisherman; a schoolboy with a flair for fashion design; the wardens of the local nature reserve; a wildlife photographer; even perhaps the woman's own sister – he begins to wonder whether anyone connected with her death can bear to tell the truth.

There are strange complications: a diary that reveals a long-guarded secret; a missing piece of lingerie that proves to be unique; a spate of stolen cars; a naked doll with a name; and, to add to his perplexities, the sinister figure of Matthew Hopkins stepping, uninvited, out of the past.

Tench feels that he could be chasing nothing but shadows, shadows on the sand, as one after another of his apparently vital clues turns out to be worthless. Nor is his task made easier by his old chief and mentor, the retired Detective Chief Inspector Lubbock, whose unconventional views about the murder are, he finds, increasingly hard to ignore.

By the same author

Where the Fresh Grass Grows (1955)
A Path to the Bridge (1958)
The Van Langeren Girl (1960)
A Touch of Thunder (1961)
A Time to Retreat (1963)
Genesis 38 (1965)
A Mission for Betty Smith (1967)
Messiter's Dream (1990)
The Cross of San Vincente (1991)
The Singing Stones (1993)
Covenant with Death (1994)

Non-fiction
Transformation of a Valley (1983)

SHADOWS ON THE SAND

Brian Cooper

Constable · London

First published in Great Britain 1995
by Constable & Company Ltd
3 The Lanchesters, 162 Fulham Palace Road
London W6 9ER
Copyright © 1995 by Brian Cooper
The right of Brian Cooper to be
identified as the author of this work
has been asserted by him in accordance
with the Copyright, Designs and Patents Act 1988
ISBN 0 09 474570 6
Set in Palatino 10 pt by
Pure Tech India Ltd, Pondicherry
Printed and bound in Great Britain
by Hartnolls, Ltd, Bodmin

A CIP catalogue record for this book
is available from the British Library

To Beth for the driving
To Miles for the steering
To Nell for the understanding

AUTHOR'S NOTE

This is a work of fiction, and those who read it should not jump to conclusions.

It makes no pretence to reflect with any accuracy the procedures of the National Trust and its wardens at Blakeney Point. Even fifty years ago.

Those readers who think they know the prototypes of Lubbock and Tench or indeed any of the characters who figure in its pages are mistaken. They are all pure inventions.

There may be some who will search for Craymere and Bradenham on their Ordnance maps. They are doomed to be disappointed. Neither exists.

Only one facet of the story has some truth. Those who live in the counties between London and the Wash will probably realize that the incidents at Bradenham have a basis in fact. They were suggested by recent happenings in and around another equally small and equally sleepy East Anglian town.

But it lies a good forty miles south of Delph Cottage.

CONTENTS

1	Death on the Marrams	9
2	Questions and Answers	36
3	Plain Ways	63
4	Considerations	93
5	The Naked Doll	123
6	Patterns	140
7	Names and Numbers	159
8	Little Things	186
	Epilogue: Time for Coffee	213

Our acts our angels are, or good or ill,
Our fatal shadows that walk by us still.

John Fletcher: *Upon an Honest Man's Fortune*

1

DEATH ON THE MARRAMS

> When you defile the pleasant streams
> And the wild bird's abiding place,
> You massacre a million dreams
> And cast your spittle in God's face.

John Drinkwater: *To the Defilers*

1

At half-past five on a warm June morning in 1950, ex-Detective Chief Inspector John Spencer Lubbock locked the door of his cottage below the church at Cley, paused to relight his pipe and then, armed with his stout cherry-wood stick, set off down the road towards the village. Swinging right past the windmill, he made his way along the coastal road, and then out on the causeway that ran across the marsh. When he reached the sea bank, he climbed to the top and stepped out towards Blakeney.

Lubbock had reached that point in his life when five or six hours' sleep were all that he needed, and on a morning such as this, what better way to drum up an appetite for breakfast than to take a brisk walk by the edge of the sea?

The morning was clear and behind him the sun was already climbing above Cromer, bringing with it the promise of another hot day. The sea was calm, lapping gently on the shingle. He knocked out his pipe on the heel of his shoe, took a deep breath of salt air, shuffled down the bank to the shingle beach and headed for Blakeney Point.

Though not as fast across the ground as he had been in his youth, and a good deal thicker round the midriff, he was still reasonably fit, and in less than an hour he was into the Marrams, the sand dunes covered with clumps of spiky grass that lay at the eastern end of the Point. He halted for a moment, leaned on his stick, and took in the prospect. To his right the sea lay sparkling in the sun, stretching away till it faded into haze; to his left, across the marshes, the flat line of the coast lengthened out, east to west, from the little hill at Beeston, through Cley and Blakeney, to the pine-covered dunes on the Holkham shore. He'd been told that from here you could count the towers of seven churches. He picked out a few: Cley and Wiveton, Morston and Wells, and almost directly opposite, rising above the village roofs, the twin towers of St Nicholas at Blakeney, the shorter one at the north-east corner reputedly once equipped with a light to guide mariners into what, centuries before, had been a thriving harbour.

He moved on between the bent tufts of marram grass. Now he could see the terneries, the breeding grounds for thousands of migrant terns that came in the summer to lay their eggs in shallow scrapes in the shingle. Slim, white birds with black crests and forked tails like swallows, they covered the sandy undulations of the Point with a fluttering, feathered carpet, the sitting birds twitchingly alert for intruders, others hovering above the creeks and diving for fish, the whole colony alive with their strident, high-pitched cries.

Lubbock kept his distance. He was sufficiently well acquainted with the warden of the Point to know that no one was permitted to disturb the birds during their nesting season. The nests themselves, mere scoops in the surface, lined with dry grass or fragments of shell, were often inconspicuous, and the colour of the eggs, a pale buff-brown, blended in with the sand. It was all too easy to tread on the eggs, even on newly-hatched chicks, and the terns were tenacious defenders of their terrain. Anyone venturing too close to the colony risked being dive-bombed by irate birds, and their sharp, pointed bills could do considerable damage.

It wasn't his intention to go anywhere near them, but something on the edge of the carpet of flapping wings happened to catch his eye. He walked forward slowly till he was sure what it was. Then, treading with care and waving his cherry-wood stick above his head to deter the swooping birds, he took a closer look.

One particularly angry bird returned to the attack time and time again, diving so low that he had to duck and weave to avoid being struck; but he'd already seen enough. Slashing the air with his stick, he stumped away across the dunes towards the old lifeboat house where the warden had an emergency telephone.

Once clear of the colony, he slowed down to his normal, phlegmatic pace. There was no need to rush. The woman was clearly dead.

He stopped to fill and light his pipe. Then, tossing away the match and leaving a trail of smoke behind him, he moved on again.

2

Mike Tench gave a groan, rolled over in bed and reached for the phone.

'Is that the Chief Inspector?'

He recognized the voice. It was Lubbock's wry way of acknowledging his young protégé's recent promotion.

He peered at the bedside clock.

'Bloody hell,' he said. 'D'you know what the time is?'

There was a pause as Lubbock consulted his watch.

'It's precisely seven fourteen and a half.'

Tench gave another groan.

'Where are you for God's sake?'

'Out at Blakeney Point.'

'At this time in a morning?'

'The sun's up, the sky's blue and the sea's all a-sparkle.'

'So what?'

'You should be down here, laddie, breathing the ozone. Do you a world of good.'

'Bed does me good. Don't you ever sleep?'

'I slept', said Lubbock, 'till the sun began to blaze through my casement window. Then I got up and took a little walk along the shore.'

'And you've rung me up to tell me.'

'No, laddie, not entirely. I thought you ought to know before anybody else.'

'Know what?'

'One simple fact. There's a body on the Point.'

'Washed up?'

'Not likely. Too far from the sea.'

'Don't tell me it's murder.'

'Looks to be, yes. So you'd better get the team out here at the double. It'll take them some time. It's low water, and you won't get a boat from either Blakeney or Morston. Only way's by the sea wall from Cley, and then along the shingle. . . .'

Tench was suddenly wide awake.

'You'd better give me some details.'

'A woman. Young, I'd say. Twenties. Looks as if she's been strangled. Could well be sexual. Skirt and knickers half-way down her legs. She's on the edge of the terneries.'

'The nesting grounds?'

'That's right. Your lads are going to need some kind of protection from swooping birds. If I were you I'd bring down a couple of tents. Reg Ledward's not going to take too kindly to being buzzed by angry terns. He's never at his best until mid-afternoon.'

Ledward was the Home Office pathologist. A humourless man with a paper-thin voice, he'd worked with Lubbock for years.

Tench took a deep breath.

'Where are you ringing from?'

'The old lifeboat house. It's the warden's summer base.'

'What's his name, the warden?'

'Langrick. Jack Langrick. And I might add, laddie, that he's none too pleased. No one's supposed to set foot near the terneries at this time of year. I've already had to warn him off. He was all for shifting the body. I told him it wasn't on. He'd just have to close his eyes for the next few hours.'

'Right. How far's the body from where you are now?'

'A good mile, I'd say.'

'Can you stay with it till we get there?'

'Looks like I'm going to have to, doesn't it? No option. I'll take a sandwich with me. Langrick's got some bacon sizzling on the burner.'

'OK. We'll be down there as soon as we can.' Tench was trying to struggle free of his pyjamas. 'Just tell me this,' he said. 'Why are you always on the spot when a murder turns up?'

'Instinct, laddie,' said Lubbock. 'When I first set my feet to the ground at five o'clock, I said to myself, "There's a body on the dunes. You'd better go and find it . . .".'

The telephone clicked and the line went dead.

He gave a little laugh. Then he dropped the receiver back on its hook.

3

Lubbock thrashed at the air with his stick. Tench, a sou'wester jammed firmly on his head, stared down at the girl.

She was lying on her back, her arms flung out beyond the sweep of dark hair that spread around her shoulders. Her face, that might well have been beautiful in life, had settled into a grotesquely twisted kind of peace: her lips were blue, there was blood round her mouth, and her tongue was clamped firmly between her white, even teeth. There was bruising on her throat, and her eyes stared back at him, as if in reproach.

Tench was still young, exceptionally young for the rank that he held, and though he'd looked down on many dead bodies, he hadn't yet achieved that clinical detachment that seemed to sever men like Lubbock from any spontaneous expression of pity.

'Poor kid,' he said.

Lubbock's trained eye was focused not on the body, but rather on the clothes: the white cotton blouse drawn up to expose two firmly rounded breasts, the short blue skirt and pink, lace-edged knickers dragged down to the knees, the white socks and rubber shoes.

'What d'you think?' he said. 'Taking a bit of exercise on the sea shore?'

'Whatever she was doing, she didn't deserve this.'

Lubbock waved his stick wildly at a lone, persistent tern.

'Not, I'd say, an assignation with a boyfriend. Not dressed like that.'

'But she must have met someone.'

'That's merely stating the obvious, laddie. She didn't kill herself. And whoever she tangled with, it must have been someone with pretty strong hands. There's no sign of ligature marks round the neck. Whoever he was, he grabbed her by the throat and squeezed the life out of her. Manual strangulation. I've seen too many cases not to recognize the signs.'

'Here?' said Tench. 'Or would you say somewhere else?'

'Well, she must have struggled, and there aren't any scuff marks around on the sand. It's my guess he strangled her some distance away and then dumped her body down among the terns.'

'But why?'

'Search me,' said Lubbock. 'To make the body more difficult to retrieve? To complicate things for your dedicated team? Or we may, quite simply, be dealing with a nut-case. Someone who's got it in for the terns.'

'That's hardly likely.'

'It's most unlikely,' Lubbock agreed, 'but when you're dealing with murder, it's always best to keep an open mind. I once knew a chap who made a hobby of killing chickens. Used to wring their necks. Did fifty in one night, on five different farms. When we caught him and asked him why, he said he didn't like them. They reminded him of his mother-in-law. Clucking all day from dawn until dusk . . . You can never tell, laddie. Keep an open mind. The incredible can always happen.'

Tench wasn't listening.

'Footprints?' he said.

'You'll be lucky to find any. They're difficult to trace on shingle like this, and the breeze across the dunes moves the fine sand and covers them up.'

'If he carried her any distance, there'd be double the weight.'

Lubbock looked around him.

'Well,' he said, 'you may be lucky. Depends how far he moved her, but there was quite a breeze last night. Apart from that, there's a devil of a lot of people tramp across this Point: Langrick, his two assistants and the daily horde of trippers. You'd be better to look for the marks of a struggle. They're more likely to survive, especially if he killed her in one of the lows.'

'The lows. You mean the hollows?'

'That's right. They're known as lows. The deeper ones as blowouts. It's the rabbits that start them off. Once they scratch the surface, the wind blows away the sand and produces a pit. They're all over the dunes, some shallow, some deep. A strong wind can shift tons of sand in a night. But if she put up a fight, you'll likely find traces, provided the lads get here soon enough.'

The terns were still circling and swooping overhead.

'I think', said Lubbock, 'it's time to retreat. My arm's getting tired.'

They withdrew fifty yards. Tench continued to stare at the body.

'I wonder who she is.'

'You'll find out soon enough.'

'You don't know her?'

'No.' Lubbock leaned on his stick. 'She's a stranger to me, but it's ten to one she's local. They usually are.'

'This chap Langrick, the warden . . . I suppose he heard nothing during the night?'

'Slept like a top and wishes he hadn't. He's a long way away.'

'So is everyone else,' said Tench. 'Whoever the man was, he could hardly have chosen a more isolated spot.'

'Nor a better one, laddie. Dump a body in the dark, and no one's likely to see it for another twelve hours. Any other morning it wouldn't have been found till the gulls had had a feast. It's lucky they haven't picked her eyes out already.'

He saw Tench's pained expression.

'Well,' he said, 'they are scavengers; but don't worry, they won't touch her as long as you're here . . . And don't even think of covering her up. Ledward wouldn't thank you.'

A cluster of men came into view, weighed down with equipment, shuffling along the shingle. He nodded in their direction.

'Team's arriving,' he said. 'I'd better be off and snatch a bite of breakfast... Where's the incident room? Have you made up your mind?'

'Blakeney,' said Tench. 'Back parlour, White Horse. Courtesy of the landlord. I've left McKenzie and Gregg there setting things up.'

'Well, you've got quite a job on here. It'll take some time.'

'It's going to take hours.'

'Patience, laddie, patience. It's the little things that count... You'll need a statement, of course. I'll call in and make one later today. Maybe by then you'll have a few clues. One thing's for sure. Someone's missing a daughter.'

'Or a wife,' said Tench.

'No wedding-ring,' said Lubbock. 'Hadn't you noticed?'

He slashed at a clump of marram, waved his stick again and stumped off along the shingle, making for Cley.

4

Tench waited to have a word or two with Sergeant Lester, the head of the scene-of-crime team, and then with a visibly disgruntled Ledward, still, so it appeared, rubbing sleep from his eyes. After that he set out across the dunes to the lifeboat house.

Jack Langrick, the warden, was in his mid-thirties, bearded, earnest and, that morning, very angry.

'Who'd do such a thing?' he said.

'At the moment,' said Tench, 'your guess is as good as mine, but we'll find him, don't worry.'

'Don't worry! From what I've heard half the eggs'll be trampled underfoot. Don't you realize the damage this maniac's done?'

'I'm sorry about that, sir. I've told the team to be as careful as they can.'

'And a fat lot of use that's going to be.'

Tench was quietly diplomatic.

'A murder's been committed, Mr Langrick. We have to search for clues.'

'But in the middle of a ternery! In the nesting season!'

'On the edge of the ternery. We'll create as little disturbance as possible.'

Langrick was far from being appeased.

'What possesses a man to strangle a girl in a colony of birds? They must have been diving down on him like Stukas.'

'It may be', said Tench, 'that isn't what he did. From the signs he may just have dumped the body there.'

'Why on earth do that?'

'I thought perhaps you might have some ideas.'

Langrick stared at him.

'Look, Inspector,' he said. 'The terns have been breeding on Blakeney Point since the eighteen-thirties. That's close on a hundred and twenty years, and it's the first time to my knowledge that anyone's dumped a body on top of their nests. How in hell's name should I know what the man was thinking?'

'Someone with a grudge?'

'Who could possibly have a grudge against birds?'

'Oh, you'd be surprised, sir,' said Tench. 'But I wasn't thinking of that. I was thinking more of a grudge against you.'

Langrick sat down on an old spindle-chair. He seemed suddenly bemused.

'Are you serious?' he asked.

'We have to consider all the possibilities ... You have two assistants who work with you here?'

'They're utterly reliable. I wouldn't have taken them on if they hadn't been.'

'You get on well together?'

'Like a house on fire.'

Tench took out his notebook.

'I'll have to know their names, of course, Mr Langrick.'

'You can take it from me, they'd never do anything to unsettle the birds.'

'That may be so, but we'll have to interview them. They may have seen something.'

Langrick gave a shrug.

'Joe Turner and Robert Phelps.'

'And where do they live?'

'Joe lives at Wiveton, and Bob down at Blakeney.'

'Can you give me their addresses?'

Langrick produced a file and read them out to him.

'But take my word for it, they've nothing to do with this.'

'I'm sure they haven't,' said Tench. 'It's just a precaution. How long have they been with you?'

'Turner for three years, Bob Phelps for two.'

'And who worked with you before that?'

'Turner took over from a lad called Hatley, Phelps from Ken Ashcroft.'

'Why did they leave?'

'Hatley got a better job somewhere up in Scotland. Ashcroft was a student. He enrolled for a course at the Royal Veterinary College.'

'They weren't dismissed?'

'No.'

'Neither of them would be likely to hold a grudge against you?'

'Not as far as I know.'

Tench nodded briefly.

'Your present assistants, Turner and Phelps. What hours do they work?'

'One day on, one day off. Is all this really necessary, Inspector?'

'Just getting a picture, sir. Nothing more than that. What time do they get here and when do they leave?'

'It depends on the tide. They come over by boat from Blakeney. When one arrives, the other goes back.'

'Does someone ferry them across?'

'No, we have our own boat.'

'You don't have a motor vehicle of any sort?'

'No, they're not allowed on the Point. They wouldn't be much use anyway in a place like this.'

'Who's on with you today?'

'It should be Phelps, but he's got a dentist's appointment. I'm on my own until Turner arrives.'

'And when will that be?'

'He'll come at high water. Round about one o'clock.'

'So you were on your own last night.'

'That's correct.'

'And you heard nothing unusual?'

'No, I wish I had.'

'No undue noise from the colony?'

'The terns are always noisy in the nesting season, but I'm at least a mile away. No, Inspector, I slept like a log.'

'You've never seen a young woman running along the shingle?'

'Running?'

'Exercising.'

'Not that I recall.'

Tench got to his feet.

'Well, thank you, sir,' he said. 'You've been very helpful. I'll send someone over to take a statement from you.'

Langrick looked up at him.

'How long are they likely to be around up there?'

'The crime team? Difficult to say. Another couple of hours? They should be clear by early afternoon.'

Langrick sighed.

'And by that time,' he said, 'God only knows what the place'll be like.'

'The Devil might know,' said Tench. 'I can't think God was much in evidence last night.'

Back at the scene, he buttonholed Lester.

'What's the score, Sergeant?'

'No signs in the hollows, sir, but marks of a struggle down on the shingle.'

'Show me,' said Tench.

They walked towards the sea.

'Here, sir,' said Lester. 'Clear signs of scuffing. The pebbles have been gouged out. The sand's been exposed.'

'So you'd say she was killed here and then carried up to the ternery.'

'Looks like it, sir.'

'Any prints?'

'What there are are round here, sir. Further up, the sand's drifted.'

'So what have we got?'

'Rubber soles, sir. Almost certainly hers. The rest are bare feet.'

'You mean he took his shoes off?'

'Wouldn't be sure, sir, but that's what it looks like.'

'Knew what he was doing.'

'Seems like it, yes . . . Oh, and we found these, sir, here on the shingle.'

He rummaged in his pocket and held out a key ring with two keys and a metal tag.

'Car keys,' he said. 'We've dusted them for prints. Two good ones, index finger and thumb. We've got them on film. They're probably hers as well . . . There's a garage name on the tag.'

Tench examined it.

'Cromer Autos.'

'Off the Runton Road, sir. They don't actually sell cars. Just do repairs and service. Reliable firm. They've done work for me.'

'You wouldn't happen to recognize the keys? Type of car?'

'Not the faintest, sir. No.'

'Well, we'll just have to find it as fast as we can.'

'Probably parked on the quayside at Blakeney, sir,' said Lester. 'That's the handiest place.'

*

They walked back to the ternery. Ledward, tight-lipped, was packing his bag.

'I suppose,' he said, 'like Lubbock, you want to know the impossible.'

'A rough estimate would be helpful.'

'It can only be rough, but I'd say she was killed between nine o'clock and midnight last night.'

'Cause of death?'

'Asphyxia. All the signs are there, but don't quote me till after I've had her on the slab.'

'She was strangled.'

'Manually. So it would appear.'

'Any sexual assault?'

Ledward gave him a glare.

'You'll have to wait for that,' he said.

'Can't you give me a hint?'

'Professionally, no.'

'Unprofessionally?'

Ledward shrugged.

'No external signs of interference,' he said. 'It wouldn't surprise me to find she was virgo intacta.'

5

Mike Tench had never been one to walk for the pleasure of walking. Route marches in the army had cured him of that. Trekking back along the shingle to Cley, he took little delight in Lubbock's sparkling waves, and chose to banish monotony by keeping his mind on the problem that faced him: an unidentified girl strangled in the summer darkness on a lonely spit of sand between the marshes and the sea.

What had she been doing out there in the dark? Reg Ledward had estimated the time of her death as between nine o'clock and midnight. Splitting the difference meant half-past ten. Still trudging along the shore, he pulled out his diary and checked the time of sunset. Twenty past nine. The light would have gone by quarter to ten. What had possessed her to be out on her own in such a desolate place with darkness coming down? Or had someone been with her? Someone she knew and felt she could trust.

From his own experience, let alone statistics, he was well aware of the fact that most murder victims knew their assailants. There was nearly always some connection between them: a connection that sooner or later became apparent. It was the minority of cases, the random killings, that posed the greatest problem. As Lubbock had often told him, random killings were the devil to solve, and the possibility that this might prove to be one of them was something he preferred to dismiss from his mind.

What he had to look for was the vital connection, and he couldn't hope to find that until he knew who she was. He fingered the car keys in his trouser pocket. The first step to take was to check on what sort of car they fitted. Then trace it and discover the name of its owner.

He began to plan ahead. Cromer Autos: they were the ones to provide some answers. How far was it to Cromer? Ten miles? A dozen? He could be there and back in less than an hour. There must be a phone box somewhere in Cley. He'd better ring the White Horse and speak to McKenzie. See if he'd turned up anything in Blakeney. If not, it was Cromer. He'd be back before the crime squad returned from the Point . . . .

As it happened, he didn't need to go there at all.

He ploughed along the shingle for another half-hour, and then climbed the sea bank. He was close enough to Cley to see the huddle of police cars parked on the gravel at the end of the causeway. Then, just as he was about to cut down the slope, the familiar figure of Lubbock detached itself from the bank and plodded towards him.

'Thought I'd better wait,' he said. 'There's something down here I think you ought to take a look at.'

Tench eyed his old chief with a mild disbelief.

'Haven't you had breakfast?'

Lubbock brushed aside the remark with his stick.

'This is more important. Breakfast's a meal I can eat at any time.' He pointed towards the cars. 'See that one, laddie, parked next to yours?'

Tench remembered it: a small, snub-nosed Morris, light grey in colour. When he'd parked his own car, he hadn't really bothered to inspect it more closely. His mind, at that time, had been on other matters.

'Saw it first thing this morning,' Lubbock went on, 'and thought nothing of it. People go walking on the shore at all hours. But it's still here, and to me that seems a bit strange. That and other things.'

'What other things?'

'There's a woman's cardigan on the back seat and a pair of high-heeled shoes.'

He led the way down the bank.

'It's been here six hours to my knowledge,' he said, 'and that's a hell of a time. Only fishermen's cars are parked for that long.'

'Well, whoever she is,' said Tench, 'she's not likely to be a fisherman.'

He reached in his pocket and pulled out the keys.

'Let's see if these fit.'

'Are they hers?'

'They could be. Lester thinks they are. He found them on the shingle.'

He chose one of the two keys and turned it in the lock. The door sprung open.

'Looks like he was right.'

Lubbock bent down.

'There's something underneath that cardigan,' he said.

Tench turned it back. Underneath was a purse: black leather with a clasp. He flicked it open and peered inside.

Lubbock growled impatiently.

'Well, what have we got?'

'A comb,' said Tench, 'a tube of lipstick, two pound notes and some coppers, and a house key – a Yale.'

He took them out and dropped them on the seat.

'Nothing else?'

'A driving licence.'

'That should be helpful . . . Name?'

'Phoebe Marriott . . . Don't tell me you know her.'

'Never heard of her,' said Lubbock. 'Where does she live?'

'Downs House, Craymere Common. Where the devil's that?'

Lubbock leaned on his stick.

'It's on the Langham road, inland from Morston. About a mile and a half the other side of Blakeney.'

'What is it? A village?'

'No, nothing so big. It's a cluster of cottages. Three, possibly four. And I think there's a modern bungalow.'

'Right.' Tench pulled out his notebook and jotted down the name and address. Then he put all the items back in the purse, pushed it under the cardigan and locked up the car.

'We'll leave it where it is for the moment,' he said. 'If it's hers, then it'll have to go to forensics, but we'd better make sure. Where's the phone box in Cley?'

'Forget the box,' said Lubbock. 'Take me back home and then phone from there. It's the least you can do for a starving man who's sacrificed his breakfast to point the CID to an invaluable clue.'

6

Detective Sergeant Andrew Gregg was young, conscientious and discreetly ambitious, but there were times when he felt there were aspects of his job that were repellent to anyone with a grain of humanity. Collecting the evidence to bring murderers to justice was fair enough, yes, but breaking the news to relatives that a loved one might be lying dead on the sands was hardly, he considered, the kind of work that he'd joined the force to do.

As he turned up the Langham road from Morston his mood was a mixture of depression and apprehension. Coping with stunned fathers and weeping mothers didn't exactly fit in with his training.

Craymere Common, as Tench had told him on the phone, was nothing but a scatter of houses half a mile up the rise: four brick-and-flint cottages with projecting wooden porches and, a hundred yards on and closer to Langham, a squat brick bungalow that appeared to be merely some twenty years old.

He had no idea which one was Downs House, but driving slowly past the cottages he'd seen no names on the numbered doors, so the bungalow seemed the most likely place. He pulled in and stopped by the side of the road, and taking a deep breath pushed open the gate and climbed the path to the door. There was, as he'd expected, a small rustic plaque that was fixed to the wall with the words 'Downs House' in a flowing white script, but the only sign of a bell was a metal chain that dangled from the bricks. He pulled it and heard a tinkling sound inside the house.

No one answered. He pulled again and waited; then he walked along the gravel path peering in at the windows. The place was comfortably furnished: no utility items as far as he could see; the furniture and fittings had clearly been bought before the war-time shortages had trimmed down choice. There was a dining-room, a sitting-room, a kitchen, two bedrooms, and a couple of glazed windows that probably concealed a bathroom and a lavatory. All appeared to be clean and tidy, apart from a number of women's magazines tossed on the floor beside an armchair; but there was no sign that anyone might be at home.

He was just about to make his way back to the car when a telephone rang somewhere inside. He guessed it was in the hall, but he couldn't be sure because the door had leaded lights. There was nothing he could do. He waited as the bell continued to ring. It rang for a long time, perhaps half a minute, then abruptly it stopped.

He gave a little shrug, walked away down the path, closed the gate behind him and made for the cottages.

He chose the nearest, Number Four. There was no bell, merely an old black knocker, but this time he could hear the tap-tap of footsteps, a key turned in the lock, the door opened slowly and he found himself facing a wizened little wisp of a woman with her white hair drawn back and pinned in a bun. She eyed him suspiciously.

'Yes?' she said.

Gregg produced his card.

'Detective Sergeant Gregg, ma'am,' he said. 'Perhaps you can help me. I'm trying to find a Miss Phoebe Marriott.'

The woman felt in her apron pocket, pulled out a pair of pince-nez, clipped them on her nose and examined the card. Then she looked up.

'Phoebe?' she said. 'She's at Downs. That's the bungalow.'

'I've been there, ma'am. There's nobody in.'

'No, there wouldn't be,' she said. 'Not at this time of day. They'll be down at the shop.'

'The shop?'

'They run a dress shop. In Sheringham. She and her sister.'

Gregg took out his notebook.

'Can you tell me what it's called?'

The woman frowned.

'They did tell me. New something-or-other.'

'New Look?'

'It could be. Something like that.'

'Whereabouts is it?'

'I wouldn't be sure about that,' she said guardedly. 'Somewhere on the main street.'

'What's her sister's name?'

She seemed undecided whether to tell him.

'I thought you wanted Phoebe.'

'I need to speak to both of them, Mrs . . . ?'

'Miss. Miss Medlicott.'

'I need to speak to both of them, Miss Medlicott,' said Gregg.

She fixed him with two eyes like gimlets.

'Strikes me, young man, you don't know what you do want . . . Her name's Diana. Diana Marriott. They're twins.'

'You know them well, Miss Medlicott?'

'As well as anyone here. I've been a neighbour of theirs since the time they were schoolgirls.'

'Then perhaps you could help me with a few more details.'

Miss Medlicott dropped her pince-nez back in her pocket.

'Young man,' she said, 'I can't stand here gossiping on the doorstep all day. I've a ginger cake in the oven... Are you to be trusted?'

'Oh, I think so,' said Gregg.

'You don't sound very sure.' She eyed him doubtfully and then stepped aside. 'I suppose you'd better come in. But I'm not answering any questions I don't want to answer.'

'I wouldn't dream of asking them, Miss Medlicott,' he said.

7

'So' – Tench was curious – 'who is this Miss Medlicott?'

The back parlour of the White Horse Hotel had been rapidly transformed into something resembling an incident room. The small bar tables had been stacked and removed to make way for three larger ones supported on trestles. These were now equipped with boxes of stationery, wire filing-trays and a couple of telephones, while a capacious wooden cupboard with a hasp and a lock had been reared against the wall.

Gregg referred to his notebook.

'Retired headmistress, five foot one, frail, eighty next month and proud of it, lives on her own and bakes ginger cakes.'

'Did you sample them?'

'It was a case of necessity, sir. She insisted.'

'And you persuaded yourself it was in a good cause.'

'Yielded to temptation, sir, I'm afraid.'

'So what did you learn, apart from this business about the dress shop?'

'Actually, sir, quite a lot.'

'Then tell me,' said Tench.

Gregg laid his notebook flat on the table.

'The Marriott girls, they're twins. Born in 1927. That makes them twenty-three. Father was a classics teacher in Norwich. He chose their names, Phoebe and Diana: the twin goddesses of the moon. Mother was a nurse. Parents built the bungalow in 1929. Both killed in a train crash, travelling back from a holiday in Scotland. That was 1945. The girls were eighteen. They were left the house and a fair bit of money, mainly from the mother, so they used it to start the dress shop. Seems they've done well. It's quite a profitable business.'

'And they're living together? Just the two of them? No one else?'

'So Miss Medlicott says. They're apparently very close. Well, they would be, sir, wouldn't they? Identical twins?'

'You didn't tell her what we'd found?'

'No, I said we thought someone might have stolen the car.'

'And she assumed both the girls were down at the shop.'

'Yes, sir, that's right.'

'Well, we know one of them isn't, and that poses a problem. If she's been lying out there on the sands since last night – and that's what Ledward says – then why hasn't her sister reported her missing?'

'Because she hasn't missed her. That's the obvious answer.'

'That raises another question. Why hasn't she missed her?'

'She couldn't have been in touch.'

'And still isn't in touch. That means she didn't spend last night at the bungalow, and she probably isn't down at the shop this morning.' Tench stroked his chin. 'You know, Andy,' he said, 'I think we've sent Mac on a bit of a goose chase.'

McKenzie had been despatched to Sheringham on his ageing Norton half an hour before to check out the dress shop.

'Well, we'll know soon enough, sir.' Gregg looked at his watch. 'He should be back any minute. That battered old wreck may be on its last legs, but it burns up the miles.'

'Mac'd burn up the miles if he was riding a push-bike.' Tench was thinking ahead. 'You didn't speak to anyone else at Craymere Common?'

'No, sir. Just Miss Medlicott.'

'D'you know who else lives there? Did she happen to mention them over the ginger cake?'

'More than mentioned them, sir. She gave me a complete rundown on the place. I think she was glad to have someone to talk to ... I made a few notes.'

'Let's be hearing them then. We can't do much else until Mac turns up.'

Gregg pulled his notebook towards him.

'Apart from the Marriotts' bungalow, there are just four cottages. Miss Medlicott's at Number Four. Next door, at Number Three, there's an elderly couple called Holland. He's retired.

Was a farm labourer. Worked at Cockthorpe, a mile inland from Stiffkey. He and his wife have a vegetable garden and keep a few hens.'

'Not likely suspects.'

'Wouldn't think so, sir, no.'

'What about Number Two?'

'A widower called Shelton. Lives there with his son. They fish for whelks from Wells harbour, and they've also got a boat moored at Morston Creek. Use it to take holiday visitors on trips.'

'That means Blakeney Point.'

'Can't be anywhere else.'

'How old are they, these two?'

'Father's in his fifties. The son must be thirtyish.'

'You haven't seen them?'

'No, sir. Didn't think it wise to make too many inquiries until we were sure.'

Tench nodded.

'Fair enough, but let's keep them in mind . . . The last cottage?'

'Number One? Strange, sir. Doesn't quite conform to the general pattern. Belongs to a farmer up at Field Dalling, a couple of miles beyond Langham. Lets it out for the summer. Seems the same family rents it every year for three months. A Mr and Mrs Leening. He's a businessman in Holt. Two children, a boy and a girl, both still at school. Plenty of money, I should think. They keep a yacht at Morston.'

'Do they? That's interesting. What did your Miss Medlicott have to say about them?'

'Charming, she said. Mother and daughter pop in to see her from time to time.'

'What about the son?'

'Clever. He's at Mountfield, the private school at Holt. Good place, so they say. On a par with Gresham's. He's a university prospect according to all accounts . . . Oh, the father stays in Holt and comes down at weekends.'

'Seems a peculiar kind of mix, this place Craymere Common. And on the edge of it two wildly attractive sisters, one of them murdered. What was Miss Medlicott's opinion of them?'

'Delightful girls, she said. The only ones she seemed to have any doubts about were Shelton and his son. Probably a bit rough. Not quite in her class.'

'She's a bit of a snob?'

'Forthright, I'd say. Seemed to think fishermen lowered the tone of the place.'

'But not farm labourers?'

'No, sir, now you mention it.'

'Wouldn't you say that was strange?'

Gregg shrugged his shoulders.

'I expect, sir, Miss Medlicott's like many old people. She nurses her own quite irrational prejudices.'

'Yes, maybe so . . .'

There was a noise that resembled a mobile machine-gun approaching from a distance; an ear-splitting rattle, and then a sudden silence.

'That's Mac,' said Tench. 'The wind-swept Pheidippides. One day he'll appear and fall dead on the threshold.'

Detective Sergeant Bill McKenzie, broad, overweight and heavily moustached, pushed open the door and collapsed on a chair.

'Well,' said Tench, 'what's the tidings from Marathon?'

'There are none.' McKenzie ran a hand through his hair. 'Not a vestige of life. Both the sisters were down there yesterday. Shop shut as usual at six o'clock. Hasn't opened this morning.'

'And no one knows anything more than that?'

'Not a whisper,' McKenzie said. 'There's a florist's on one side and an ironmonger's on the other. They hadn't even noticed the place was closed.'

Tench scratched his head.

'We need to trace this sister. What's her name? Diana?' He turned towards Gregg. 'You'd better get back to Craymere. You go with him, Mac. See if anyone there knows anything about her. Where's the nearest phone box?'

'Morston,' said Gregg.

'Then keep in touch. If you come up with a lead, then give me a ring. I'd better get forensics on to that car.'

'Right.' McKenzie heaved himself up. He looked across at Gregg. 'You coming with me?'

'You must be joking,' said Gregg. 'I've a wife to consider. I wouldn't trust myself to that smoke-spitting death-trap if you offered me a fiver and tied it up with red ribbon.'

McKenzie raised his black eyebrows.

'Well, please yourself, but she's in tip-top condition. Flies like a bird.'

'I get air-sick,' said Gregg. 'I'll see you down there.'

8

It was McKenzie who saw the taxi.

Coasting to a stop by the first of the cottages, he dragged the Norton on to its stand and flagged down Gregg, who braked the police car to a halt behind him and wound down the window.

McKenzie leaned in and pointed up the road.

'Is that the Marriotts' place?'

'That's it,' said Gregg. 'The bungalow.'

'There's a taxi just driven away towards Langham.'

'Who was in it?'

'No one but the driver. Reckon he'd already dropped someone off. Would it perhaps be our missing sister?'

'We'd better go and find out.' Gregg sounded reluctant.

McKenzie knew his young colleague. He clapped him on the shoulder.

'It's all right,' he said, 'Andy. Leave this to me. I've had to do it more times than you've had eggs for breakfast. All you have to do is stand by with the smelling-salts. That's your job.'

He led the way up the path and tugged at the bell chain.

Gregg kept his gaze fixed firmly on the door. It opened an inch, stalled for a second and then swung back. The woman who stood there was delicately slim. Dark hair flowed round her shoulders. She wore a white silk blouse and a long tan skirt. She was, he thought, undeniably beautiful, but it was her eyes more than anything that caught his attention. They were puzzled, then fearful, perhaps even frightened.

She said nothing. Just stood there.

McKenzie held up his card.

'Detective Sergeant McKenzie,' he said, 'and this is Detective Sergeant Gregg. Are you Miss Marriott?'

'Yes.' That was all.

'Miss Diana Marriott?'

She nodded. 'There's something wrong, isn't there?' She was plainly apprehensive.

McKenzie didn't answer.

'May we come in, Miss Marriott?' he said.

She led them into the sitting-room: the one that Gregg had seen. The magazines still lay scattered on the floor. She gathered them up – an automatic gesture – shuffled them together and dropped them on a coffee-table. Then she folded her arms and hugged herself tightly as if she were cold.

'Where is she?' she said.

'Please sit down, Miss Marriott.' McKenzie's gruff voice was unusually gentle. He looked round for a seat.

She jerked out a hand towards the settee, and he perched on the edge.

'Tell me,' she said. 'Where is she?'

'You mean . . . ?'

'Phoebe. My sister. Something must have happened. That's why you're here, isn't it?'

'What makes you think that?'

'She was supposed to meet me in Norwich. I've rung the shop. She isn't there. And now she isn't here.'

She looked first at McKenzie and then up at Gregg.

'Please tell me,' she said.

'We're not exactly sure what's happened, Miss Marriott.'

'We need your help,' said McKenzie. 'Do you and your sister own a car?'

She nodded her head again.

'Is it a Morris Minor? Registration number' – he drew out his notebook – 'CL 8524?'

'There's been an accident, hasn't there?' There was a catch in her breath. 'Where is she? In hospital?'

McKenzie was quietly, blandly deliberate.

'Is that the number?'

'Yes,' she said, 'it is.'

'Have you any idea why the car should be parked by the sea bank at Cley?'

'Oh, God.' She put her hand to her mouth. 'It's not been there since last night?'

'That's what we think. Did your sister drive down there?'

'She said she was going to do some running on the beach . . .' Her voice petered out. She sat there, twisting her hands in her lap.

'She's dead, isn't she? You've come to tell me she's dead.'

'We've found a young woman's body on the shore, Miss Marriott. We don't know yet whether or not it's your sister.'

She tossed her head savagely. All of a sudden there were tears in her eyes.

'No!' she said. 'No!' She looked from one to the other, pleading with them to disavow the truth. Then, without any warning, she snatched the handkerchief tucked in the bracelet at her wrist, pressed it to her lips and ran out of the room.

Gregg made to follow her, but McKenzie stopped him.

'No,' he said. 'Leave her. If you want to be useful, then make some tea. Hot, sweet and strong. And while you're doing that, ring up Mike Tench. Tell him she's here, and we're bringing her in.'

Gregg glanced towards the door.

'Is she fit to go?'

'D'you want to sit here while she sobs her socks off?' McKenzie's voice, for the first time, was rough. 'No, you damn well don't. So listen and learn another trick of the trade. There's one infallible rule in a case like this. Question them right away, if you possibly can. Don't give them time to think up a story.'

'You aren't suggesting . . .?'

McKenzie cut him short with a wave of the hand.

'No,' he said, 'I'm not, but I've been in this game far too long to trust anyone. She's probably, like all of us, got something to hide. Now shove off for the moment and leave her to me.'

9

Tench, it was evident, had never subscribed to the McKenzie book of rules.

He regarded the elegant young woman in front of him with both approval and sympathy.

'Miss Marriott,' he said, 'I have to ask you some questions, but if you don't feel up to it, I am prepared to wait.'

She was clearly still struggling to come to terms with what had happened, but she shook her head.

'No. Please carry on.'

'You're sure?'

'Quite sure.' She tucked her handkerchief back in her bracelet and straightened her shoulders. 'What is it you want to know?'

'Will you tell me exactly what happened yesterday?'

'I had to go up to London.'

'Why was that?'

'There was a show of autumn fashions. I went to place some orders.'

'Where was it held?'

'In the Burnton Galleries in Oxford Street.'

'I see. And what time did you go?'

'I caught the 1.30 train from Norwich. Phoebe drove me there. We closed the shop at twelve. She dropped me off at the station, then she set off back to Sheringham.'

'To open up again?'

'Yes, until six.'

Tench nodded slowly.

'Did she say what she was going to do after that?'

'She was going home to get a meal. We usually did that together.'

'And after that?'

'She said she'd probably drive down to Cley and take a run along the shore.'

Tench frowned.

'Was this something she did regularly, Miss Marriott?'

'In the last few weeks, yes. Since petrol rationing was taken off. We couldn't do it before that.'

'You went with her?'

'Sometimes. Not always. There were times when I had to stay and check the shop accounts.'

'What time did you normally go?'

'It depended on the weather. We usually went before we had a meal. About half-past six. But yesterday was very hot. Phoebe said she thought she'd leave it until things had cooled off.'

Tench leaned back in his chair. He was watching her closely.

'You want me to keep going, Miss Marriott?' he said.

'Yes, I'm all right.' She pulled out the handkerchief and dabbed at her eyes.

Tench gave her time.

'You stayed the night in London?'

'Yes, at a small hotel in Sloane Street. The Winstanley. I always stay there when I'm in town.'

'And this morning?'

'I did some shopping. I bought . . .' The tears came again.

Tench waited.

'Yes, Miss Marriott?'

'I bought an underset for Phoebe.'

'Then you caught the train back?'

'Yes, the 10.35. It was due into Norwich at 1.15.'

'And was it on time?'

'It was five minutes late. I'd arranged with Phoebe to be at the station to meet me . . .' She closed her eyes, bit her lip.

'She wasn't there?'

Miss Marriott took a deep breath.

'No,' she said. 'I waited outside. There was nothing else I could do. I suppose I must have waited a quarter of an hour. Then I rang the shop, but of course it was shut. And when I rang home, there was no reply, so at last I took a taxi. I'd just got back and was wondering what to do when your sergeants arrived.'

Tench seemed to hesitate.

'Do you have any relatives, Miss Marriott?' he asked.

'No,' she said, 'none. We lost both our parents five years ago. Neither of them had any brothers or sisters. Phoebe and I were the only two left.'

'You realize, of course, that we're not yet certain this woman is your sister?'

She nodded again, mutely.

'And we need to be sure.'

She looked straight at him.

'You want me to see her?' Her voice was a whisper.

'I'm sorry, Miss Marriott. It seems the only way.'

'Where is she?'

'In Norwich.'

She gripped the seat of the chair and pushed herself up.

'Then we'd better go, hadn't we?'

Tench eyed her doubtfully.

'You want to go right away? Wouldn't you like a couple of hours to rest and recover? All this must have come as a considerable shock.'

'No,' she said. She was quite decisive. 'If it has to be done, then I'd sooner get it done. Let's not waste time.'

Tench reached for the phone.

'I'll drive you there myself,' he said. 'Give me five minutes. There's a washroom through the bar if you feel you need to use it. You know Sergeant Gregg. He'll show you where it is.'

10

He waited till Gregg had steered her towards the bar; then he dialled the operator and asked for a Norwich number. There was a pause while he drummed his fingers on the table. Then a youthful voice answered.

'Lock?'

Detective Constable Desmond Lock was manning the phone at the CID office.

'Sir?'

'Get on to the mortuary. Tell them I'm bringing someone in to do an ID on the Blakeney body. And have Sue Gradwell standing by there. I'm going to need her.'

'Right, sir.'

'And get through to Records. I want a list of all known sex offenders who live within a ten-mile radius of Blakeney . . . Oh, and warn the Chief Super I'm coming in for a word.'

'I'll do that, sir.'

'Good.'

Tench replaced the phone and turned to McKenzie.

'We can't afford to wait,' he said. 'You and Gregg get back to Craymere. I want everyone there interviewed. You don't need to tell them the grisly details if they haven't heard already. Just say the girl's missing, and we need all the help they can possibly give.'

'You think it is the sister?'

'I've seen them both, Mac. They're identical twins. I don't think there's any doubt. So find out what you can about both of them, and weigh up the residents. Gregg's got all the names. It may be a local job. Let's hope that it is.'

'If it isn't,' said McKenzie, 'we're going to need a bloody long boathook, so keep your fingers crossed.'

If it had been at all possible, Tench would have crossed them. His mother, though a self-reliant Lancashire matron and the redoubtable wife of a Church of England minister, had always taught him, much to his father's disrelish, to walk around ladders and throw salt across his shoulder; but the trouble was, as he'd realized early on in life, that unless you were double-jointed or a devotee of yoga, you could never keep them crossed for a long enough time. And to do it while driving at fifty miles an hour through the twists and turns of the Norfolk roads was to court disaster.

For that and other reasons he gripped the wheel firmly as he drove towards Norwich, and inhibited by the presence of the girl at his side, refrained from even breathing a silent prayer that the process ahead would provide no complications.

It was, for the most part, a silent journey. Diana Marriott sat gazing blankly at the windscreen, her fingers curled round the small lace handkerchief resting in her lap. From time to time she dabbed at her eyes. Once she blew her nose, but apart from that she sat soundless, intent, so it seemed, on holding her emotions for the moment in check.

It wasn't until they were approaching Horsford, on the outskirts of the city, that he ventured at last to break in on her thoughts.

'I'm sorry to have to put you to this ordeal, Miss Marriott.'

She gave a little shrug of the shoulders.

'You haven't any option. Neither have I.'

'It's still very hard.'

'It's my turn,' she said.

'Your turn?'

She nodded.

'Phoebe did it five years ago when Mum and Dad were killed. She insisted. She said she was older than me . . . Well, now it's my turn to do it for her.'

Tench felt it might be wise to keep the talk flowing.

'Tell me about your sister, Miss Marriott,' he said.

'There's nothing to tell. We're twins. You see her, you see me.'

'Then she can't be a great deal older than you.'

'Three and a half minutes. Enough, I suppose.'

'Are you very much alike?'

She looked down at her handkerchief; twisted it round her fingers.

'Physically, yes. People who don't really know us can't tell us apart, but we're altogether different.'

'In what way?'

'She's artistic, a dreamer. I'm very much more practical.'

'A good business partnership?'

'Yes, we work well in tandem. She has an eye for fashion, and she's a very good seamstress. I'm the buyer and seller. I keep the accounts.'

'It's a profitable business?'

She shifted in her seat.

'Reasonably so. We had our problems with rationing like everyone did. But now that that's gone we're hoping for better things . . . or, at least, we were.' She brushed away a tear.

Tench glanced at her.

'We'll make it as easy as we can, Miss Marriott.'

She gave a wan smile.

'Don't worry,' she said. 'I won't faint on you, Inspector. I'm not that type.'

Tench drew to a halt in the mortuary compound, and made his way across to another police car parked in a corner.

He rested an arm on the roof and leaned down to the driver.

'You got the message then, Sue?'

Detective Constable Susan Gradwell was the first woman to be recruited for the Norwich CID. Bright, intelligent, fair-haired and self-possessed, she'd proved her value on more than one occasion.

'Yes, sir,' she said. 'D'you want me inside?'

'Let's hope not.' Tench crossed two fingers on the rim of the window. 'If I need you, I'll call. Just hang on here. When we're through, I want you to drive Miss Marriott back to Craymere Common. It's the other side of Holt, on the road to Morston. Check on your map. And she's not to be left alone. You're to stay with her till I get there.'

'Understood, sir.'

Tench walked back to his own car, opened the door, helped his passenger out and then led the way up the mortuary steps.

'This way, Miss Marriott,' he said.

He pushed open the double doors, and they trudged side by side down the long, bleak corridor till they reached the bare, white-tiled room at the end.

The attendant stood waiting. On a hospital trolley, covered by a sheet, lay a slim, inert form.

Tench touched the girl's elbow.

'Are you ready?' he asked.

'Please get on with it.' She was tense.

The attendant drew back the sheet, but all she needed was a glance.

'Yes,' she said, 'that's Phoebe.' The tears welled in her eyes.

Tench led her out. She looked up at him, pleading.

'Why?' she said. 'Tell me. Why on earth would any man do such a thing?'

The eternal, unanswerable question. He sighed.

At least he could be honest.

'I don't know,' he said gently. 'Once we're able to find him, we may learn the truth. But thank you for helping. There's a car outside waiting to take you back home.'

She stared down the corridor towards the daylight at the end.

'Home?' she said. 'No. Hardly that, Inspector. Home is where the heart is. I don't know whether mine can find a place there any more.'

2

QUESTIONS AND ANSWERS

Questions are never indiscreet. Answers sometimes are.

Oscar Wilde: *An Ideal Husband*

1

Detective Chief Superintendent Hastings laid down his pen and leaned back in his chair.
'So,' he said, 'tell me about this Blakeney case.'
Tench gave him the details.
'Local, d'you think?'
'No real idea, sir. Not at the moment.'
'If it isn't, then you're likely to need quite a team.'
'I think we're going to need that, sir, anyway. To begin with. There's a hell of a lot of checking to be done.'
'Right, so what are you going to do? Leave Darricot here?'
Detective Inspector Graham Darricot was a recent addition to the squad from the Met. Young and keen, he was a city-wise copper, and it hadn't taken long for Tench to size him up. Capable, yes, but once out in the sticks he was still inexperienced.
'I think so, sir,' he said. 'He's at home here in Norwich, but he's still a lot to learn about rural Norfolk. He's a bit like I was when I first started here.'
'You had a good teacher.' Hastings was swift to acknowledge the fact. 'It's up to you to do for him what John Lubbock did for you.'
'Oh, we'll train him,' said Tench. 'He'll pick things up soon enough, but this is a case where we've got to move fast. I need men on tap who already know the ground. McKenzie and Gregg know the coast up there between Cromer and Wells. They've clocked up more miles in and out of the villages than anyone else. They know what to expect when they knock on a cottage door, and they won't be baffled by the Norfolk speak. If Darricot was told that someone

was shanny or all up at Harwich, he wouldn't know what was meant. He'd be sending someone down into Essex with a map.'

Hastings nodded.

'Point taken. So who do you propose to use?'

'Immediately, Lock and Ellison. Possibly Rayner.'

'Ellison? Why Ellison?'

Detective Constable Robert Ellison was the youngest and latest recruit to the CID.

'He knows the coast, too, sir. Did his National Service at the ack-ack battery on the marshes at Cley. Knows a lot of the locals. He could be very useful.'

'Right. So what's the programme?'

'We're checking out all the residents at Craymere Common and the wardens at the Point. Sex offenders in the area. Hotel guests at Blakeney. And we'll need to have a sweep through Cley and Morston. If we reach a dead end or get a lead somewhere else, we'll have to widen the net.'

'Ransome?'

'Hasn't shown up yet, sir, but no doubt he will.'

Dave Ransome was the crime reporter on the *Eastern Daily Press*. Tench knew him well. They had a working arrangement.

'He could be helpful in this case,' Hastings said.

'I've got him in mind, sir.'

'Good. If I were you, I'd use him . . . This murdered girl . . .'

'Sir?'

'What about boyfriends?'

'No sign of any at the moment, sir, but it's one of the first priorities.'

'You say she was attractive?'

'More than that, sir, I'd guess. Something of a stunner.'

'Then there must have been someone. The sister's the one to know.'

'She's pretty shocked by what's happened. Sue Gradwell's looking after her. She needs a little time.'

'You're seeing her again today?'

'Yes, sir. Later on.'

'The sooner the better, Mike. You know what they say. The first forty-eight hours in a murder case are crucial . . . They were twins, very close and living together?'

'Yes, sir, that's right.'

'Then she's likely to know more than anybody else. Go for her first of all. I would in your place . . . Who found the body? Was it one of the wardens?'

'No, sir.'

'Who then?'

Tench gave a wry smile.

'Hazard a guess, sir. Cley's the nearest land point.'

Hastings's eyes opened wide.

'Don't tell me it was Lubbock.'

'Had to be, hadn't it?'

'Out on Blakeney Point? At half-past six in a morning? What the devil was he doing there?'

'According to him, he swung his legs out of bed when he first saw the sun and said to himself, "There's a body on the dunes. I'd better go and find it."'

The Chief Super shook his head in bewildered amusement.

'He always did have a nose for a murder . . . So he's staked a claim already?'

'I'm afraid so, sir, yes.'

'It's his case, is it?'

'He's an indispensable cog in the investigative team,' Tench said drily, 'or at least he seems to think so.'

'No signs of this new disease, metal fatigue?'

'Just a cherry-wood stick.'

Hastings picked up his pen.

'Well, Mike,' he said, 'there's no one knows the Norfolk ground better than he does. Let him sniff around. He may come up with something useful. But always remember what I said once before. Keep him on a leash, and don't, for God's sake, let him catch you off balance. If you do, you could find yourself chasing a hare.'

'Not likely, sir, nowadays.'

'No. Perhaps not . . . Well, you'd better get on. If you need any help, you know where to come. Keep me posted on progress.'

'I'll do that, sir,' said Tench.

It was all very well, he thought, as he drove towards Blakeney, to talk about leashes. The trouble was that he wasn't dealing with some dozy-eyed bloodhound. This particular breed was more of a bull-mastiff. It stood five foot eight, weighed fourteen stone and was notoriously tenacious.

Added to which, it had taken the scent and was hot on the trail.

From past experience, holding it in check might well prove a difficult balancing act.

2

Bill McKenzie made a fist, and rapped on the door of Number One, Craymere Common.

The girl who opened it was fair-haired and freckled. She wore a white blouse, unbuttoned at the neck, and a green knee-length skirt that was clearly a part of her school apparel. Tossed aside somewhere in the house, no doubt, were a blazer and tie to match. She had a tip-tilted nose and wide grey-green eyes. Aged thirteen, maybe fourteen, she was slim but already showing signs of maturity. He noted with approval the swell of her breasts as they thrust against her blouse.

'Hello, love,' he said. 'Is your mother at home?'

The girl turned towards the stairs that ran up from the hallway.

'Mum,' she called. 'There's someone to see you.'

The voice that answered back was cheerful, unconcerned.

'Who is it?'

The girl faced him.

'Who shall I say?'

McKenzie pulled a card from his inside pocket.

'Detective Sergeant McKenzie, Norwich CID.'

She looked at him with interest.

'You a detective?'

'Yes, love,' he said. 'Don't I look like one?'

'Not much.' She was frank. 'It's the police, Mum,' she called, louder than before; then again to McKenzie, 'She's just out of the bath.'

He'd have had to be a moron, let alone no detective, to fail to note that much. The woman who came tripping down the stairs was swathed in a bath robe and had a towel twisted nonchalantly round her head. She was her daughter, grown up: the same tip-tilted nose and freckles, the same grey-green eyes, the same thrusting breasts. She looked worried, but then they all did. A policeman knocking on the door made you wonder what had happened.

'Mrs Leening?'

'Yes.' The worried look on her face swiftly turned to misgiving. 'What's wrong? It isn't Duncan . . .?'

'There's nothing wrong, Mrs Leening.' He was quick to reassure her. 'We think you may be able to help us with some inquiries we're making. One of your neighbours is missing and we need some information.'

'Missing?' she said. 'Who?'

'A young woman called Phoebe Marriott.'

'Phoebe?' She was puzzled. 'But I saw her last night.'

'Perhaps I could come in, Mrs Leening,' he said.

She stood aside to let him pass, opened a door on the right, and showed him into a room that wasn't exactly cluttered; more lived-in and littered. His eyes took in photographs, wooden boxes and ashtrays, a tin of biscuits, a tennis racket reared against the wall, a couple of dirty glasses, a bottle of lemonade and three tattered copies of *Picture Post*. A white cotton frock was draped across the arm of a leather settee, a pair of white rubber shoes lay discarded on the rug, and, as if to confirm his capacity for detection, a dark green blazer and a tie hung askew from the back of a cane-bottomed chair.

Mrs Leening ignored them all except for one *Picture Post*. She swept it up from an armchair, dropped it on the floor and then sat down. McKenzie chose the settee.

'Phoebe?' she said. 'You say that she's missing?'

'I'm afraid so, Mrs Leening.'

'Since when?'

'Since last night.'

'But I saw her,' she said.

'When was that?'

'Oh, about eight o'clock. I'd been across to Grace Medlicott's to pick up some scones. When she bakes, she always does some for me. It was when I was coming back. Phoebe passed me in the car and waved.'

'Which way was she going?'

'Down towards Morston.'

McKenzie made a note.

'You're sure about the time, Mrs Leening?' he asked.

'Not exactly to the minute, but it was round about eight.'

'You don't know where she was going?'

The woman shook her head.

'I haven't any idea.'

'How well d'you know them, she and her sister?'

She shrugged.

'We're neighbours. We speak from time to time.'

'D'you ever visit them?'

'You mean go inside the house? No, not really . . . Giles knows them better than anyone else.'

'Giles?'

'My son. He's very good at art. Wants to be a dress designer. Needless to say, his father disapproves... Phoebe knows a lot about fashion. She's been helping him with sketches, giving him some ideas.'

'He's still at school, Mrs Leening?'

'Yes,' she said, 'at Mountfield.'

'How old is he?'

'Seventeen. Duncan wants him to try for a scholarship at Cambridge.'

'He doesn't want to?'

'No, he thinks it'll only be a waste of time. He wants to go to art college.'

'Is he at home?'

She nodded.

'Yes, he's up in his room. Doing his homework. He always starts it as soon as he gets back from school.'

'I'd like to meet him,' McKenzie said. 'He may be able to help.'

3

She walked across to the door, tightening the towel round her head as she went, and called up the stairs.

'Giles.'

A voice must have answered, but too indistinctly for McKenzie to hear.

'Come down here a minute, will you? There's someone wants to see you.'

A pause, perhaps a query.

'Just come down,' she said.

She turned back into the room.

'Have you any children, Sergeant?' she asked.

McKenzie could truthfully have said he wasn't sure, but he took the easy way out.

'I'm not married, Mrs Leening.'

'Then you don't know what it's like. You think as they get older... They're more trouble in their teens than when they were small.'

He didn't have the chance to ask her what sort of trouble. Feet clattered on the stairs, and he turned to see a tall, gangling boy wearing horn-rimmed glasses and a look of irritation. He stared first at McKenzie and then at his mother.

'Yes?' he said. 'What is it?'

'Sit down, Giles,' she told him. 'You're too big to lounge about. You make the place look untidy.'

McKenzie saw the flash of anger, almost disbelief that crossed the boy's face. Then it was gone just as swiftly. He gave a little shrug as if to say 'What's the point?', pulled out the cane-bottomed chair, straightened his sister's blazer neatly around the back, draped the tie across it and then sat down.

'Giles,' his mother said, 'this is . . .' She realized she didn't know McKenzie's name.

'Detective Sergeant McKenzie.'

'Detective Sergeant McKenzie. He wants to ask you some questions about Phoebe Marriott.'

The boy's eyes narrowed.

'What about Phoebe?'

'Apparently she's missing.'

He stared at her in silence, then turned to McKenzie.

'I'm sorry,' he said, 'but I don't understand. What d'you mean? Missing.'

'According to your mother,' McKenzie said, 'she drove off in her car about eight o'clock last night. She hasn't been seen since.'

'You mean she didn't come back?'

'Of course she didn't come back,' Mrs Leening said. 'If she had, the police wouldn't be searching for her, would they? Really, Giles!'

'All right,' he said, 'all right.' He raised a hand. 'Have you tried the shop in Sheringham?' he said to McKenzie.

'She didn't open the shop this morning. It's been closed all day.'

'Then she must have gone up to London to be with Di.'

McKenzie seized on the point.

'You knew her sister was in London?'

'I knew she was going. Phoebe told me she was.'

'When did she tell you?'

'The night before last. I came back and told Mum.' He turned to his mother. 'Didn't I?'

She nodded at McKenzie.

'That's right. He did. That's how I knew it was Phoebe in the car.'

'So she must be in London.' Giles was insistent.

'I'm afraid not, son.' McKenzie shook his head. 'Her sister hasn't seen her. She was supposed to turn up in Norwich today to meet the train, but she didn't arrive . . . Have you any idea where she might have been going when your mother saw her driving away last night?'

The boy looked worried.

'I suppose she might have been going down to Cley.'

'Why would she do that?'

'She sometimes goes for a run along the beach. They both do, she and Di.'

'You think she may have gone there on her own?'

'She could have done. They usually go earlier.' The boy threw out his hands. 'I really don't know.'

'Well, at least that tallies,' McKenzie said calmly. 'We found her car abandoned by the sea bank at Cley.'

'Oh, no.' It was no more than a whisper from Giles. He stared at McKenzie. 'You don't think . . .?'

'We don't know anything yet, son. Not for sure.'

The boy wrenched himself up and ran a hand through his hair. He was suddenly wild-eyed, almost hysterical.

'No,' he said vehemently. 'No. Not Phoebe.'

'Giles!'

Mrs Leening stretched out a hand towards him, but he swept it aside.

He faced McKenzie.

'She's dead,' he cried, 'isn't she? You know she is. You've found her.' And without waiting for an answer, he turned and ran from the room.

Mrs Leening, with a lift of her eyebrows, went after him, her bath robe swinging wide.

There were voices on the stairs and then the girl sidled in, looking back across her shoulder. She'd changed her skirt for a pair of shorts.

'Oh, hello,' she said cheerfully. 'You still here?'

McKenzie could only admit that he was.

'And what's your name?' he asked.

'Barbara,' she said, 'but you can call me Babs . . . What's up with Giles? He zoomed past me like a rocket. Nearly knocked me down.'

'I think he's a bit upset.'

'That's nothing new.' She dismissed him with the usual sisterly contempt. 'Mum said something about someone being missing. Who is it?'

'One of the girls from the bungalow. Phoebe Marriott.' McKenzie wondered whether he was in for another bout of hysterics, but all she did was give a sigh.

'That explains it,' she said.

'Explains what?'
'Giles.'
'Then explain it to me.'
She was even more scathing than she had been about her brother.
'You're not much of a detective,' she said, 'if you didn't guess . . . He's soppy about her, isn't he? Has been for months.'

4

McKenzie knocked on the door.

There was no response.

'Giles,' he called.

'Go away.' The voice was tense, overwrought.

'Come on, son. Let me in. We've got to have a talk.'

There was a sound of reluctant footsteps. A bolt was drawn back. He listened for a second, then he turned the knob and pushed the door open.

The boy was facing away from him, head down, hands clenched.

'Why can't you leave me alone?' he said stormily. 'I don't want to talk.'

McKenzie looked round the room. There was a small single bed with a blue chintz cover, a table and chair with its back to the window, a chest of drawers surmounted by a mirror, a three-tiered bookshelf and a tall, narrow wardrobe. On the table were a drawing-board, angled on a stand to catch the light, a clutch of pencils, a paint box and a medley of brushes. Everything, as he'd expected, was neat and arranged with an utter precision. The pencils and brushes were carefully aligned, the spines of the books on the bookshelf were levelled, a comb and a hairbrush were symmetrically placed in front of the mirror, and all the drawers and the door of the wardrobe shut fast. The place was a complete contrast to the carefree disorder that prevailed downstairs; but it was the walls more than anything that caught and held his attention. They were covered with sketches, immaculately framed and hung, small in size, drawn in pencil and then water-coloured. There must have been at least fifty, each of them depicting the same luminous, dark-haired woman, but in a variety of poses and an equally wide variety of feminine attire.

McKenzie strolled around the room, examining them with interest.

'Did you do these?' he asked.

The boy slumped behind the table. His hands gripped the edge.

'Yes,' he said.

'They're good.' McKenzie peered closer. He inspected a skirt that rode up to mid-thigh.

'A bit short, this one, isn't it?' he said.

Giles picked up a pencil and tapped it on the table.

'It'll come,' he said, 'soon.'

'You think so?'

'Phoebe says so.' He made the statement as if quoting an oracle. 'We've got longer, fuller skirts now that rationing's gone. But the fashion won't last once the novelty's worn off. They'll get shorter and shorter.'

'This short?' McKenzie laid his finger on the woman's upper thigh.

'Even shorter than that.'

'Well, I hope I live to see it.'

'You will,' Giles said. He seemed suddenly more at ease, almost amused.

McKenzie looked round the walls.

'The model's the same in all of them?'

'Yes.'

'Is it Phoebe?'

The boy nodded. He stared at the pencil.

McKenzie sat down on the edge of the bed.

'She must be something special.'

Giles looked up.

'Tell me the truth,' he said.

'The truth?'

'Is she dead?'

McKenzie wished he could say yes. He wanted to say, 'Yes, son, she's dead. She's been murdered, and you're the one who can help us to find the man who did it.'

'We don't know, lad,' he said. 'We've found a body on the beach, but until it's been identified . . .'

'You think it's Phoebe?'

'We think it may be,' McKenzie said.

The boy closed his eyes. A tear trickled down his cheek and he brushed it away.

'Was she drowned . . . this woman?'

'No.' McKenzie weighed his words. 'I'm sorry to say she wasn't.'

'Sorry?' Giles frowned. His face showed confusion, then a dawning comprehension. 'You mean . . . ?'

'She was murdered,' McKenzie said. 'Strangled.'

'Oh, God.' The boy buried his head in his hands. 'Phoebe . . . That's awful . . . It's obscene.'

'All murder's obscene, lad.' McKenzie was grim. 'So is the man who did it. He may do it again. We have to find him quickly. We need you to help.' He paused, willing the boy to look at him. 'Tell me about her.'

Giles raised his head. His eyes were filled with tears.

'What d'you want me to say?'

McKenzie heaved himself up and made a circuit of the pictures.

'She's a very attractive woman.'

'Yes.'

'She must have had men friends.'

'No,' said Giles. 'No.' The words came out fiercely.

'I find that hard to believe.'

'It's the truth,' he said. 'I swear it.'

McKenzie looked down at him.

'Then answer me this, lad. What makes you so sure?'

'I just know.' The boy was sullen. 'If she had, she'd have told me.'

5

Gregg chose Number Three where Joseph Holland, the retired farm labourer, lived with his wife.

He lifted the knocker and banged it down heavily a couple of times. There was a pause, then a hand-bell rang from upstairs.

He waited. Feet tramped along the passageway inside, and the door was wrenched back by an elderly, grey-haired, bent-backed man with a day's growth of beard.

He looked at Gregg with curiosity.

'Dorn' know you,' he said.

The sergeant produced his warrant card and held it out.

'Detective Sergeant Gregg.'

The man gave it no more than a cursory glance.

'Dorn' have no truck wi' police,' he said. 'We ent done nothin' wrong.'

'Mr Holland?'

'Aye.'

'There's no need to worry, Mr Holland,' said Gregg. 'We're just making inquiries about someone who's missing, and you may be able to help.'

A woman's voice shouted from somewhere up above.

'Who be tha', Joe?'

'Naught to wittle about, lass . . . It's th'wife,' he said to Gregg. 'She be bed-bound. Rheumatics. Ye'd best come upstairs or she'll be moitherin' herself.'

Gregg closed the door and followed him up. In a room at the front a large, red-faced woman with straggling white hair seemed to overflow the bed.

Holland nudged him forward.

'It's police,' he said, 'Amy.'

She eyed Gregg up and down.

'He dorn' look like police.'

'I'm in plain clothes, Mrs Holland. I'm CID.'

'An' what the hell be tha'?'

'We investigate crimes.'

'Then what be you a-doin' of here?' she said. 'We ent done no crimes.'

Gregg sighed, but persisted.

'Someone's missing, Mrs Holland. We need some help.'

'Who be tha' then?' She fixed him with eyes that glittered like beads.

'Phoebe Marriott from the bungalow.'

'That ent much to fret on,' she said with contempt. 'They be all roun' th'place like kittywitches, both on 'em. Winter an' summer. Flittin' up an' down i' tha' motor o' theirn.'

'You see them often, Mrs Holland?'

'Every mornin',' she said, 'an' most every night. See 'em through th'winder. Not a lot else to do.'

'Did you see them last night?'

'See th'motor.' She tipped her head towards the road. 'It go off down to Morston.'

'D'you remember the time?'

'Three minutes gone eight,' she said very firmly.

Gregg blinked.

'8.03?'

'Tha' be right. On th'dot.'

'You made a note of the time?'

'Dorn' need to,' she said. 'It be right there, ent it?' She pointed to a washstand at the foot of the bed. Apart from a bulbous, blue-veined jug reposing in a bowl, the only other thing it held was a large brass alarm-clock.

'Has it there so she can allus see th'time,' her husband said. 'Gets her milk an' biscuits at a quarter gone eight . . . Every night,' he added.

Gregg still wasn't entirely convinced.

'You see a lot through the window, Mrs Holland?' he asked.

'Most everythin',' she said, 'save when I be sleepin'.'
'D'you remember the precise time that everything happens?'
She hunched her shoulders.
'Can't say tha' fer sure. I'd be romentin' like.'
'Then how come you recall the exact time last night? Three minutes past eight.'
'Why, 'cos it dorn' be right.'
'How d'you mean? It wasn't right.'
Mrs Holland surveyed him in some exasperation.
'It be wrong,' she said, 'ent it?'
'Yes.' Gregg was patient. 'But why was it wrong?'
'That ol' motor,' she said, 'it go down to Morston regler-like roun' half arter six. Last night it be late. I be watchin' fer it goin'.'
'Did you see who was in it?'
'From up here?' she said. 'Tha mus' think I'm got eyes like a Cyprus cat. 'Twere out o' sight in a flash ... But I see other folk.'
'Who?'
'Number One were comin' in.'
'Mrs Leening?'
She nodded.
'Aye. That'd be right. An',' she added darkly, 'she be furrin. Not Norfolk.'
'She saw the car too?'
'She ent blind, not her.'
'I suppose not,' said Gregg. 'Where was she coming from?'
'Reckon as she be mardlin' wi' ol' Grace Medlicott, an' tha' be nothin' new ... Arter that, I see th'lad.'
'Lad? What lad?'
'Her lad, o' course. Him tha's straight up an' down like a yard o' brand ale.' She turned to her husband. 'What his name be, Joe?'
Joe frowned and thought.
'Ent it mebbe Giles?'
'Aye,' she said, 'Giles. Furrin sort o' name ... He be off on his bike, same road, down to Morston.'
'What time was that?'
Mrs Holland, once again, was unflinchingly precise.
'A quarter gone eight.'
'You looked at the clock?'
'Not a lot o' cause ter do tha',' she said. 'He be just out o' sight, pedallin' like mad, when Joe there, he be in wi' me milk an' biscuits.'
'She gets 'em every night, same time,' said Joe. 'I ain' never missed a night in all o' five year.'

Gregg chose not to comment.

'Did you see him come back?'

'Not afore it were dark,' Mrs Holland said. 'Joe, he pulls curtains at twenty to ten, an' he dorn' be back then.'

'Was there anyone else who went down that way?'

'On'y young Moses.'

'Moses?'

'Moses Shelton. Him from next door.'

'What time did he go?'

'Same as every time. Just afore seven. But tha' dorn' be right neither.'

'Why not, Mrs Holland?'

'He tek off same way.'

'You mean down to Morston?'

'He allus go to Morston?'

'Most every night,' said Holland. 'He be off there till closin' time, an' tha's fer sure.'

Gregg fought against a growing sense of confusion.

'Then what was wrong about last night?'

'He tek off on a bike same as th'other one, dorn' he?' Mrs Holland made it clear that she regarded Gregg as well below par when it came to intelligence.

'And didn't he do that normally?'

'Wha'? Moses?' she said. 'I' th'state he come back! It tek him all his time to stand up on two legs. Gi' th'bugger two wheels an' he be arse-uppards in a delf.'

'So he walks, and last night he went on a bike. Why would that be?'

'Happen fer once', said Holland, 'he be goin' some place else.'

'Aye, happen he be,' said the old woman grimly. 'He've a bag on his back. Reckon th'ol' stewpot be a-steamin' today.'

'You didn't see him come back?'

'Dorn' never.' She tossed her head. 'Hear him though, some nights. Like as not midnight. He come a-rorpin' up th'path an' trip on tha' scraper they'm got by th'door. Then he gi' it a ding an' swear like it ent any right to be there. He be one o' they dispomaniacs, be Moses. Show him a pot of ale an' it be gone a deal quicker ner Jack Mellon's ol' bull tek ter spit a game cow, an' he be no slouch.

'He dorn' never wait fer no invite,' she added. 'Nor do Moses, I reckon. There be more ner one little Shelton roun' Wells they be sayin', an' that ent far wrong.'

6

As Gregg retreated down the path towards the Hollands' front gate, he reflected, somewhat wryly, that if Joseph and Amy Holland could be struck off the list of possible suspects, a certain Detective Chief Inspector, searching for a point of surveillance in Craymere, might do far worse than adopt their front bedroom. Not only would he have unrivalled command of the comings and goings of its handful of residents, he'd also have access to expert opinion on their characters, timings and likely destinations.

Turning at the gate, he surveyed Number Two, the Shelton cottage. There was no sign of life and the curtains at an upstairs window were closed, but, taking good care to avoid the metal scraper set firm in the flags, he marched up the path with some resolution and rapped on the door.

There was no response. He waited and knocked a second time.

A bed creaked up above; he heard a voice swear with a good deal of vehemence; then the curtains were flung back, the window jerked open, and a heavily bearded man in a fisherman's jersey leaned out and looked down.

'Why the hell ye makin' all tha' rattle?' he said.

'Mr Shelton?'

'Right. Wha' the devil d'ye want?'

'Mr Moses Shelton?'

'Right agen. So wha'?'

'It's the police, Mr Shelton. Please come down and open up.'

'Open up thiself. I got other things to do.' The head was withdrawn and the window slammed shut.

Gregg hesitated a moment, then he turned the knob and pushed. The door was unlocked. It swung back to reveal a claustrophobic lobby, lined with scarred linoleum and furnished with an old mahogany hatstand hung about with oilskins, topped by sou'westers and buttressed at the base by discarded gumboots.

'Mr Shelton,' he called.

The only reply was a sound of running water from somewhere above, then lumbering footsteps, followed, once again, by the creak of a bed.

Gregg made for the stairs, took them two at a time, turned along the landing and into the bedroom. Then he halted and stared.

Shelton lay on the bed, his hands behind his head. He was naked apart from the jersey, which was short.

He grinned.

'Find yer way up then, did ye?' he said.

Gregg, who'd been raised to observe the social niceties, viewed what he saw with considerable disfavour. He took an instant dislike to Mr Moses Shelton. The man, he decided, was no more than a lout, and the best form of defence against louts was attack. He wasted no time.

'Mr Shelton,' he said, 'where were you between nine o'clock and midnight last night?'

Shelton seemed unmoved.

'What's it to you?' he asked cheerfully enough.

'You were seen riding off on a bike towards Morston at seven o'clock. So where did you go?'

'None o' your affair.'

Gregg pulled up a cane-bottomed chair and sat down.

'Mek yerself at home,' Shelton said. He closed his eyes.

'You had a bag on your back.'

'An' what if a did?'

'I'd like to know what was in it.'

'Why be tha' then?'

'I'm interested,' said Gregg.

'Then ye'd best find out.'

'Oh, I'll find out, Mr Shelton, sooner or later. I just thought you might possibly be willing to help.'

'Then think agen, manny.'

'I'm thinking, Mr Shelton. I'm thinking you may be in serious trouble.'

'Don' tell me tha'. I ent in no trouble.'

'You will be unless I get answers to my questions. Where did you go last night with a bag on your back?'

Shelton reached out to a bedside table, closed his hand on a packet of cigarettes, lit one and blew a cloud of smoke to the ceiling.

'Tha' be my know, not yourn.'

'Poaching, Mr Shelton?'

'An' what if a were?'

'Where were you poaching?'

'I be tekkin' a few rabbits. Ent that enough?'

'It depends where you took them.'

'I be down at Holkham Meals.'

'That's private land, Mr Shelton.'

'It be all bloody private. Every grain o' sand atween Yarmouth an' Lynn.'

'You set snares?'

'Ent sayin'.'

'You know it's an offence to set snares on private land?'

'Then bloody well charge me, but get it done quick. Let a man get his rest.'

Gregg wasn't to be deflected.

'You were out late last night?'

'Same as every night, reckon.'

'What time did you get home?'

'Mebbe midnight. Thereabouts.'

'You set off at seven, rode to Holkham Meals and got back at twelve? Don't tell me you were four hours rabbiting on the dunes.'

'Course I bloody weren'.' Shelton was scornful. 'Went to th'pub, didn' I?'

'You mean the one at Morston? What time did you get there?'

'Half-pas' nine mebbe.'

'How much did you drink?'

Shelton took a deep breath.

'Five or six jars. Could a bin seven. Wha' th'hell do it matter?'

'And then you rode home?'

There was a snort from the bed.

'D'ye think I be shanny?'

'I wouldn't like to venture an opinion, Mr Shelton.'

'Well, I ent.'

'So you didn't ride home. Then what did you do?'

'Went walkin' a pace.'

'You had seven pints of beer and then you went walking?'

'Said so, didn' I?'

Gregg leaned forward.

'I don't believe a word of this, Mr Shelton.'

The man gave a shrug.

'Please yer bloody self.'

'Where did you walk to?'

Shelton sat up, swung his legs off the bed and stubbed out his cigarette on the table. He glared across at Gregg.

'Wha' th'hell be all this?' he said. 'Why should I be tellin' you all o' my know? What's ter tekkin' a rabbit? There be thousands o' th'little buggers out there i' th'Meals.'

'Where did you walk to?'

'Out Cockthorpe Common. An' you dorn' never tell me there be laws agen tha'.'

'Did anyone see you?'

'Aye. Jenny Muckloe. Reckon she must a seed me.'

'Who's Jenny Muckloe?'
'She live down o' Morston.'
'And where did she see you?'
'It be up Garret Hill by Jack Mellon's barn.'
'Did you speak to her?'
'Reckon a did. Aye.'
'What did you say?'
'Ye want gospel?'
Gregg took out his notebook.
'Every single word.'
Shelton heaved himself back on the bed and lay flat. He lit another cigarette. Gregg waited, pen poised.
'Ye're sure ye want gospel?'
'Certain, Mr Shelton.'
'Right then. Ye want gospel, gospel ye'll get.' He raised himself on one elbow and looked straight at Gregg. 'It were like this,' he said. 'We be lyin' there kiddlin' i' Jack Mellon's barn – handy tha' be – an' I say to her, "Jen, tha be tight as a drum. Shift ower a piece an' spread thi legs a mite wider, else tha'll be nippin' me off at th'root." An' Jenny, she say . . .'
Gregg closed his notebook. Then he closed his eyes.
'Never mind, Mr Shelton.'
'It be good wha' she say. Worth mekkin' a note. "Reckon as it need a bit o' prunin'," she say. "It shoot out o' they breeches winter an' summer like as it might be gaspin' fer breath." ' He paused. 'You got all tha' down?'
Gregg stood up. He replaced the chair.
'I'll not have any trouble remembering it,' he said.
Shelton lay back. Then he stretched his arms and yawned.
'Happen ye'll be off then . . . An' shut th'bloody door. I ent partial ter folk as come moseyin' aroun' an' I be abed.'

7

'Great,' said Tench. 'We've got two compulsive curtain-twitchers, an infatuated schoolboy who designs women's clothes and a sex-mad dipsomaniac. All in the space of four small cottages. It's a comfort to know Craymere's a normal sort of place.'

He was standing with Gregg and McKenzie at the gate of Downs House.

'Any sign of those men friends?'

'No one's mentioned any so far, sir,' said Gregg.

'And', McKenzie added, 'young Giles swears she had none.'

'That's the schoolboy?'

'Correct.'

'Well, if he had a crush on her, he would swear that, wouldn't he? But he has to be wrong, Mac. A girl like that? There must have been scores of men ready to drop on their knees and plead with her for favours.'

'You'd think so, wouldn't you?' McKenzie frowned. 'Trouble is they seem to be damned elusive.' He jerked his head towards the bungalow. 'The sister's the one to know. If she doesn't, no one does.'

Tench nodded.

'My turn to do the talking. You go back to Blakeney. Get it all written up . . . Have you checked Shelton's story?'

'Couldn't confirm it with his father, sir,' said Gregg. 'He's apparently out at Wells, working on the boat. We're going to check on the way back, down in Morston.'

'D'you know where this woman – what's her name? Jenny Muckloe? – d'you know where she lives?'

'According to Shelton, she's a barmaid at the pub.'

'So we'll see the landlord first,' McKenzie said, 'and then we'll see her. Shelton says he got there round half-past nine, and he must have left with her at closing time.'

'You don't know anything about her?'

'Not yet, but we will.'

'How d'you rate Shelton?'

'He's a slob, sir,' said Gregg. 'His days and nights revolve around drink and women.'

'Well, he's not alone in that. The real question is, is he capable of murder?'

'More than likely, I should think.'

'Suspect Number One?'

'At the moment, sir, yes.'

'Right,' said Tench. 'If you don't get confirmation, you know what to do. Bring him back to Blakeney, with or without his pants. Let's give him a grilling.'

He waited till they'd turned and driven away to Morston, McKenzie in the lead. Then he walked up the path to Downs House and tugged on the bell chain.

Sue Gradwell let him in.

'How is she?' he asked.

'She had a good weep, sir. Seems better now.'

'Up to answering questions?'

'She's expecting them, sir. I told her you'd need to see her.'

'I want her sister's room searched. That's your job, Sue. But we'll speak to her first. You go ahead.'

Gradwell opened a door.

'It's the Chief Inspector, ma'am.'

Diana Marriott was curled up on the settee. She'd changed into a lemon-coloured button-through dress. Her eyes were red, but she seemed composed.

'Come and sit down, Inspector,' she said.

Tench took the edge of a deep armchair.

'I'm sorry to have to trouble you again, Miss Marriott. How are you feeling?'

She gave a weak smile.

'Stricken,' she said, 'but I suppose I'll survive.'

'I have to ask you some questions. There are things I need to know.'

'I realize that, Inspector. I'll do my best to help.'

Tench waited a moment.

'Have you any idea', he said, 'who might possibly have done this?'

She shook her head very firmly.

'No idea at all.'

'Did your sister – Phoebe – did she have any men friends?'

'Not in the sense that you mean, Inspector.'

'No one who was particularly close?'

'Not recently, no.'

'What exactly d'you mean by "recently", Miss Marriott?'

'Not for two or three years.'

'She *was* a very attractive young woman.'

'Yes.' The word was whispered.

'Surely there must have been men who were interested.'

'Business acquaintances, Inspector. That was all.'

'Did she go out with any of them?'

'Not to my knowledge.'

'This boy, Giles Leening . . .'

'He's only a schoolboy.'

'But she does seem to have made quite a deep impression on him.'

'She helped him, yes.'

'Nothing more than that?'

'Of course not, Inspector. Phoebe was a woman. He's just an adolescent.'

'There have been stranger relationships, Miss Marriott,' Tench said gently.

'Not in this case, Inspector. You can take my word for it.'

'Then I'm perfectly willing to accept it.' He paused. 'I'd like Constable Gradwell to take a look at your sister's room. Have you any objection?'

'No. None at all.'

'You have the right to go with her.'

'No.' She tossed her head. 'I don't think I could face Phoebe's room at the moment.' She turned. 'It's the one at the back. Please do what you have to, Constable. On your own.'

Tench looked at Sue Gradwell. She slipped quietly outside.

He waited. Miss Marriott seemed to hesitate.

'D'you mind if I smoke, Inspector?' she said.

'Not at all. Please do.'

She swung her legs down, flicked open a wooden box on the table beside her, took a cigarette, and lit it with a gold-plated lighter from her pocket. Then she leaned forward, elbows on her knees and stared at the carpet.

'Can I ask *you* a question, Inspector?'

'Of course. Why not?'

'Am I right in thinking that, when there's a murder, a doctor examines the body before it's moved?'

'Normally, yes.'

'And he estimates the time of death?'

'Roughly. As best he can.'

'Did that happen in Phoebe's case?'

'Yes, it did.'

'What time did he say she died?'

Tench studied her carefully.

'Miss Marriott,' he said, 'there's really no need . . .', but she waved him aside.

'What time did he say?'

'He thought somewhere between nine o'clock and midnight last night.'

There was another long pause before she spoke again.

'This may seem a stupid question, but tell me, Inspector. Did birds have anything to do with what happened?'

'As a matter of fact, yes. The terns on Blakeney Point.'

She nodded her head three times very slowly.

'He was right, then,' she said. 'It was twenty past nine. I looked at my watch.'

8

She leaned back on the settee and curled her feet underneath her.

'How much d'you know about telepathy, Inspector?'

Tench shrugged.

'Does anyone know much about it?' he said.

'Oh, yes. Its existence was first acknowledged by a man called Barrett – William Fletcher Barrett – more than seventy years ago. The word itself was coined in 1882 by a poet, Frederic Myers. He described it as "the communication of impressions of any kind from one mind to another independently of the recognized channels of sense". It's sometimes known as transference of thought.'

'You seem to have made quite a study of the subject.'

She nodded.

'More than most people, I suppose. It often occurs between identical twins like Phoebe and me. We could always tell when something was wrong, even though we might have been miles apart.'

'And something happened last night?'

'Yes,' she said, 'it did. In the Burnton Galleries. You have to understand, Inspector, that it's more likely to happen in times of crisis. You're suddenly aware of danger. Not to you. To your twin. The warning can come in any number of ways: dreams, visions, hallucinations, or simply just a vague feeling that something's amiss.'

'And which was it in this case?'

She took a deep breath.

'I suppose you'd have to call it a vision,' she said. 'I was sitting there in the Galleries watching the models on the catwalk, and all of a sudden I saw this cloud of birds. They rose up into the air, all beating their wings, and I could tell they were making a frightful noise. They were only there a moment and then they were gone, but the image was so vivid I knew it must have something to do with Phoebe, and it troubled me so much I slipped out of the room and made a phone call to Craymere. Of course there was no reply, and by the time the show had finished I knew she'd be in bed and probably asleep. I didn't have the chance to ring up again this morning, and I hadn't heard anything from her, so I just assumed that what had happened couldn't be serious. Then I got to Norwich, and she wasn't there to meet me...'

She took a handkerchief from her pocket and dabbed at her eyes again. Tench gave her time.

'You say you looked at your watch?'

'If anything like that happens,' she said, 'I always do. Over the years it's become something of a habit. I always check the time.'

'And it was twenty past nine.'

'Just after,' she said. 'Perhaps a minute after.'

Tench made a note. She watched.

'Is it helpful?'

'Any snippet of information's likely to be helpful, Miss Marriott,' he said. 'If we can pinpoint the time, we're a step on the way ... You saw nothing else in this vision of yours? Nothing that might provide us with a clue to this man?'

'No,' she said. 'I'm sorry. I only wish I had. The impression was just of a flight of birds. They looked like gulls. Wheeling and screaming. The whole thing was over in a matter of seconds.'

Tench laid his notebook and pen on the table.

'You say you've had this kind of experience before, Miss Marriott?'

'Oh, yes, more than once.'

'And Phoebe? Was she just as receptive?'

'I think she was even more susceptible than I am.'

'Was there a reason for that? Anything you can think of?'

'There are theories, Inspector. Most receivers ...' She broke off as the door opened behind her, and Sue Gradwell moved quietly back into the room.

Tench waited.

'Yes, Miss Marriott?'

'Most receivers are women, and researchers seem to think it's because they're more intuitive and more closely linked to their emotions than men. Phoebe was more emotional than I am. And more intuitive. Perhaps that's the answer.'

'You say she was more emotional. What d'you mean by that?'

'She was far more aware of other people's feelings. She could put herself in their place, feel with them and for them. She had ... what's the word?'

'Empathy?'

'Yes, that's it. Empathy.'

Tench seemed to be mulling over what she'd said.

'Was that how she felt about young Giles Leening?'

There was a pause. Then the answer came, blandly enough.

'She believed he was very gifted. She felt she had to help him develop his talent.'

'And you're absolutely sure that was all, Miss Marriott?'
She sighed.
'I've already said so, haven't I, Inspector?'
'And on his side?'
'I don't really know him well enough to be able to say.'
Tench picked up his notebook; clipped his pen back in his pocket.
'He seems to have been very much in love with her, Miss Marriott.'
'At his age? I doubt it. Perhaps a schoolboy crush.'
'Such feelings can often be very intense. If, as you say, she was tuned in to other people, then she must have been aware of them.'
'Possibly, yes.'
'But she never encouraged them?'
Diana Marriott looked him straight in the eyes.
'Not Phoebe,' she said. 'She'd never have done that.'

He waited till they were outside before he spoke to Sue Gradwell.
'Find anything?' he asked.
'This, sir.' She took it from her pocket and handed it to him: a small leather-bound book with a blue ribbon marker.
'What is it?'
'A diary. It has to be Phoebe Marriott's. It was tucked away with her underclothes inside a drawer.'
'Does it give us any clues?'
'I think you'd better read it for yourself, sir,' she said. 'It looks very much to me as if someone's been spinning us a whole web of lies.'

9

Jim Thober, the landlord of the Black Dog at Morston, was large, round and cheerful, and his protruding paunch bore witness to either a love of good food or a less than prudent addiction to the ales for which his tavern was rightly renowned.

His assessment of Moses Shelton was none the less candid.

'If ye want my thinkin',' he said, 'he's a dishcloth. Needs a good wringin' out every night, does Moses. Mops it up like a pint mug's no more than a thimble. He'll be smitten wi' the shakes afore he gets to middle age, an' tha's naught but a fact.'

'Good for trade, though,' McKenzie said.

'Helps keep the books in balance, tha's true.' Thober planted two plump hands on the bar for support. 'But he gets to be a bloody nuisance late on. Have to chuck him out mos' nights. Come ten o'clock an' he be ready to tek on anyone. God only knows how he gets that ol' boat across the Wells Bar. One o' these days he'll be runnin' her aground, ye can tek it from me.'

'We've met him,' said Gregg.

'Stroppy, was he?'

'Stroppy's the right word.'

'Allus is,' said Thober, 'till he downs another pint. Then he's full o' the joys o' spring fer mebbe an hour. Arter that he turns sour.'

'We're interested', McKenzie said, 'in what he did last night.'

'Can't help ye much there.' Thober swayed back on his feet. 'Weren' in here fer long. No more'n half an hour.'

'He says he got here about half-past nine. Would that be right?'

Thober shook his head.

'He'm a worse bloody liar than Ananias. Gets here at seven. Out sharp at ha'-pas'. Never seed him again.'

'D'you know where he went?'

'Mebbe the Crown at Wells or the King's at Blakeney. Wouldn' rightly know.'

'He says he was out taking rabbits at Holkham.'

'Wouldn' put it past him. He weren' here, tha's fer sure.'

Gregg intervened.

'Apart from you, Mr Thober, who was on duty last night in the bar?'

'Jus' Meg Rooney an' me.'

'Not Jenny Muckloe?'

Thober was suddenly seized by a fit of coughing. He clutched at the bar, and tears streamed down his face. Pulling a large red handkerchief out of his pocket, he blew his nose noisily.

'Did ye say Jenny Muckloe?'

'Isn't she one of your barmaids?'

Thober wiped his eyes.

'I'd look well havin' Jenny Muckloe pullin' pints. Not as it wouldn' be an eye-catchin' business. Reckon folk'd turn up fer miles jus' to garp.'

'Why would they do that?'

'Look, son,' said Thober. 'There be only one Jenny Muckloe as live down i' Morston. She be ninety-two come Michaelmas an' blind as a bat fer th'las' twenty year.'

McKenzie looked at Gregg.

'Is she now?' he said. 'And what about Meg Rooney?'

'What about her?'

'How old would *she* be?'

'Twenty-one las' week. Ye want a word wi' her?'

'Yes,' McKenzie said. 'I think we'd like to meet her.'

Thober turned to the door.

'Meg!' he called. 'Come in here . . . She be doin' out the snug,' he added, 'ready fer tonight.'

Meg Rooney was a slim, full-busted girl with a visible cleavage. She faced the two detectives with her hands on her hips.

'What d'ye want?' she said. 'I'm busy.'

'Miss Rooney,' McKenzie said, 'you were behind the bar last night?'

The girl looked at him, then at Gregg.

'Yes,' she said. 'What of it?'

'Did you see Moses Shelton after half-past seven?'

'No, never a sight.'

'You're quite sure about that?'

'Not likely to miss him, am I?'

'You didn't take a walk with him after closing time?'

'Moses?' she said scornfully. 'No, I damn well didn't. I'd as soon take a walk with a two-legged pig.'

Outside, McKenzie halted.

'Someone's dropped us in a bed of bloody nettles,' he said.

'Back to Craymere?'

McKenzie swung a leg across the Norton. He drew a deep breath.

'Back to Craymere,' he said. 'And if Moses Shelton still hasn't got his pants on, I'll string him to this bike of mine by his balls and drag him to Blakeney.'

10

Lubbock was suffering no such frustrations.

Once Tench had made his phone call and driven away to Blakeney, he fried himself two strips of off-ration bacon and an off-ration egg, thoughtfully provided by his only sister who ran a restaurant by the side of the Wensum in Norwich. He then munched his way through a slice of blackened toast, brewed a pot of strong Darjeeling tea – once again the yield of sisterly benevolence – sat down in the one armchair he possessed and reached for his pipe.

His small side-table held everything he needed for a comfortable smoke: pipes, matches, tobacco pouch, a battered tin ashtray won years before at a fairground in Yarmouth, and a multi-purpose knife with a spike, a tamper and a blade, long since blunted, that he used for scraping the bowl of his briar.

Rolling the tobacco between the palms of his hands, he filled the long-surviving pipe that Tench had once described as a corroded old menace, lit its contents, tamped them down, then leaned back, crossed his legs and blew smoke at the ceiling.

He smoked contentedly for a full half-hour, at the end of which time he picked up his spiker and poked inside the bowl with some dissatisfaction. Then he knocked out the dottle, laced up the shoes that he'd loosened for comfort, and made his way out to the old brick storehouse he used as a garage.

Backing his Morgan three-wheeler with inches to spare between the rickety gateposts, he drove off into the village and, short of the windmill, turned left on the coastal road that led to Blakeney. Finding the incident room at the White Horse deserted except for Detective Constable Rayner, he made his statement, signed it and then stumped away down the slope to the quay.

He spent a considerable time there studying the tide-tables and making odd notes which he jotted down on a crumpled wad of paper. After that he climbed the steps to the Blakeney Hotel and sought out one of the waiters who was apparently an old acquaintance. They stood together in the lounge looking down at the road that ran beside the quay, and Lubbock could be seen to nod his head once or twice and then ask a further question.

He drove back from there to Cley, turned down past the mill and knocked on the doors of several cottages, engaging the residents in earnest conversation; while mid-afternoon saw him climbing more steps, this time to the old battery observation post where the coastguards had their look-out.

An hour later he was back in his own cottage parlour where, having enjoyed another meditative pipe and a second pot of tea, he settled down in his chair, put his feet up on a stool and promptly went to sleep.

3

PLAIN WAYS

> The way is all so very plain
> That we may lose the way.
>
> G.K. Chesterton: *The Wise Men*

1

Tench and Sue Gradwell drove away from Downs House in opposite directions: Gradwell back to Norwich, and Tench towards Morston and the incident room at Blakeney.

He hadn't gone more than a quarter of a mile before he met McKenzie's Norton followed by Gregg's police car returning to Craymere. All three of them stopped. Tench got out and crossed the road.

'Shelton?' he queried.

'The man's a lying bastard,' McKenzie said savagely.

'He wasn't at the pub?'

'Vanished in a puff of bloody smoke at half-past seven. God knows where he went.'

'What about Jenny Muckloe?'

'She's ninety and blind. If he'd been tarted up with fairy lights she couldn't have seen him.'

'So where is he now?'

'He'd better be still in bed. We're off back to check.'

'Right. Lead on,' said Tench. 'I'd like to meet Mr Shelton.'

McKenzie was only too eager to lead.

He wasn't in any mood to follow social conventions or rules of procedure. Flinging open the door of the Sheltons' cottage, he bounded up the stairs and into the bedroom.

'Hell's bells,' he said.

Tench was right behind him.

'No one at home?'
'Looks like he's skipped.'
'Check the other rooms, Andy.'
Gregg went down the landing, opening doors.
'Nothing,' he said.
'He could be downstairs.'
They clattered down, then halted as the front door opened. A burly figure in an oilskin stared up at them from the hall.
'Who th'devil are you?'
The voice held more of menace than frank curiosity.
Tench moved forward.
'Police.' He pulled out his card. 'Detective Chief Inspector Tench.'
The man took no notice. He continued to stare.
'What d'ye want here?'
'Are you Aaron Shelton?'
'Aye. What's it to you?'
'We need to talk to your son, Mr Shelton.'
'Fer wha'?'
'D'you know where he is?'
'Ent he in?'
'He doesn't appear to be.'
'Then he'll be down at th'Black Dog, like as not, I reckon.'
'We've been there,' McKenzie said.
'He ent there?'
'No, he's not.'
'Then ye know as much as I know. Could be in any o' half a dozen pubs. He'll be in one, tha's fer sure.' He hung up his oilskin. 'Wha's th'gret lummox bin a-doin' of this time?'
Tench waved McKenzie back.
'We need to know where he was last night, Mr Shelton.'
'He weren' here, an' tha's a fact.'
'What time did he go out?'
'Same as every night. Sevenish.'
'We know he left the Black Dog on his bike at half-past seven. Have you any idea where he might have gone after that?'
Shelton shook his head.
'He dorn' tell me much.'
'He had a bag. Was he rabbiting?'
'Could a bin.'
'Where?'
'No good axin' me. He ent one fer tellin' me all of his know.'
'What time did he get back?'
'Reckon it were late.'

'How late?'
'Three, four o'clock mebbe.'
'Does he usually come home that late?'
'Time to time, aye.'
'Did you see him?'
'Heard'n.'
'But you haven't the faintest idea where he'd been?'
'Like as not sleepin' it off in a barn. Wooden as a pump, Moses. Allus were.'
If Tench was frustrated, he gave no sign.
'You said he might be at any of half a dozen pubs. Can you give me a list?'
Shelton reeled off five without a great deal of thought.
'An' if ye find him,' he said, 'then lock th'bugger up. He'm as much use ter me as a dead duck in a delf, an' that ent far wrong.'

Tench thumped the roof of Gregg's car with his fist.
'I want him picked up,' he said, 'if it takes all night. I'll be waiting at Blakeney. Just give me a ring as soon as you find him.'

2

He watched them drive away towards Morston; then walked back to the car and sat for some time with his hands on the wheel, staring up the road at the Marriotts' bungalow.
'Someone's been spinning us a whole web of lies,' Sue Gradwell had said.
There was only one person she could possibly have meant, yet he found the accusation difficult to credit. Diana Marriott hadn't seemed to be a devious person. Taking into account the shock of her sister's death and her inevitable grief, she'd faced up to his questions remarkably well. Her answers had been straightforward, unambiguous. And yet . . .
And yet, what?
He reached across the wheel, unlocked the glove compartment at the side of the dashboard and took out the diary Sue Gradwell had found.
About four inches by five, bound in blue leather, with a ribbon marker of identical colour, and on the front in gold script the single word 'Diary'. Otherwise unexceptional. No gilt-edged pages. No

fancy designs. The kind of book that could well have been bought in Norwich at any of a dozen shops.

He flicked it open at random. May 14. Sunday. Two days to a page, the four-day spread covered with close, neat writing.

He read the first sentence, and then the second.

'Good God!' he said softly.

He read both pages, then turned back to the beginning and worked steadily through to the point where the entries finished: the day before Phoebe Marriott had died.

Sue Gradwell was right. Others in Craymere, apart from Moses Shelton, had been hiding the truth. Why they had, he didn't know, but the diary proved it.

What he'd read was erotic, almost pornographic. It was Solomon's Song rewritten by a twentieth-century woman. A paean to sex, to the joys of a love repeatedly fulfilled. A bible of contact, passionate contact day after day, between two bodies.

He stared at the last words.

'Today was sheer rapture. The very best of all. Our love is like a stream that flows wider and deeper till it breaks of a sudden into the sea. Then the warmth of water, a wonderful peace, and I wake to my lover's hand on my breast.'

'My lover's hand.' The phrase was plain. It brooked no denial. Her sister had said there was no one that close, had been no one at all for two or three years; but Phoebe Marriott had had a lover. And by her own admission. She'd shared her bed with someone: someone who'd slept with a hand on her breast. And not once. Many times.

Reg Ledward had been wrong. This girl was no virgin. And her sister must have known. She could hardly not have known.

His first impulse was to go straight back to Downs House. Confront Diana Marriott. Show her the diary. Demand an explanation. Then he told himself, no. No, not yet. He needed time to reflect.

He closed his eyes. Tried to rethink his conception of the case.

Someone had been Phoebe Marriott's lover. But who?

He turned back through the pages, searching for a name, knowing he wouldn't find one. 'My lover,' she'd written, 'my love, my beloved, my dearest one.' But her lover was nameless. There wasn't even an initial to yield up a clue . . .

It couldn't have been Shelton. That was beyond belief. Yet what had Lubbock said, only that morning? 'Keep an open mind. The incredible can always happen.'

He tried to imagine it happening, and shook his head. No, not in this case. It was inconceivable.

Then who was this lover she'd chosen not to name?

Could it, after all, be the boy? Giles Leening?

When he'd mentioned him, Diana Marriott had been dismissive. 'Phoebe was a woman,' she'd said. 'He's just an adolescent.'

But adolescents had feelings. He'd told her that. Feelings that could be just as intense.

How old was Juliet? Thirteen, fourteen? And Romeo? Tybalt had called him a boy. Was he as old as Giles?

And Diana Marriott had been determined, only she knew why, to cover up the truth.

This boy had told McKenzie much the same tale. There'd been no one, he'd said. Phoebe would have told him.

He was either ignorant of the truth, or he, too, was lying.

And . . .

One thing more.

He'd gone out on his bike last night. He'd followed her down to Morston . . .

He closed the book; put it back in the glove compartment.

Then he crossed the road again and knocked on the door of the Leenings' cottage.

It was time he took a look at Master Giles Leening and made his own assessment.

He was still young enough to remember what it was like to be seventeen.

McKenzie was in his forties. Perhaps he'd forgotten.

3

The fair-haired, freckled girl stood in the doorway and surveyed him.

'You're a detective,' she said.

Tench raised his eyebrows.

'How can you tell?'

'You look like one,' she said. 'The other one didn't.'

'The other one?'

'The fat one.' She looked him up and down. 'Corblimy . . . You married?'

Tench gave her a winning smile.

'I'm afraid so,' he said.

'Just my luck.' The girl swept back her hair. 'All the ones I fancy are snapped up already . . . You want to see Giles?'

'I really should see your mother first of all.'

'You can't do that. She's out. Over at Mother Medlicott's. Won't be back for ages . . . Is it true that Phoebe Marriott's dead?'

Tench professed ignorance.

'Who told you that?'

'No one,' she said. 'I guessed. Giles is locked in his room, sobbing his socks off. I think I must have an analytical mind. D'you think I'd make a good detective?'

'You might. It's a bit too early to say.'

'You mean you'd need to know me better?'

'Something like that.'

'Would I work with you?'

'You could. In course of time.'

She nodded.

'Then I'll give it some thought.' She stepped to one side. 'You'd better go up and see him. The fat one did. Got a hanky on you?'

'A hanky?' Tench was baffled.

'You'll need one,' she said, 'for Giles. All his must be sopping wet.'

Tench looked at her gravely.

'I think you'd better take me up and introduce me,' he said. 'My name's Tench. Detective Chief Inspector Tench.'

'What's your first name?'

'Mike.'

'Super-duper,' she said. 'That's my favourite name. Come on then. Let's go and see Weeping Willie.'

She knocked on the door.

'Giles,' she called.

No answer.

'Giles!' This time louder.

A chair scraped on the floor.

'What d'you want?'

'Just to talk.'

'I don't want to talk.'

'I'm not going away.'

'Stay where you are then. Leave me alone.'

'I'll keep on knocking. You'll have to let me in.'

There was a sigh from inside and the bolt was drawn.

She pushed the door open.

'About time,' she said. 'You turned into a hermit all of a sudden?'

'Can't you understand?' The voice was petulant: brother to younger sister. 'I just want to be on my own.'

'Well, you can't be,' she said. 'There's someone here to see you.'

'Who is it?' Wearily.

'His name's Mike. He's a detective.' She beckoned to Tench. 'And you'd better watch out,' she added very darkly. 'You're under suspicion.'

Giles was standing with his back to the window. He clearly hadn't been expecting anyone but his sister. His face was stained with tears. His glasses dangled from one hand. The other clutched a crumpled white ball of handkerchief.

Tench stepped forward.

'Detective Chief Inspector Tench. And don't take any notice of what your sister says. She's a strong imagination.' He turned to the girl. 'Outside, miss,' he said.

'Can't I stay?'

'Not permitted. If you want to be a detective, you've got to learn the rules.'

She read the look in his eyes.

'OK,' she said. 'I'll go. He wouldn't want me anyway. I mess things up too much.'

Tench watched her down the stairs; then he closed the door.

'So you're Giles,' he said.

The boy nodded dumbly.

'Well, let's put it this way, Giles. I need some help.' He looked round the room. 'D'you mind if I sit down?'

Giles gestured to the bed.

'Was it her?' he said. 'Was it Phoebe on the sands?'

'Yes, I'm afraid it was.'

'Then . . . she's dead?'

'Yes, she's dead.'

The boy replaced his glasses. He sat down very slowly and leaned forward on the table, his face between his hands. He didn't look at Tench.

'She was beautiful,' he said.

'Yes, she was.'

'How can anyone destroy beauty? How can they ever bring themselves to do such a thing?'

'Jealousy?' suggested Tench. 'Perhaps whoever it was hated his own ugliness.'

Giles shook his head.

'All the more reason to cherish beauty in others. It's a rare thing, beauty. It shouldn't be disfigured.'

'Yet it is. All too often. The world's a strange place . . . You were fond of her, weren't you?'

The boy raised his eyes.

'I wasn't fond of her. I loved her.'

'Love needs reasons, Giles. What was it made you love her?'

'She understood,' he said.

'Understood what?'

'What I wanted to do. She was the only one who did.'

'Don't your parents?'

'No. Father hates the idea. Mother goes along with him. She doesn't want trouble.'

'What about your sister?'

'Babs? She's just a kid.'

'But Phoebe was a woman, and she said you were right.'

'She helped me,' Giles said simply. 'Now she's gone and there's no one.'

Tench got up from the bed. He strolled round the room, examining the pictures.

'You've got talent,' he said. 'Don't waste it. If this is what you want, then fight for it. Don't give in. You'll win in the end.'

'You make it sound easy.' Giles's tone was bitter.

'Well, it isn't,' said Tench. 'It's damnably difficult. Take it from me . . . What does your father want you to do?'

'He wants me to try for Cambridge.'

'And you don't want to.'

'It's just a waste of time. What can I do at Cambridge that'll help me with this?' He waved a hand at the pictures.

'Academically,' said Tench, 'perhaps not a great deal, but take a tip from one who's been through the mill. My dad went to Cambridge. He wanted me to go, but I knew what I wanted to do even then. I told him I wasn't going. He didn't like it one bit. "Go, Mike," he said. "Do your three years. If, after that, you're just as determined to choose the police, I'll not argue about it . . . But go. You'll find that it's worth it." '

'And you went?'

'For two years. I'd have done all three, but then the war came and claimed me for five. I'd lost too much time, so I didn't go back. But I don't regret those two years. I'd do them again . . . Go to Cambridge, Giles, if you possibly can. Don't throw away the chance. Drink in its beauty, pick its best brains, meet the avant-garde. Then design your clothes. You'll be better equipped. And that's not a lecture. It's sound common sense.'

The boy bit his lip.

'Phoebe said that.'

'If she did, she was right.'

'She said to go somewhere quiet and have a good think.'

'And did you?'

Giles nodded.

'Last night,' he said.

'Where did you go?'

'There's a windmill. It's empty. Doesn't work any more. It's the other side of Stiffkey, on the road to Wells.'

'Breckmarsh Mill,' said Tench.

'I don't know what it's called, but there's a window that's broken. You can get in quite easily. I've been there before. You can climb up the ladders and get to the top. It's quiet up there, and you can see all the coast.'

'How long did you stay there?'

'An hour. Perhaps a bit more. I got home about half-past ten.'

'Did anyone see you?'

'I don't think so. They never do. The place is out on its own. Nothing anywhere near. That's what I like about it. I just sat on the floor and stared out to sea. It was peaceful. At least, so I thought. And all the time, Phoebe . . .' He looked up at Tench. 'What time did it happen?'

'We don't know for sure. We think it was round about twenty past nine.'

'I was sitting up there,' he said. 'Everything was still.' He brushed away a tear with the back of his hand. 'If only she'd said she was going, I'd have gone along with her. Then it wouldn't have happened.'

He thumped the table with his fist. The pencils jumped and rattled.

'Why?' he said. 'Why Phoebe?'

'That's the question we've got to answer.' Tench watched him intently. 'Could she have arranged to meet someone down on the beach?'

Giles didn't hesitate.

'No,' he said. 'Not Phoebe. She wasn't like that.'

4

Outside the Leenings' gate Tench looked at his watch. It showed half-past seven, and the sun, though sinking, was still high in the cloudless sky over Wells.

He walked across to the car, opened the glove compartment, took out the diary and dropped it in his pocket. Then he made his way up the path to Downs House and pulled on the bell chain.

She came to the door, still in her lemon-coloured, button-through dress, but she'd washed off her make-up, and without it, Tench thought, she looked vulnerable, less in control of herself.

'It's hardly fair of me, Miss Marriott, to trouble you again,' he said, 'but there's a problem I think you can help me resolve.'

'A problem, Inspector?'

'Something that needs clearing up straight away.'

She looked at him, puzzled, then stepped to one side.

'You'd better come in,' she said. 'I've just made coffee. Would you care for a cup?'

Tench, at that moment, would have cared for nothing more than a strong black coffee. He resisted the temptation.

'Not for me, thanks,' he said, 'but you carry on.'

He sat where he'd sat before, on the edge of the armchair, and waited as she poured.

'You must be ready for that. It's been a long day.'

'An . . . unusual day.'

'Not one to be repeated.'

'One that can't be repeated, Inspector. Ever.'

'No,' he said. 'Of course.'

She added milk and sugar, and stirred the coffee slowly.

'You said you had a problem?'

'Yes, Miss Marriott.'

She waited. Tench seemed reluctant to begin.

'Well,' she said. 'What is it?'

'I wouldn't like you to think I was questioning your word . . .' He paused again.

'But . . .'

'Something's come up that I don't understand.'

'Something about Phoebe?'

'Yes.'

'Then perhaps I can explain.'

'If you can, I'd be grateful.'

She took a sip of her coffee.

'Then what is it that's troubling you, Inspector?'

'I'm afraid there's a conflict of evidence, Miss Marriott.'

'You mean something I said doesn't seem to make sense?'

'It conflicts with something else.'

She frowned.

'What exactly?'

Tench took the diary from his pocket and held it up.

'This,' he said. 'Constable Gradwell found it in one of Phoebe's drawers. Have you seen it before?'

'I never go in Phoebe's drawers.'

'Then I think you'd better read it.' He handed it to her.

She opened it at the marker and read the last entry. Then she turned back, one by one, through the pages.

He watched her, expecting to see shock, confusion, perhaps even guilt; but she didn't seem surprised. She nodded from time to time. Once he thought he almost detected a smile.

At last she looked up.

'This troubles you?' she said.

'Shouldn't it?'

'Not if you knew Phoebe.'

'Then maybe that's the trouble, Miss Marriott. I didn't. I take it that that's her writing?'

'Oh, yes, it's hers.'

'She writes about a lover, in quite explicit terms. Yet, when we spoke before, you denied all knowledge of any such connection.'

She nodded.

'Yes, I did.'

'Wouldn't you call that a conflict of evidence, Miss Marriott?'

She handed back the diary.

'I would if that was evidence, Inspector, but it isn't.'

'Then what would you call it?'

'It's fantasy,' she said. 'Phoebe was a dreamer. I told you she was.'

'You mean these are dreams?'

'They have to be. What else could they possibly be?'

'Are you telling me your sister had erotic dreams, night after night, and then wrote them down?'

'No, of course not,' she said. 'They're day-dreams.'

'Day-dreams? For Adults Only? In Glorious Technicolor?'

'They're hopes, Inspector, wishes, fancies, reveries. Don't tell me you've never had them. Surely you've dreamed of taking some girl to bed. Undressing her slowly, fondling her breasts. All men do that.'

'Well . . .'

'Admit it, Inspector. There's nothing shameful about it. It's perfectly natural. We all of us do it. Women have their fantasies, just as men do.'

'But they don't write them down in such detail, Miss Marriott.'

'Don't they?' she said. 'Forgive me, Inspector, if I sound a bit sceptical, but how can you say? Diaries are secret things, tucked away in drawers, locked in trinket boxes, hidden under floorboards. They're intimate, private, not intended to be read by anyone else. And believe me, ones like that aren't as rare as you think. You'd be surprised at the thoughts that run through girls' minds, and what are diaries for if not to record them?'

Tench pursed his lips. He weighed the book between his fingers.

'Then you say this means nothing?'

'Nothing except that Phoebe was like hundreds and thousands of other young women. She fantasized about love. Is that such a crime?'

'And you still maintain there was no man in her life?'

Her answer could well have come from Giles Leening.

'If there had been, Inspector' – her gaze didn't waver – 'can you honestly believe that I wouldn't have known?'

5

If Tench was making the disconcerting discovery that plain ways in Norfolk were likely to develop unexpected twists and turns, McKenzie and Gregg were meeting equal frustration as they sought to track the elusive Moses Shelton through the convoluted byways between Blakeney and Wells.

It was an evening's excursion that made no appeal to Bill McKenzie. Nearer fifty than forty, a detective sergeant of long experience who made no secret of his healthy disdain for promotional ladders, he was normally a man who was happy in his work; but two things were calculated to unravel his equanimity. One was the need to chase villains across roofs: he'd suffered from vertigo all his life. The other was having to chase them round pubs when duty precluded the sinking of a pint.

His temper was therefore under some strain.

Starting from Blakeney, where he'd left his trusty Norton outside the White Horse, he and Gregg had plotted a winding course that embraced, among others, Aaron Shelton's five widely separated taverns. Turning inland, they made first for Wiveton, and then drove on to Langham. From there they cut back to the coast at Stiffkey, and followed that by swinging further inland to Binham and Wighton. From Wighton they turned north again to Warham, and ended up at Wells where they combed the snugs and taprooms without a single sighting of the man they had to find.

By the time they reached Langham, McKenzie was fretting. By Warham he was fuming, and when at last they halted on the quayside at Wells, he swore to Gregg that once he laid hands on Moses Shelton he'd break every bone in his bibulous body.

'Where the hell's the bugger got to?'

'You tell me,' said Gregg.

'Rabbiting again?'

'Could be.'

They trailed all the way down to Holkham Gap. On the sand below the pines a man was walking his dog.

'Seen anyone about?' McKenzie asked him.

'Rabbits,' the man said. 'Plenty o' them around.'

They waited till he'd disappeared through the Gap.

McKenzie stared at the long wall of pines and swore.

'Any ideas?' he said.

'Could be under a hedge or even in a ditch.'

'What about that barn he mentioned to you?'

'Jack Mellon's barn? I suppose it's worth a try. He said it was a handy sort of place for a bit of slap-and-tickle.'

'From what I've heard of Moses Shelton, he'll be tickling with more than his fingers,' McKenzie said. 'Whereabouts is it?'

'Garret Hill. This side of Morston.'

McKenzie turned towards the Gap.

'Come on, then,' he said. 'Let's go and take a look. It'd make my day to interrupt the sod when he's touching up some poor deluded maiden from Morston.'

The light was already fading as they drew to a halt on the coastal road, and picked their way down the side of a field towards the barn. Outside they stood and listened. There was a rustling from somewhere deep in the hay.

McKenzie nudged Gregg, and they crept forward together. It was difficult to see in the semi-darkness below the kingposts and tie-beams, but McKenzie had a nose for bucolic lechery. He stopped of a sudden and cupped his hands round his mouth.

'Come in, Moses Shelton! Your time's up!' he bellowed.

There was a scuttering in the hay and a figure detached itself from the gloom and raced for the doorway. They saw a flash of bare shanks and Gregg dived towards them. His headlong tackle brought the man down, but a wildly flailing fist knocked him over backwards. McKenzie didn't hesitate. Before the scrambling figure could get to its feet, he planted a large foot firmly on its chest.

He peered down at his writhing victim.

'Moses,' he said, 'you're nicked. I think you'd better do the honours. Introduce me to this peerless young virgin you've ravished.'

Half an hour later, in the bleak electric light of the incident room, Tench inspected the sullen, swaying, trouserless Shelton with visible distaste. He looked from him to Gregg's rapidly blackening eye.

'Take him back to Norwich,' he said. 'Rayner'll do the driving. And when you get him there, charge him. Drunk and disorderly, wasting police time, indecent exposure, resisting arrest, assaulting an officer. Throw the book at him. And give him back his trousers, Mac, now that I've seen the evidence. The mere sight of it scares me. God knows what that girl imagined she was getting. What did you say her name was?'

'Maisie Thaxton.'

'Where is she?'

'Took her back to her mother,' McKenzie said. 'She's only fifteen.'

The look of distaste on Tench's face changed to one of disgust.

'Indecent assault,' he said. 'Add that to the charges. He wasn't raping her, was he?'

'Not according to her.'

'Pity,' said Tench, 'but I'll need some convincing that he didn't snare those rabbits last night on Blakeney Point.'

6

He heard them drive away: the revving of Rayner's car, then the crackle of the Norton.

On the table in front of him, Rayner had left his message pad. He flicked it open. Not that he expected any startling revelations, but there might just be something to tie the threads together . . .

He ran his eye down the top sheet.

Message from Lock.

He'd phoned from Norwich with the list of sex offenders.

Tench glanced through them. There were a dozen local men with recorded convictions, but five were locked away, still serving their sentences. Of the seven that remained, two were no more than flashers, and three had indecently assaulted young boys.

He ruled those out straight away. None of them were likely to have murdered Phoebe Marriott. The two cases of attempted rape were more relevant, but, on closer inspection, neither appeared to be likely suspects. One had been convicted twenty years before, at the age of thirty-nine, and had not offended since; while the other, drunk in a pub at Edgefield, had tried to rape his girlfriend under a haystack. That had been back in 1946. He'd served eighteen months, and had then returned to live with his parents at Felthorpe.

Tench shook his head. It was too far away: the other side of Holt, almost in Norwich.

He turned to the next sheet.

Steve Harris, the resident copper at Blakeney.

He'd done a round of all the local hotels, checking the registers. No guests had made sudden, unexplained departures.

That simply signalled another dead end.

What else?

Dave Ransome, the crime reporter.

Rayner had scribbled a note to say he'd been around. Would the Chief Inspector please give him a bell? Tench looked at his watch. No, the Chief Inspector wouldn't. It was too damned late. He'd have to wait till the morning.

The sheet that followed was blank. That, it seemed, was the lot, apart from Lubbock's statement about finding the body. He dropped it in a file and stared at the pad.

Had he made any bloody progress at all?

Where were the clues that he needed, the links?

They must be hidden away somewhere, but where did he start to look?

Phoebe Marriott's diary?

Was there something he'd missed?

Or maybe something he'd . . . what exactly? Wilfully ignored?

He pulled it out of his pocket, laid it on the table and unscrewed his pen.

'January 1, Sunday. Oh, the gentleness, the mystery. When we make love I feel I'm beautiful, desirable, the most desirable woman in the whole wide world. I know that I'm wanted. Delicate fingers. Tracing my hair, my face, my neck, my breasts. Running down my body . . .'

He imagined it happening; felt a stirring inside him, and told himself sternly to read every word with a clinical, analytic detachment . . .

He read on; read the whole thing through from beginning to end, slowly, methodically, jotting down dates and phrases as he went. It took him half an hour. Then he looked at what he'd written.

At what she'd written.

He frowned at the words, concentrating hard, closing his eyes, admitting what he hadn't wanted to believe. Accepting the thought which, because of all its disruptive possibilities, he'd pushed more than once to the back of his mind: the idea that there could be another explanation. Not Diana Marriott's; not Giles Leening's; but one that, in a way, coincided with both.

He turned back to the dates he'd noted, the phrases that had seemed to him strangely contrived.

Read in a different light, all the evidence was there.

It repeated itself, day after day.

It wasn't the words themselves. It was the fact that words were missing. Deliberately excluded. Ruthlessly scythed away from the text . . .

Checking the time again, he reached for the phone and asked for Lubbock's number.

He heard the bell ring. There was no reply, but he sat and let it ring, his ear clamped to the receiver.

At last he heard a voice.

'Cley double two.'

'Did I get you out of bed?'

'No, laddie, you didn't.' The response was gruff as usual. 'I was leaning on the gate, smoking a pipe and giving some thought to an urgent problem.'

'What problem was that?'

There was a sound that meant Lubbock was mildly amused.

'Detective Chief Inspectors.'

'Why should they be a problem?'

'They're never around when you want them.'

Tench felt a quite irrational sense of relief.

'Put the coffee on,' he said. 'I'm already on the way.'

Lubbock's cottage, Umzinto, named after one of the ships that had traded with Cley when the place was still a port, had always been for him a retreat from the daytime bedlam of Norwich: a refuge where, in the evening, he could settle down and think. When he'd still been at work, the back room of his sister Meg's Riverside Restaurant in the heart of the city had always been the place where he and his team had thrashed out their problems without interruption, fuelling their discussions with haddock and egg, Lubbock's customary choice, and Meg's seemingly inexhaustible supplies of tea and coffee. But, since his retirement, Umzinto had, in a sense, replaced it, and it wasn't the first time that Tench, faced with an apparently intractable case, had laid its details before his old chief inspector and talked them through in the parlour in the hope of finding some kind of an answer. If more than one Norfolk murderer had owed his conviction to Lubbock's sense of fulfilment as he'd lounged in Meg's chair and watched the smoke wind away from the bowl of his briar, there were others, more recent, who'd ended up in the dock because Tench had spent an evening, breathing in the pungent fumes of tobacco, drinking Lubbock's coffee and listening as the old boy dissected his problems.

It was a familiar process, repeated that night without variation.

Tench poured the coffee. Lubbock poured his own tea. Then he relit his pipe, leaned back in his chair and stretched out his legs.

'So, laddie,' he said. 'What have we got so far? Any possible suspects?'

'A couple.' Tench paused. 'But that's all they are: just possibles, not probables.'

'Who are they?'

'One's a schoolboy.'

'Doesn't sound to be a likely candidate for murder. What's his name?'

'Giles Leening. He's seventeen. His family rents a cottage at Craymere for the summer.'

'And what's his connection with this girl, Phoebe Marriott?'

'She and her sister run a dress shop in Sheringham.'

'Yes, I've gathered that much. Had a chat with Rayner. So where does the boy come in?'

'He designs women's clothes as a hobby. Wants to make it a career.'

Lubbock bit on his pipe.

'Does he now? That's unusual. The Marriott girl encouraged him?'

'Yes, he's gifted. There's no doubt about that.'

'Then why should he want to murder her?'

'I never said he did.'

'But what?'

'He's intense, emotional. Claims he was in love with her. He was out on his own last night, and he hasn't exactly got a watertight alibi.'

Clouds of smoke billowed up to the rafters of the parlour.

'Seems a pretty thin case against the lad,' said Lubbock. 'Where does he say he was?'

'Down at Breckmarsh Mill.'

'Breckmarsh? It's derelict. What was he doing there?'

'Thinking, so he says. He goes there on his bike when he wants peace and quiet. Gets in through a broken window and climbs to the top. Works out his problems.'

'And no one saw him last night?'

'According to him, not a soul.'

'Well, they most likely wouldn't. The nearest cottage must be at least a mile away . . . You told him the girl was dead?'

'Yes.'

'What was his reaction?'

'Disbelief. Floods of tears.'

'Sounds genuine to me. An emotional adolescent with a crush on an older woman. They do strange things at that age . . . D'you think she was flattered?'

'Like enough,' said Tench.

'Enough to lead him on?'

'Her sister says no, not the slightest chance.'

'Rayner said they were twins. Were they close?'

'Very close.'

'Well, she should know . . . Who else is in the frame?'

'A fisherman from Wells with a cottage at Craymere. Name of Moses Shelton.'

'Why him?'

'He's a drunkard, a lecher, a liar and he's violent.'

'Sounds to be a much more likely proposition.'

'He is. I've inked him in . . . But there's a slight complication.'

'What's that?'

'This,' said Tench. He held out the diary.

7

Lubbock took it; eyed the inscription on the cover.

'Whose is it?'

'Phoebe Marriott's. Our WDC found it in her room.'

A nod. Lubbock opened it, read the first lines and then riffled through the pages.

'You want me to read it?'

'Yes, I think you should.'

The old man picked up his knife and tamped the tobacco down in his pipe.

'Then go away,' he said. 'Take a stroll round the Green. Sniff the evening scents. There's nothing more disconcerting than someone sitting opposite you watching you read . . . Go on. Get off. Vanish. Give me ten minutes. Take that coffee with you and lean on the gate. Let the silence of the stars console your troubled mind.'

'You think it will?'

'Never fails,' said Lubbock. 'Now, d'you want me to read this rubbish, or not?'

Tench leaned on the gate and looked at the stars. He tried to pick out the Plough, the only one of the constellations that he knew. He found it at last, traced the Pointers to the Pole Star, and told himself that someday he really must learn a bit more about the sky. What was the Latin name for the Plough? Ursa Major. That was it. The Great Bear. Some called it Charles's Wain. Well, it did look like a cart. The Yanks in Italy had called it the Big Dipper, though God only knew why.

He found the Pole Star again. Polaris. Strange to think that mariners had once steered by that, finding their way into Cley by the stars. Stranger still to think that, as Lubbock had told him, this Green had once been a busy quayside where ships from the Low Countries and Hanseatic ports, from bleak northern coasts and the Mediterranean – ships with biblical names: *Matthew* and *James* – had discharged their cargoes. Vegetable oil from Greece, spices from the Levant, fish from Iceland, coal from Newcastle and bricks from Flanders: all to be stored in the dockside warehouses, then loaded on to waggons for transportation inland. Where the Green stretched away to the narrow stream of the Glaven, there'd been a wide-spreading estuary with teeming wharves where cartloads of barley and oats and malt, and thousands of sacks of wool had lain waiting to be stacked in the holds of the *Gifte of God* and the *Trynite*.

The *Umzinto*, nosing in centuries later, would have docked half a mile away by the windmill, or lain up in Blakeney Pit while lighters had ferried her cargo to shore. Now the marshes spread a mile beyond the mill to the shingle bank. The sea was constantly retreating from Cley.

He swung the gate open and walked round the Green, searching for the slow-moving trickle of the river. Then he turned and looked back.

Beneath a sky strewn with stars, the dark hump of the church with its short, squat tower, its long nave and clerestory, rose on its eminence above the lighted cottage windows. All was still. A lone, tall tree stood like a feather duster behind Umzinto. The sound of the sea as it dragged on the shingle was too distant now to break the silence that held the ancient port in its grip.

Cley was dead, but at peace.

Lubbock had chosen well.

He began to walk back, the sound of his shoes as they brushed through the grass louder than the waves that once, long ago, had lapped against the quays.

8

Lubbock was deep in concentration. The diary lay open, but upturned, on the table.

'Well, have you read it?'

'Enough of it, laddie.'

'And what's your impression?'

Lubbock laid down his pipe.

'Before I answer that,' he said, 'let me ask you a question ... This girl, Phoebe Marriott. Who were the men in her life?'

Tench gave a shrug.

'You mean apart from Giles Leening? That's a bit of a problem. Nobody seems to know.'

'No other names have surfaced?'

'Not a single one, so far.'

'Hasn't her sister mentioned anyone?'

'No, she says there's been no one around for years. At least, no one serious.'

'And what does young Giles have to say about that?'

'Exactly the same. He says if there had been, Phoebe would have told him.'

'Maybe, maybe not. Hope springs eternal in the adolescent breast ... But then I'm a cynic. You need to be one if you work as a detective.'

'You don't believe him?'

'Immediately, no. Neither him, nor the sister ... What's her name?'

'Diana ... Goddess of the Moon.'

'Or moonshine,' Lubbock said. 'Let's look at the facts. If I'm to credit what I've read, this girl had a lover. One that she found more than adequate. He was gentle. She talks about delicate fingers. That, I'd imagine, rules out your fisherman.'

'Right from the start.'

'But it doesn't rule out the schoolboy.'

'No, I'm not convinced that it does.'

Lubbock was undeterred.

'Then let me do a bit of convincing, laddie. How old did you say he was? Sweet seventeen? Hardly into long trousers . . . This lover of hers is a damned sight older. He knows far too much for a boy of seventeen. He's a practised hand. She's not the first he's made love to. I doubt if she rates among the first baker's dozen . . . You've read this, haven't you? Come on, Mike. Be honest. Wouldn't you agree?'

'With one reservation.'

'And what would that be?'

Tench poured another coffee.

'It's possible young Giles could have learnt a lot from her.'

'That assumes she was a very promiscuous young woman. You've no evidence for that. It's all to the contrary. Your witnesses seem to think she behaved like a nun.'

'OK. Point taken . . . So there must have been some other man in her life.'

'Perhaps.' Lubbock picked up the diary. 'Does the sister – Diana – does she know about this?'

'Yes, I tackled her about it.'

'And what did she say?'

'Said it was all fantasy. Phoebe was a dreamer. Dreamt of being ravished by a handsome young man, and wrote it all down. Not unusual, she said. Hundreds and thousands of young women did it. I'd be surprised at the fancies that girls indulged in.'

'Well, I wouldn't know,' said Lubbock, 'but if this is a sample, there must be a whole horde of sex-obsessed maidens positively yearning to be robbed of their virginity. It all sounds most unlikely to me. First she says her sister's led a chaste life for years, and then she comes up with the random excuse that these erotic descriptions are nothing but the fruits of a fevered imagination. Well, I'm sorry, Mike, but I just don't believe her. She can't have it both ways. The entries are far too explicit for that. The girl who wrote this was no blushing novice. She was a seasoned sophisticate as far as sex was concerned.'

'You think the entries are true.'

'The substance of them, yes.'

'Then that means she really did have a lover.'

'Must have had one, I'd say, and for quite a long time. But that's simply my feeling. I just can't accept that everything I've read is merely make-believe.'

'I can understand that.' Tench gave him a nod. 'So we're faced with another question. If this lover of hers wasn't Moses Shelton and he wasn't Giles Leening, then who was he?'

Lubbock unscrewed the stem of his pipe, pushed a cleaner through it and held it up to the light.

'Let's take a closer look at the evidence, laddie . . . This pornographic idyll.' He tapped the diary. 'If it does reflect the truth, then this girl must have been having a pretty torrid affair. She was sharing a bed with someone more or less every night, if not every day. What does that suggest to you?'

Tench wasn't to be drawn.

'I want to know what you think.'

'It suggests to me', said Lubbock, 'that this was a lover who was readily available.'

'I thought that, too.'

'Of course you did. It's obvious.' Lubbock peered at him shrewdly. 'You're just stringing me along, laddie, aren't you?' he said. 'You didn't dash down here from Blakeney in a mist of confusion. You already know the answers. You've worked them all out.'

'I've got my own ideas. I want to know whether yours coincide with mine.'

'Don't you trust your own logic?'

'Perhaps . . . not entirely.'

'Why?'

'Because, on the face of it, the answer's grotesque.'

'But not incredible.'

'No.'

'Didn't I tell you this morning to keep an open mind when you're dealing with murder? The incredible can always happen. I emphasized the point . . . Well, this isn't incredible. To quote your own turn of phrase, it's merely grotesque. All the more reason then to accept it.'

'Maybe I do,' said Tench, 'but I need to hear your logic.'

'You want it step by step?'

'Just imagine I'm not very bright in the head.'

'Fair enough, laddie, if that's what you want.' Lubbock struck a match, relit his pipe and blew out a cloud of smoke that all but eclipsed him.

He wafted it away. Then he held up the diary.

'Let's go back to this, shall we?' he said.

9

'First point to be noted. There's one glaring omission. The name of her lover. That's never mentioned. Has to be deliberate ... Now for the next. Let's take a date at random. You suggest one.'

'Shall we say May the sixth?'

'May the sixth it is.' Lubbock turned to the entry, ran his eye down the page and then handed the book to Tench.

'Read it, laddie,' he said, 'but not out loud. It hardly bears repetition.'

Tench read.

'May 6. Saturday. Last night we bathed together, then we lay on the bed. Playing with my hair, kissing my breasts, loving the shape of them, the softness. Touching me where I needed to be touched, knowing exactly where I needed to be touched. Tongue brushing across my nipples, finger tips slowly caressing my legs, moving up, stroking. Then a steady rhythmic friction gathering between us, and at last our bodies twisting and arching together. Both at the same time. Breathless perfection. And later, lying still, pressed against me, whispering. Telling me I'm lovely, that I'm loved every minute of every day. That's true for me, too. There can never, never be anyone else.'

It was the third time he'd read it. He looked up at Lubbock.

'OK. Carry on.'

'First of all, forget the crude physical mechanics. Concentrate on the words. There are still more omissions, significant ones. I'm intrigued by the absence of certain pronouns. You get "I", "me" and "my" and "we", "us" and "our", but no "he", "him" and "his". Nor can I find the words "she" and "her". And it's not just in this particular entry. It's the same all the way through. That's why I asked you to choose a date at random. It wouldn't have mattered where you'd told me to look.'

'And so?'

'These omissions. They seem to me, like the first, to be deliberate. This girl seems intent on concealing not merely the name of her lover, but also the sex. And add to that something else. She describes her own body in intimate detail. An artist, once he'd read through this diary, wouldn't need her to pose. He could sketch her in the nude accurately and without a great deal of trouble. And yet – note this – there are no similar descriptions of her lover. You're continually conscious of a physical presence, but only in a very limited sense. The lips, the tongue, the fingers: those parts of the body that touch her and rouse her. It's as if she's purposely contracting the picture, cutting out her lover, so that no one shall recognize just who it is. That makes me ask a question. Why all this persistent, calculated reticence?'

'And what's your answer?'

'The same as yours, I fancy. That first impressions can be wrong.'

'And that means?'

'Quite simply, that this lover may not be a man after all. There's a strong possibility that it could be a woman.'

'You're too cautious by far.' Tench was dismissive. 'It has to be a woman. And that means we're dealing with a lesbian affair.'

Lubbock seemed amused.

'They exist, you know,' he said. 'They've been polishing their techniques ever since the time of that Greek poetess. What was her name? Sappho?'

'Burning Sappho.'

'Burning is right.'

'So tell me the rest.'

Lubbock raised his eyebrows.

'What else d'you want to know?'

'Who the other woman is.'

'You mean who I think it might logically be.'

'If you want to put it that way.'

'I do. I can't be sure and neither can you. We can only look at the evidence and say that it points in a certain direction.'

'But pretty firmly.'

'I'd say so.'

'Well, go on,' said Tench. 'Who does it point to?'

Lubbock knocked the dead ash from the bowl of his pipe.

'We both know the answer to that one, don't we?'

'The sister? Diana?'

'They were twins, laddie, weren't they? Identical twins? You said they were close. They lived together. One of them, Phoebe, was anxious to hide not merely the sex, but the name of her lover. Then there's the schoolboy, this lad, Giles Leening. He swore she had no men friends. Well, he could, after all, have been telling the truth. So could the sister. You asked her about the men in Phoebe Marriott's life, and she said there were none. It could have been a truthful answer. As far as I know, you didn't ask her whether there happened to be a woman . . . And there's a bit of confirmation, for what it may be worth. I had a word this afternoon with old Walter Bates at the Blakeney Hotel. He's one of the waiters. I've known him for years. According to what he told me, the Marriott girls were in there quite often. Called in of an evening. Always sat at the same table, always on their own. Spoke to no one else. He never remembers seeing a man in their sights.'

Tench frowned.

'Two sisters? Wouldn't that be incest?'

'Incest?' Lubbock shrugged. 'I don't know whether you could call it that, or not. Incest's a misdemeanour. It carries a heavy penalty. Penal servitude for anything from three to seven years. But it's usually men who get sent down for that. It's a sentence that can be passed on a woman, but I can't say I've ever met with such a case. Sexual intercourse within the prohibited degrees of kindred. Well, what went on between these two girls was certainly within the prohibited degrees, but was it sexual intercourse? I don't know the answer to that one, Mike. What is sexual intercourse? The law's pretty vague in a case like this ... I'd forget all about it. It's not going to help you lay hands on whoever killed Phoebe Marriott, and that's your job.'

Tench was restless.

'But the whole affair's unnatural. You've got to grant that.'

'Is it?' Lubbock said. 'I wouldn't even be altogether sure about that. Identical twins, robbed of their parents, left on their own, living in the same house, clinging to one another. What could be more natural? I'm a grizzled old hand at this game of detection, laddie, so take my advice. Accept this business simply for what it is: a variation on an all too familiar theme. Consign it to the files. You're looking for a murderer, and I can't somehow think that Diana Marriott strangled her sister. She was in London, wasn't she? That means those delicate fingers of hers would have needed to stretch a devil of a way.' He tossed the diary across to Tench. 'If I were you, I'd lock that away. Put it out of your mind. It could prove to be nothing but a dangerous distraction. There's only one possibility it does open up.'

'What's that?'

'That this Marriott case could be a crime of passion. The motive could be jealousy, and the killer a woman.'

'Or a man.'

'Or a man.'

'Or even a random maniac.'

'Why not?' Lubbock reached for his matches. 'At least you could hardly class that as incredible. It happens somewhere every day in this perverted world.'

Tench took a deep breath.

'We're not getting very far, are we?' he said.

10

'Oh, I wouldn't say that. How long is it since I phoned you this morning?' Lubbock peered at the clock. 'Sixteen hours, thereabouts. It's early days yet. Listen and learn, that was always my motto. Listening's half a detective's work. Let people talk, and something at some time'll drop into place. Would you like me to give you a couple of leads?'

'I'd be delighted to get one lead, let alone two.'

'Well, I think I can maybe rustle up two. You see, laddie, this afternoon I've been letting people talk. It's surprising what you learn, if you're only prepared to listen... Didn't you say Giles Leening cycled down to Breckmarsh?'

'Last night? So he said.'

'But nobody saw him?'

'Mrs Holland, who lives two doors away, saw him set off. That was round about quarter past eight. Apparently she said he was pedalling like mad.'

'But no one saw him after that.'

'He doesn't think so. Why d'you ask?'

Lubbock blew out a rolling thunderhead of smoke.

'And this lecher-cum-drunkard, Moses Shelton. Where does he say he was?'

'Swears he was snaring rabbits down at Holkham Meals.'

'Believable?'

'No.'

'How does he say he got there?'

'Same way as young Giles. Went on his bike. That's confirmed by Mrs Holland. She saw him go off just before seven.'

'Remarkable woman, this Mrs Holland.'

'Bedridden,' said Tench. 'Watches everything from an upstairs window... We know he was down at the pub at Morston soon after that. And, according to the landlord, he left at half seven.'

'Bound for Holkham Meals.'

'That's his tale.'

'No witnesses?'

'We haven't been able to trace any yet.'

'So,' said Lubbock, 'we've got two suspects, both out on bikes. One says he was communing with himself in a windmill, the other that he was having a few quiet words with a handful of rabbits, and neither can produce a witness to verify his claim.'

'As things stand, no.'

'And, as far as you're concerned, things don't stand too happily.'

'That's a bit of an understatement.'

'Then stow this away in your memory bank, laddie. I've been chatting to one or two people in Cley, who just might have noticed something odd last night.'

'And did they?'

'Well, that's up to you to judge, but what they said may perhaps be worth following up . . . I called in on Sam Curl. He lives in one of the cottages down by the mill. Sam likes to call himself a conchologist. Makes a study of shells. He's got quite a collection. You'll usually find him at low water scouring the shingle. I checked the tide-tables at Blakeney. Low water last night was at 18.42. That's roughly a quarter to seven.'

'He was down there?'

Lubbock gave a nod.

'Went down at half-past seven. Was back in his cottage when the light began to fade. Round about half nine.'

'And he saw someone?'

'No. Unluckily for us he was working east along the beach, towards Salthouse. And anyway, when he's searching for shells, he's got his nose to the shingle. The rest of the world recedes into distance. No, he didn't notice much about comings and goings, but on the way back he saw the girl's car parked below the bank. He described it well enough. A light grey Morris Minor. He'd seen it there a number of times before. But he said there was another car parked just beyond it. A green one. Didn't bother to look at it closely. He wasn't all that interested, but it seemed to him, he said, to be a sports car of some kind. And there was a bicycle.'

'Was there now? Whereabouts?'

'Tossed down against the bank, very close to the cars.'

'Was he able to describe it?'

'Only glanced at it in passing. Said it was just an ordinary black bike. But it certainly wasn't new. Looked as if it had had a good deal of hammer. So it might be worth checking the two bikes in question: the schoolboy's and Shelton's.'

'Well, it's worth a try,' said Tench. 'I'll get Gregg to take a look at them first thing tomorrow. But the way things are going, they'll probably both be clapped out and black.'

'More than likely.' Lubbock peered into the bowl of his pipe, frowned and then knocked it out in the ashtray. 'Which makes my second lead worth a few questions. It may be nothing but another dead end, but it'd pay to make sure. I thought I'd better try to find out a bit more about this second car that Sam Curl had mentioned, so I took a walk down to the coastguard station to see Dick Woodford. I knew he'd been on duty part of last night. Not that he'd have looked for folk walking on the shingle. The sea's more his province. But he's something of a car fiend, and he's genned up on sports cars. He keeps a pre-war Bentley in a barn up at Kelling, and spends all his spare time buffing it up. So I reckoned if he'd seen this mystery car, he might be able to add a little something to what we knew already.'

'And he did.'

'Yes, he did. And more than a little. He spotted it first about half-past eight, and swears it wasn't there half an hour before that. Once he'd finished his turn of duty at nine, he went down to have a look at it before he went home. Said it was quite distinctive: a 1935 Lagonda M45 Rapide, low-slung, open-topped with massive headlamps and wide-spreading mudguards. Encyclopaedic, Dick's knowledge of cars. He gave me all the details. Apparently this model had a Meadows six-cylinder, four-and-a-half-litre engine, though I don't suppose you find that altogether fascinating.'

'Did he get the number?'

'Unfortunately not, but then again why should he? It was the car that intrigued him, not the number-plate. But he did say it was local. The registration letters were CL. That's Norwich. So it shouldn't take much tracing. There can't be many fifteen-year-old Lagondas still around.'

Tench nodded.

'I'll have it checked out.'

'Do that,' said Lubbock. 'It may have no connection with the Marriott girl, but in murder cases . . .'

'You never can tell.'

'Never. The oddest things can provide the vital clue: a screw, a ticket, a cigarette stub. I've even known a patch of cow dung provide all the answers.'

'Cow dung?'

'Cow dung. That chap who went around wringing chickens' necks. We only caught him in the end because he trod in a cowpat and carried half of it into the local pub. The landlord remembered.'

'Lucky that he did.'

'Lucky for us that he was what he was. Ex-army type. Stickler for spit and polish. Whitewashed everything down to the chain on the privy. If he'd kept any chickens, he'd have whitewashed them, too ... So remember, laddie. That spruced-up Lagonda could well be your own special patch of cow dung.'

He stretched and yawned.

'And now,' he said, 'get off back to Norwich and let me go to bed. Even retired DCIs need a few hours' sleep. Leave the case to simmer. It'll come to the boil in its own good time. Do what I used to do. Forget it till morning.'

'What time? Seven o'clock?'

Lubbock chuckled.

'Not tomorrow. Unless, of course, I find another body.'

'God forbid,' said Tench.

He spoke the words with some feeling.

11

He didn't take the direct route from Cley to Norwich. He followed the coastal road through Blakeney to Morston, and turned up to Craymere.

Just why he did so he was loath to admit, even to himself; but, pressed for a reason, he might have confessed to a sullen reluctance to let the case simmer as Lubbock would have done.

Approaching the line of cottages he slowed to a crawl. They were all in darkness. The Leenings, the Hollands, Aaron Shelton, Grace Medlicott: all of them, it seemed, had retired to their beds and locked out the world.

Even Downs House showed no glimmer of light. The curtains were closed, sealing it away from inquisitive eyes.

He switched off the engine and let the car roll gently to a halt.

Craymere.

This time last night he'd never heard of the place.

Four cottages and a bungalow. Each on the outside quite unremarkable, yet behind their walls ...

Like turning a stone and finding beneath it ... what? A dead butterfly? A host of other disconcerted residents?

But these were very odd residents indeed.

He counted them off one by one in his mind.

Miss Medlicott, eighty years old, twittering and baking her trays of ginger cakes; the gross Mrs Holland, eyes like a pair of long-focus lenses trained on the road; her self-effacing husband bearing milk and biscuits to the shrine where she sat, perpetually enthroned; Moses Shelton, lurching from pub to pub, copulating in the grass like the rabbits he snared; his father, censorious, out of patience with the self-indulgent monster he'd reared. And the Leenings: young Giles, shedding tears for a murdered girl, surrounded by the sketches that were all he had left; his sister, uncomplicated, searingly dismissive; and the mother, vague and haphazard, fractiously failing to cope with the tensions.

And then Diana Marriott . . .

Who was Diana Marriott? What kind of a woman was she? What had happened behind those curtains to strip her sister half-naked, robbed of life on a shingle bank by the sea?

Anything? Or nothing?

Was Phoebe, after all, just another random victim of some deranged killer?

He shrugged, and then, with a sudden decisive movement, started up the car and drove off towards Langham.

It had been a long day.

A hell of a long day.

For the moment he'd had enough. The case could bloody well simmer. Grow cold for all he cared.

He was going home to bed.

He drove fast, as if, for this night at least, he needed to put all the distance he could between himself and the complex conundrum that was Craymere.

4

CONSIDERATIONS

Ah, take one consideration with another,
A policeman's lot is not a happy one.

Sir W.S. Gilbert: *The Pirates of Penzance*

1

The Chief Super sat back and interlaced his fingers underneath his chin.

'Suspects, but no firm leads.'

'Not so far, sir,' said Tench.

'What's Ledward got to say?'

'Preliminary report, sir. Came in this morning. Estimates death took place between nine and ten in the evening. Manual strangulation. No signs of recent intercourse, but the girl wasn't a virgin.'

'No mutilations?'

'Apparently not.'

'But there's still nothing to say that this wasn't a random murder.'

'I'm afraid not, sir. We need a good deal more evidence before we can rule it out.'

'This relationship between the girl and her sister . . .'

'It's just conjecture at the moment. We can't prove anything.'

'So it may be non-existent, or even immaterial.'

'That's possible.'

'But not probable?'

Tench gave a shrug.

'It's only my opinion, but I think there was a sexual connection between them. Whether it has any bearing on the case, that's another matter.'

'Then better to press ahead and eliminate the suspects.'

'That's what we're intending to do right away.'

'So who's doing what?'

'Gregg's off to Craymere to examine the two bikes, and Rayner's checking out the number-plate on the Lagonda. Lock's already out at Blakeney Point. He's taking a statement from the warden and interviewing Turner, the assistant who's out there. Ellison's seeing the other man, Phelps. He lives in Blakeney. Then he's going down to Cley to see Curl and Woodford. Spurgeon's on duty at the incident room, and we've got the girl's clothing back from the lab. Sue Gradwell's returning it to the sister in Craymere.'

'And asking one or two pertinent questions?'

'She may do, sir, yes. As woman to woman she may get the answers we can't hope to get. I've told her to weigh things up. Her opinion may be useful.'

'And you and McKenzie?'

'We're going to tackle Moses Shelton.'

Hastings nodded.

'Ruling out the lesbian connection,' he said, 'he's your main suspect?'

'He has to be, sir, yes. He's been telling us a pack of lies about where he was at the time of the murder. There's obviously something he doesn't want us to know.'

'You've got him here, in the cells?'

'Yes, he's facing a number of charges already. I think we've got enough on him to squeeze out the truth.'

'Have you seen Ransome yet?'

'Yes, sir. Spoke to him this morning. I've given him a description of the girl and her car. He's putting out an appeal for witnesses in the *EDP*. I also gave him all the details about the Lagonda, but told him to hold his fire till we'd interviewed the driver. We should know who that is as soon as Rayner's done the check.'

'I suppose he could just be an innocent visitor strolling on the beach.'

'He could be, sir, yes, but even if he was, he may have seen something. He was there at the right time.'

The Chief Super seemed to be thinking.

'Lock ... You say he's out at the Point?'

'Yes, sir. Spurgeon ran him down to Cley at eight o'clock this morning. If it hadn't been low water, we'd have arranged with one of the boatmen to take him.'

'And how will he get back?'

'He'll walk along the shingle to Cley, and Ellison'll pick him up. It was either that or waiting for the next high tide, and that's not till half-past two.'

Hastings frowned.

'I'm not too keen on this reliance on local boatmen. Apart from anything else it's a waste of time. You'd be better off having access to a boat of your own. Something a bit faster. You never know. You may need to whip out there at speed.'

'That's more than a possibility.'

'You need a boat on tap in case of an emergency. One that'll get you out there and back while these crab boats are waiting to fill up with visitors.' He stroked his chin. 'You wouldn't remember Larry Cotterill? No, before your time. Great pal of mine. Chief Inspector at Lynn. Retired just after the war and went to live at Glandford. Keeps a speedboat at Blakeney. He's the chap to help. Leave it to me. I'll give him a ring.'

'It'd certainly be useful.'

'Need to muster all the resources we reasonably can. And save time where we can.' He paused. 'These two sisters. They were twins.'

'Identical twins.'

'Physically alike.'

'Very much so. Diana Marriott said that people who didn't really know them couldn't tell them apart.'

'Then there's another possibility you should perhaps be awake to.'

'What's that, sir?'

'The chance', said Hastings, 'that someone set out to murder one of the sisters and got the other by sheer miscalculation. Mistaken identity. It's happened before; and out on Blakeney Point, in a fading light, it could have happened again.' He smiled. 'It's just a thought, Mike, but bear it in mind ... Have you talked again to Lubbock?'

'Had a word with him last night, sir.'

'What's his view of the case?'

'He suggested we might have to look for a woman. Had a notion there might be a lesbian triangle.'

'And he could well be right,' the Chief Super said. 'I've known it happen with men, so why not with women? Murder's an irrational crime. People act from the most peculiar motives. We had a chap once who went round killing chickens ...'

'Really, sir?' said Tench.

He did his best to sound surprised, but discretion proved costly.

It was another ten minutes before he made his escape to the interview room.

2

Moses Shelton, dishevelled, unshaven and still bleary-eyed, proved as obdurate as he had been the day before.

Tench faced him across the table in the interview room. McKenzie lounged against the wall. A constable sat in the corner, armed with a notebook and pencil.

'Sit down, Mr Shelton.'

Moses grudgingly swung back the chair and lowered himself on to it. He sat with his legs apart, glowering at Tench.

'What d'ye want o' me now?' he said.

'I have to remind you', said Tench, 'that you're still under caution. Anything you say may be given in evidence.'

'Ye can give it to Jack Mellon's pigs fer all I bloody care.'

'You're facing serious charges, Mr Shelton, and there may be more to come, so think carefully before you answer.'

Moses muttered darkly. Tench looked him up and down with obvious disrelish.

'You said something, Mr Shelton?'

'Said I ent heard a single bloody question as yet.'

'You will. If you listen.'

'Then get on wi' askin'. Ye're wastin' yer breath.'

Tench raised his eyebrows.

'Where would you like me to begin?'

'Tek yer bloody pick. What the hell do it matter?'

'Shall we say last Tuesday evening? Half-past six? Where were you then?'

'I' bed, like as not.'

'But you went out, Mr Shelton.'

'Aye. Mebbe so.'

'What time was that?'

'Sevenish, I reckon. Mos' nights it be seven.'

'And where did you go?'

'Said already, ent I?'

'Not to me, Mr Shelton.'

'Ye want it all agen?'

'I want a truthful account of how you spent every minute of the time from when you left Craymere to when you got back.'

Moses turned even more sullen than before.

'Went to th'Meals, didn't I?'
'Holkham Meals?'
'Aye.'
'That's close on eight miles. How did you get there?'
'Well, I didn' bloody walk.'
'I wasn't suggesting you did, Mr Shelton.' Tench was all smoothness.
'Went on me bike, didn' I?'
'You own a bicycle, do you?'
'Reckon I'd not be ridin' it else,' Moses said. 'You shanny, or wha'?'
'Just trying to get at the truth, Mr Shelton. This bike of yours then. How old would it be?'
'Three year, mebbe four.'
'D'you use it a lot?'
'When I don' walk.'
'Look after it, do you?'
Moses raised his eyes to the ceiling.
'Now wha' th'bloody hell be tha' supposed ter mean?'
'Clean it? Polish it?'
'When it be mucky.'
'What colour is it?'
'Black. Least it look black ter me. An' there's a lamp, an' a bell, an' one o'they things at th'back as shine red. What else d'ye want ter know?'
'When you got to Holkham Meals, what did you do?'
'Were rabbitin', weren' I?'
'How long were you there?'
'Mebbe an hour.'
'And after that, what?'
'Come back ter Morston.'
'The Black Dog?'
'Aye.'
'What time did you get there?'
'Half nine, I reckon.'
'And left when?'
'Soon as ol' Thober shut up th'bar.'
'Half-past ten?'
'Musta bin.'
'And then you did what?'
'Went walkin'.'
'Where to?'
'Out Cockthorpe way.'

'On your own?'
Exasperation showed on Moses Shelton's face.
'Gorblast it, no. Why'd I be tekkin' a walk on me own?'
'You had someone with you?'
'Aye.'
'Who was it?'
'Said already, ent I?'
'Then say it again, Mr Shelton, just for me.'
'It were Jenny Muckloe, weren' it?'
'And where did you go?'
'Went i' Jack Mellon's barn.'
Tench sat back and looked him straight in the eyes.
'You're asking me to believe that you took Jenny Muckloe into Jack Mellon's barn?'
'It's God's honest truth. An' don' you be tellin' me they be passin' laws now agen two folk a-kiddlin'.'
There was a pause.
'So you kiddled Jenny Muckloe in Jack Mellon's barn. What time did you get home?'
'Reckon it were mebbe midnight. Why you axin' all this squit? Tuesday night I were tekkin' rabbits. Ent nothin' so very fearsome i' tha'. What's to a couple o' rabbits? Meals is all coney land. There be more o' th'little buggers there ner flies on a muck field.'
Tench glanced towards McKenzie. The sergeant shrugged himself off the wall and sat down behind the table. The two of them stared at Shelton.
'Moses,' McKenzie said, 'you're a fisherman, aren't you?'
'Aye. What's it ter you?'
'What d'you fish for?'
Moses scowled at him.
'Fish fer whelks, wha' d'ye think.'
'Not cod?'
'Ye mus' be right dawzled. Why bloody cod?'
'Because in the last ten minutes' – McKenzie leaned forward – 'you've talked a bigger load of codswallop than I've heard in ten years. You're a liar, Moses, aren't you? You lie in bed, you lie in ditches, you lie in barns, and now, to cap it all, you're lying to us here to try and save your own skin.'
Shelton was still determined to brazen it out.
'Ye're romentin',' he said. 'If ye think I be lyin', then you bloody prove it.'
Tench turned to McKenzie. He was deceptively casual.

'I think we'd better start again, don't you, Mac?' he said. 'Before we charge him with murder.'

3

To say that Moses Shelton was shocked into silence would be falsifying fact. He was stung into further protest.

'What ye bibblin' about?' he said. 'I ent done no murder.'

'You can hardly expect us to believe that,' said Tench. 'You've shown no respect for the truth up to now.'

'Murder? Wha' murder?'

'At some time between eight o'clock on Tuesday night and six o'clock on Wednesday morning, a young woman was strangled. You refuse to tell us truthfully just where you were between those two times. We can only conclude that you've a great deal to hide.'

'I were down at Holkham Meals, then at th'pub, an' arter that i' Mellon's barn.'

'So you say.'

'But we can prove', McKenzie said, 'that you're a downright liar.'

'Then ye'd best get on wi' it.'

'And you'd better listen.' McKenzie's voice was suddenly sharp. It had an edge like a razor. 'You've lied to us, Moses, on four separate counts. According to you, at seven o'clock on Tuesday, you rode direct to Holkham Meals. We know that isn't true. We've spoken to Thober. At seven o'clock you were in the Black Dog, and you didn't leave till half-past.'

'Wha's ter say he ent romentin'?'

'To be fair with you, nothing. But if it comes to a choice between accepting your word against that of Mr Thober, you've about as much chance as a celluloid rabbit tossed into hell.'

'Tha's bloody good, that is. Ye talk o' bein' fair . . .'

'Second count,' McKenzie said. 'You tell us you got back to the pub at half-past nine and you were there till closing-time. That's another lie. Neither the landlord nor the barmaid, Miss Margaret Rooney, set eyes on you at all. They certainly never served you a drink. Are you telling me you sat in the bar for an hour without having a jar? I find that hard to believe. Have you taken the pledge?'

'No, an' I ent seen any pink bloody rabbits.' Moses's temper was showing audible signs of wear. 'Tha' Meg Rooney she allus be shanny. Dorn' know a bee from a bull's arse, she dorn'.'

'Seemed a bright enough girl to me.' McKenzie was clearly enjoying himself. 'What was it she called you? Oh, yes, that was it. A two-legged pig.'

'Slummockin' gret mawther. She be thick as a hedge.'

'And some hedges, Moses, are thicker than others. Some are so thick you can't see through them straight. Like yours last Tuesday. Old crows look like goslings.'

'An' goslings like kittywitches. Aye. Mebbe so. Wha' th'hell is all this? Ye're slarverin' on lak a winnickin' babby.'

'What I'm moving towards smoothly,' McKenzie said, 'is count number three. You told Sergeant Gregg you were seen by Jenny Muckloe up at Garret Hill, and she went with you to Mellon's barn for a bit of slap-and-tickle. You did say that, didn't you?'

'What if a did?'

McKenzie shook his head sadly.

'You're so much of an idiot you must think we are too. We know Jenny Muckloe.'

Moses feigned surprise.

'Weren' it her?'

'No, it wasn't. And you know damn well it wasn't.'

'Musta got it wrong then. Got wax in me lugs.' He poked a finger in his ear.

'I'll ignore that.' McKenzie was curtly dismissive. 'Count number four. You said you got home at midnight. That's another lie.'

'There were a clock strikin' twelve . . .'

'Not according to your dear old dad. He says it was nearer four.'

'So,' said Tench, 'it's like this. You've lied your way through from seven o'clock Tuesday evening to four on Wednesday morning. That's nine vital hours, and for eight and a half of them we don't know where you were. What are you trying to hide from us? Tell us that, Mr Shelton.'

'Ent hidin' nothin'.' The response was just as churlish as ever.

'Then tell us where you were, and make it the truth, and fast.'

Moses scowled at the floor.

There was silence.

Tench waited. Then he pushed back his chair and stood up.

'Take him away and charge him, Mac. This time with murder.'

'Ent never done no murder.'

'That's another lie, is it?'

'No, it bloody ent.' Moses suddenly came alive. 'Mebbe I seed her. But there ent no crime i' lookin'.'

Tench sat down again.

'Are you telling me now that you saw the murdered girl?'

'Aye, ten foot away. Not a deal more'n tha'.'
'Where was this?'
'Mebbe it mighta bin out Blakeney Point.'
'And did she see you?'
'Reckon not.' Moses grinned. 'She'd have a job. She were dead.'

4

It took them another half-hour to unravel Moses's latest version of events.

He'd apparently intended to ride straight to Holkham, but passing the Black Dog and seeing the door to the bar standing open had reminded him that he'd developed a thirst. He'd popped in to quench it and stayed for half an hour, at the end of which time he'd set off for the Meals. He'd reached Holkham Gap about quarter past eight, hidden his bike among the pine trees and worked round his snares. That had taken him something like an hour; then he'd ridden back to Wells and called in at the Norfolk Wherry. He knew the landlord well, and he'd promised to let him have a couple of rabbits. He'd handed them over, had a pint in the snug and then made off to Morston.

At that point McKenzie sniffed and said it was all a load of old bolsom. He frankly didn't believe that Moses could leave a pub after only one pint.

Moses himself was indignant. He were tellin' th'truth, weren' he? One pint, that were all, an' then he were off. They could go an' ask Bill Bastable. He were the landlord.

And had he bribed this Bastable with something more than a couple of rabbits?

No, he bloody hadn'. Why would he do tha'?

Then why hadn't he stopped at the Wherry till it closed?

He were aimin' ter get back an' have one or two at th'Black Dog, weren' he?

Then why didn't he?

Because far side o' Stiffkey there were a nail on th'road. Ran over it, didn' he? Burst his tyre. Had to push th'bloody bike all th'way into Morston, an' by tha' time owd Thober'd rung his bell an' called time. Th'pub were locked up.

And what time was that?

Reckoned it musta bin round about eleven.

That, Tench pointed out, still left a full five hours unaccounted for. Why hadn't he gone straight home?

He'd had other things ter do.

What other things?

Check his snares at th'Point.

Was he saying he had snares out on Blakeney Point?

Aye. Thousands o' rabbits there. Best place o' th'lot.'

And he was checking them at midnight?

Had ter wait fer th'tide.

But at midnight? In the dark? Didn't he and his father ferry visitors to Blakeney Point during the day? Why not check them then?

Had done, till a year back. But it were tha' bugger Langrick.

The warden?

Aye. Cetched him at it, didn' he? Said he'd have him locked up if he found him there agen.

Did he mean to say that the warden had warned him off?

Too bloody true, he had. Botty little bastard. Fer two pins he'd a gan him a ding roun' th'lug.

So since then he'd always checked his snares at night?

Had to, hadn' he?

And that was what he'd done at midnight on Tuesday? Taken the boat to Blakeney Point on the tide?

Aye. That were what he'd meant ter do, an' that were what he'd done. Moored at Pinchen's Creek an' then checked his snares. He'd been all but finished when he'd seen there were a body.

Tench still seemed unconvinced.

'And what exactly did you see?'

'It were this young lass, weren' it?'

'Go on.'

'She were down among th'kittywitches, tits all bare an' most else as well.'

'Did you touch her?'

'Not a bloody chance. Jus' took one look, an' off back ter th'boat.'

'Why didn't you report what you'd seen?'

'I'd a looked well, wouldn' I? An' Langrick waitin' ter get me wi' a chopper.'

'So you thought the best thing was to lie about being there?'

'What would you a done, blast it?'

'You realize you've been withholding information, Mr Shelton? That's another charge against you.'

Moses shrugged his shoulders.

'So bloody wha'?'

'Did you recognize the girl?'

'Tha's bloody likely. Ten foot away, i' th'dark, wi' all they birds? It weren' any time fer lookin' tha' close.'

'Then for all you knew, she might not have been dead.'

'Flat on her back at two o'clock of a mornin', smothered i' birds an' her knickers in a twist?' Moses was scathing. 'Course she were bloody dead.'

Tench gave him one last disparaging look; then he turned to McKenzie.

'Take him back to the cells, Mac,' he said. 'I've had enough of Mr Shelton for one bright morning.'

He sat there, deep in thought, till the sergeant returned.

'Well,' he said, 'what d'you think?'

'No dice,' said McKenzie. 'What's your opinion?'

'Well, Gregg's out at Craymere tracking down his bike. Not that that's likely to tell us a deal. If he did run over a nail, he's probably fixed it. The man we need to check with is this chap Bastable, the landlord at the Wherry. If he's a credible witness and he says that Shelton was there at half-past nine, then we'll have to rule him out. There's no way he could possibly have been at Blakeney Point between nine o'clock and ten.'

'So where does that leave us?'

'Up Morston Creek, I'd imagine,' said Tench, 'and stuck in the mud.'

And, it seemed, without a paddle.

Rayner was waiting in the CID room.

'This car, sir. The Lagonda.'

Tench pulled out a chair and sat down at his desk.

'Tell me about it.'

'It's registered to a Richard James Crawley. Lives at Upper Sheringham. Repton Lodge.'

'Then we'd better have a word with him.'

'That's not all, sir,' said Rayner. 'It was reported stolen on Tuesday evening.'

'Stolen?' Tench stared at him. 'Stolen where from?'

'The Blakeney Hotel.'

'And has it been found?'

'Yes, sir. Yesterday morning.'

'Where, for God's sake?'

'On the edge of a wood near Bradenham.'

'Oh, marvellous,' said Tench. 'We've got a car that was parked right next to the murdered girl's at exactly the time when somebody killed her, and now we find it was pinched and we don't know who the bloody hell it was that was driving it.'

McKenzie jerked his head towards the door.

'D'you want me to go and see this chap Crawley?'

'No, Mac.' Tench pushed himself up from the desk. 'I think both of us had better take a look at Mr Crawley.'

5

Upper Sheringham was not, as its name suggested, a more exalted section of the seaside town. It lay a mile inland, tucked away in a fold of a wooded ridge that rose to the dizzy Norfolk height of three hundred feet, and revealed itself as an old-world village of blue shingle cottages clustered round a fourteenth-century church.

McKenzie, who knew it well, regarded its charms with a jaundiced eye – he preferred the bright lights to rustic simplicity – but Tench, whose journeys to Cromer and beyond had always confined themselves to main roads, was predictably impressed. It wasn't what he'd expected.

Nor was Mr Crawley.

Inquiries in the village produced first the response that Repton Lodge was out towards the Hall, on the edge of the park, and second that they must be looking for Colonel Dick.

'Colonel Dick?' said McKenzie. 'Army man then, is he?'

'Looks like it.' Tench nodded. 'Probably one of those young tearaways who got quick promotion during the war. Gets a kick out of pounding the Norfolk lanes in a high-powered car.'

His prediction was considerably wide of the mark.

Repton Lodge was indeed on the edge of the park, a large Georgian house set back from the road, hidden by trees and approached by a winding drive that only revealed it at last by a steep dramatic swing between walls of rhododendrons.

The Lagonda was clearly visible, parked on a gravelled terrace in front of the pillared porch, and standing beside it, armed with a hosepipe and spraying the wheels, was a tall, straight-backed man with a shock of white hair, plus-fours and a hacking jacket.

Hearing the sound of the police car crunching the gravel, he turned towards them, disclosing a swarthy face seamed like a tessellated pavement and a waxed moustache the points of which extended to the line of his cheeks.

He then raised a hand, strode firmly to a large conservatory on the edge of the terrace, turned off a tap and made his way back with an equally decisive step.

'Ha!' he said. 'Police. About Mirabelle, is it?'

'Colonel Crawley?' said Tench.

'Brigadier actually. But that was thirty years ago. Long gone and forgotten.' The moustache points quivered, but more in amusement than anything else. 'Call me Dick. All the Shannocks do.'

'Shannocks?' Tench was baffled.

'Folk who live in the village. Damn it all, man, you never heard of a Shannock?'

'I know I should have done, sir . . . '

'But you haven't. Never mind. Doesn't matter. Now's the time to learn. This is Upper Shannock. Down there' – he waved a hand vaguely towards the sea – 'that's Lower Shannock. Has been since way before I was born, and that's eighty years back . . . Mirabelle, is it?'

'Mirabelle, sir?'

'The car.' He laid an affectionate hand on one of the spreading mudguards. 'Call her Mirabelle. Always have. Named her after a girl I met once in Amiens. That was back in '16. She had deep, lustful eyes and lips that sucked you in like a vacuum cleaner. Married to a Frog, of course. Most of 'em were. Come in and have a drink.'

'Sorry, sir. On duty.'

'Oh, be blowed to duty. Always shot better on a couple of snifters. Nothing like a dram of Scotch to steady the trigger finger. What's your name?'

'Tench, sir. Detective Chief Inspector, and this is Detective Sergeant McKenzie.'

'Well, you'll have to come inside, Tench. It's time for my morning sundowner. Not to be missed on any account. Not even for Rosie.'

'Rosie, sir?'

'The Chief Constable. Young Will Rosebery. You know him, I suppose.'

'Not intimately, sir.'

'Not to worry,' said the brigadier. 'Step this way.'

He led them through the porch and down a high, wide hall lined with animals' heads: wild boar, tigers, koodoos, impalas and numerous other species Tench couldn't identify; and then, turning left and doubling back along a couple of corridors, into a small, square room hung with mildewed prints of regimental groups. The only furniture it contained was a low coffee-table stranded in the centre; three easy chairs set at angles around it; and a steel filing cabinet bolted to the wall beside a narrow sash window.

The cabinet had two drawers. He pulled open the top one, extracted three whisky glasses and placed them on the table. From the bottom one he took out a bottle of Scotch, and poured three large measures. He handed one to Tench, another to McKenzie, and then raised the third.

'The King,' he said, and tossed it back.

'The King.' McKenzie also downed his at a gulp.

The brigadier poured him another tot and one for himself. Then he flopped into one of the chairs and stretched out his legs.

'Sit down,' he said. 'Make yourselves at home. Relax and be merry. Can't think what the devil you've come for though. Thought I'd given all the dope to that sergeant chap at Bradenham.'

'I'm sure you did, sir,' said Tench. He set down his glass. 'But since then, I'm afraid, the situation's changed.'

'Changed? In what way?'

'We think your car could have been used in the commission of a crime.'

'You mean to make a getaway?'

'Possibly, sir, yes. You may have heard that a girl was murdered on Tuesday night out at Blakeney Point.'

The brigadier nodded.

'Damned abominable business. Don't know what the country's coming to.'

'Well, sir, it's like this. At the time of the murder the Lagonda was seen at Cley, parked next to the girl's Morris.'

'You telling me Mirabelle's been harbouring a killer?'

'We don't know that for certain, sir, but we need to trace the thief. So perhaps you'd be good enough to repeat to us what you told the police at Bradenham. It seems you left the car outside the Blakeney Hotel.'

'That's right. I did.'

'You had business there?'

'No. Went there for dinner.'

'On your own, sir?'

'Yes and no. Drove there alone. Had dinner with friends. Randy Merrick and Ollie Osborne. Always meet 'em there. Celebration do.'

He drained his second whisky.

'Mafeking,' he said.

6

'Mafeking?'

'Relief of. We were there, all three of us. Celebrate every year.'

Tench, whose time at Cambridge had been spent reading History, was, on this occasion, more puzzled than baffled.

'With all due respect, sir, wasn't that in May?'

'Damned right it was.' The brigadier growled. 'May the seventeenth. Final of the billiards tournament at the club. Won by Blinky Southworth, or was it Dasher Potts? Immaterial anyway. We've always met in June. Don't ask me why. Special do this year. Fiftieth anniversary. Had to be there on time.'

'What time, sir, exactly?'

'Nineteen-thirty. Twenty hundred hours dinner.'

'And whereabouts did you park the car?'

'Side of the Blakeney. Always do.'

'And that was the last you saw of it?'

'Never gave her a thought till twenty-three hundred. Far too busy till then. Drinks first and then dinner, coffee in the lounge, a couple of brandies, and we had a long palaver about old times: chaps like Dusty Rhodes and Mad Boy Mallalieu. Broke up at last: it was yawning time. Paid the score. Went out. Looked for Mirabelle. Gone. Not a damned trace. So rang your lads in Norwich.'

'And no one at the Blakeney had seen the car taken?'

'Asked a few questions. Not a glimpse of the scoundrel. Wish there had been, old boy. Sort of feller needs blasting from the mouth of a cannon.'

'Must have been stolen soon after you got there,' McKenzie said. 'It was spotted at Cley around half-past eight.'

'The devil it was!' The waxed moustache bristled. 'Drove her away in broad daylight, did he? Damned thieving blackguard. Pity we didn't see him. We'd have frog-marched him down to the quay and tossed him in the mud. Might have saved that girl's life.'

Tench shook his head.

'We can't assume a connection yet, sir,' he said, 'but we need to examine the car for forensic evidence. Perhaps you'd lock it in the garage till our men can get out here.'

The brigadier waved a dismissive hand.

'No point,' he said cheerfully. 'Had to get her spruced up. Big day today. She's been washed down, dusted, vacuumed and polished. Up at the crack of dawn and no effort spared. You won't find a speck of dust inside or out, let alone a fingerprint.'

'All the same, sir . . .'

'Can't be done. Not a chance. Sorry, old boy. Promised young Dolly Dearing I'd pick her up at twelve. Officer's word's sacrosanct, even in peacetime.' He pulled a heavy, gun-metal watch from his pocket, held it to the light and sprang to his feet. 'By Jove!' he said. 'Is it that time already? Have to dash, I'm afraid. Must get togged up. And Mirabelle needs ribbons. Wouldn't like to help by any chance, would you? No, perhaps not. Other things in mind.'

'The car should be locked up, sir . . .'

The brigadier stood firm.

'Not on, Tench,' he said. 'My apologies to Rosie, but it just can't be done. Gal's getting spliced. Have to drive her to church. Marrying another Upper Shannock, of course. They always do that. Wouldn't be seen dead in the aisle with a foreigner. Be good chaps and let yourselves out.' He was already in the doorway. 'Two right turns and a sprint down the hall. Don't need a compass.'

With that he disappeared, only to thrust his head back again round the door jamb.

'Reception, Red Lion, thirteen-thirty. No need to dress up. Working clobber accepted. Come as you are. Everyone welcome. Barring Lower Shannocks. You're not from there, are you? No? Thought not. Come as friends of the bride. First drinks are free. Find me at the bar.'

He vanished a second time.

Tench gave a sigh.

'Helpful,' he said.

'Quite a character, though.'

'One of a rapidly diminishing breed. The English eccentric. Trouble is, Mac, we're still up Morston Creek.' He gave a shrug of frustration. 'Well, we're doing no good here. Let's go and take a look at the car.'

They circled round Mirabelle. She positively gleamed. Tench looked inside.

'Reckon he was right. If we called in the boffins, they wouldn't get much joy.'

'Waste of time and resources,' McKenzie said. 'Rosie wouldn't approve.'

'Then there's only one thing to do.'

'We could go to this reception. Cheer ourselves up. Honorary Shannocks.'

'Tempting, but no. We'd better check with Bradenham. They must have sniffed around the car before they handed it back, and we need to take a look at the spot where they found it.'

'Last time I was in Bradenham,' McKenzie said gloomily, 'it rained cats and dogs.'

Tench looked up at the cloudless sky.

'Not this time, Mac,' he said. 'It's Dolly Dearing's day. I've a feeling we're going to get something more festive.'

'Like what, for instance?'

'Pennies from heaven? Newly minted, like a set of fresh clues?'

McKenzie seemed to sink deeper into gloom.

'You'll be lucky,' he said. 'I once bought a packet of fags in Bradenham. Got a couple of Irish coins in the change.'

7

Sue Gradwell was expecting no such blessings. As she drove into Morston and turned up the road to Craymere, her feelings were much the same as Gregg's had been when he'd followed the same route the morning before. Returning a murder victim's clothes to a grieving relative wasn't exactly the kind of job she'd joined the force to do. It was almost as unpleasant as actually breaking the news of a death to the next-of-kin.

It wasn't that she was squeamish. Three years on the beat had inured her to death in many different forms. She didn't faint at the sight of blood, or when sheets were drawn back from battered mortuary bodies. She'd attended post-mortems and stayed on her feet, but she still felt, like Gregg, that bringing grief to the living demanded a degree of inhumanity that she didn't possess, and which, moreover, she'd no desire to acquire.

Not that she expected Diana Marriott to show much emotion at the sight of her sister's clothes. As the only woman member of the Norwich CID, there'd been numerous occasions when she'd had to hold the hands of bereaved wives and mothers till some relative or close friend had come to relieve her. She'd tended weeping sisters, but she'd never known one who'd recovered her composure quite so swiftly. There'd been tears from her, yes, but they'd been few and brushed away brusquely with a small pocket handkerchief.

No, she'd said, she didn't want anyone to stay with her. She preferred to be on her own. Then she'd straightened her back, changed her clothes, combed her hair and emerged from the bathroom to face the Chief's questions with an equanimity that Sue Gradwell had felt was unnatural. It just hadn't been genuine. The responses had been just a little too prompt, the explanations too plausible. They'd made her suspicious, and so had the diary. She'd been certain then, and she was quite as certain now, that there was more to Diana Marriott than her apparent self-control had seemed to imply.

She braked the car to a halt in front of Downs House, took the black plastic bag from the passenger seat, carried it up the path and pulled on the bell chain.

Miss Marriott let her in and replaced the phone on its hook. She was wearing the same long tan skirt that she'd worn the day before, but her hair was swept up and secured by a comb. She looked elegant, immaculate.

'I've been trying to get hold of Inspector Tench,' she said, 'but he seems to be out. When am I likely to have the car back? Perhaps you can tell me.'

'It shouldn't be long, ma'am. I'm sure the Chief'll ring you as soon as he hears from the lab.'

'Can you make some inquiries? It's very inconvenient. I have to open the shop, and it's difficult to get to Sheringham and back without it. In this part of the world, the buses hardly run with a businesslike efficiency.'

Her tone was a little too sharp for Sue Gradwell, but experience had taught her that soft words often smoothed away frustration.

'I can try to find out, ma'am, and I do have instructions to take a look at the shop. I'm sure the Chief wouldn't mind if I ran you down to Sheringham.'

Miss Marriott smiled. The tension relaxed.

'That really would be helpful,' she said. 'The thing is: there'll be customers wondering what's happened.'

'Oh, I'm sure they'll have heard, ma'am. They're bound to make allowances. People understand.'

'Perhaps they do, yes. But I'll be happier at the shop. You know how it is, Constable. At times like this, you're better doing something than moping around. I have to get back to work. I'm doing myself and others no good stuck out here at Craymere . . . You wanted to see me?'

'Yes, ma'am.'

'More questions?'
'No, not this time.'
'Then what was it you wanted?'
Sue Gradwell held up the plastic bag.
'I'm sorry to have to do this, ma'am, but it is routine.'
Diana Marriott stared at the bag. She seemed reluctant to touch it.
'Phoebe's clothes?'
'That's right, ma'am. We'd like you to check them. Make sure there's nothing missing.'
'How could there be?'
'Well, ma'am, there have been cases . . .'
'You mean whoever killed Phoebe could have walked off with something?'
'It has been known to happen, ma'am. And it is important. If there is something missing, it could provide a clue.'
'Yes, of course.' Miss Marriott still stared at the bag. She made no move to take it. 'You'd better bring it to the table.'
She cleared a vase of flowers from the polished top. Sue Gradwell dropped the bag on the table, untied the neck and began to count out the contents, item by item.
'One pair of rubber shoes . . . I presume they are Phoebe's, ma'am?'
Miss Marriott glanced at them.
'Yes, they're hers.'
'One pair of white socks . . . a blue skirt . . . a white blouse . . .'
'Yes, they're all Phoebe's.'
'And a pair of pink briefs.'
There was a pause.
'Is that all?'
Sue Gradwell looked inside the bag.
'That's the lot, ma'am.'
'Let me see.'
Miss Marriott took the bag, turned it upside down and shook it. She handed it back.
'Then there is something missing.'
'There is?'
'Where's her bra?'
'Perhaps she wasn't wearing one.'
Miss Marriott shook her head.
'Not Phoebe,' she said. 'She'd never go running on the beach without a bra.'

8

'It had been a hot day, and it was still very warm. Maybe she left it off.'

'No, she wouldn't have done that. Not when she was running. She needed the support. She wasn't happy without it . . . Could it have been missed?'

'When the squad searched the area? No, ma'am, most unlikely. They're always very thorough.'

'Then where is it?'

Sue Gradwell bit her lip.

'I don't know, ma'am, but we do need to find it.' She took out her notebook. 'You'd better give me some details. What make of bra was it?'

'A Berlei Undalift. We both wear the same.'

'What size?'

'A 34B. But this one was different.'

'Different, ma'am?'

'Yes. It was a special design.'

'Special in what way?'

'Phoebe had adapted it.'

'You mean it was a Berlei as bought in a shop, but she'd made some alterations?'

'Yes, that's right.'

'What had she done, exactly?'

'She'd made it more dependable.'

'Dependable?'

'Yes. You know the trouble with bras. The shoulder-straps slip. Yours must have slipped. Then there's no support. You may as well not be wearing one. For Phoebe and me it was quite a problem. We've got sloping shoulders. When we went out running, we were continually hitching the damn things up. Phoebe said it only needed a simple adjustment. She couldn't understand why the manufacturers hadn't designed one and put it on the market. She was sure it would sell. Women running or playing tennis. You know the sort of thing.'

Sue Gradwell nodded.

'It sounds a good idea. So what did she do?'

'She unpicked the straps at the back and crossed them, but that didn't seem to work. They still seemed to slip, so she lengthened them and then linked them at the back to make a letter X. She said that solved the problem. She was going to do mine in just the same way.'

'How many of her own had she done?'

'Only the one. She was trying it out.'

'So the one she was wearing was quite distinctive.'

'In the sense that there wasn't another one like it, it must have been unique.'

'And you're sure she was wearing that particular bra?'

'I haven't checked in her drawers, but she must have been, yes.'

'Can you look and make sure?'

'I think we'd both better look,' Miss Marriott said. 'Then there won't be any doubt.'

They riffled through the drawers.

'No, it's not here. She must have had it on.'

'And there isn't another.' Sue Gradwell frowned. 'That makes things awkward.'

'How does it do that? I'd have thought it was a help.'

'Well, in a way it is, but I'm pretty sure the Chief'll want to run an appeal for information in the *EDP*. As it is, we can give them a verbal description, but that's about all. It'd have been far better if we could have let them have a photograph or even perhaps a drawing. You know what I mean, ma'am. Visual communication.'

Miss Marriott closed the drawers.

'Well, there is one person who might have a drawing.'

'Who would that be, ma'am?'

'The Leening boy. Giles. He and Phoebe were working together on the project. I know he made some sketches.'

'And you think he'll still have them?'

'He must have them, yes. They were hoping to sell the idea to one of the manufacturers. Phoebe had a notion it might be worth money. If it turned out that way, we were aiming to buy a bigger shop, or open another one somewhere else. Maybe in Norwich.'

Sue Gradwell was brooding.

'I think', she said, 'I'd better see Giles Leening.'

'He'll be out at school now.'

'That's at Holt?'

'Yes, at Mountfield.'

'What time does he get home?'

'I think round about five. He goes on his bike.'

'It's a long time to wait.' She looked at her watch. 'I'll have to talk to the Chief. You've a phone at the shop?'

'Oh, yes.'

'Then I'll run you down to Sheringham and ring him from there. He should be back by then. Will that be all right?'

'Perfectly all right. And you'll mention the car?'

Sue Gradwell breathed deeply, but, she hoped, inaudibly.

'I'll ring the lab myself, ma'am. If they've finished, you can come back to Norwich with me and we'll pick it up there.'

'That's very good of you, Constable.' Miss Marriott smiled at her again. 'I didn't know the police could be quite so accommodating.'

'It is your car, ma'am.' Sue Gradwell was bland but discreetly unresponsive. 'We borrowed it. It's our duty to see that it's returned. I'm quite sure the Chief Inspector would approve.'

She turned towards the door.

'Shall we go, ma'am?' she said.

9

Tench and McKenzie weren't having much luck.

It hadn't rained in Bradenham, but neither had clues dropped out of the sky.

The duty sergeant there confirmed that the Lagonda had been found at Primrose Spinney, a mile and a half out on the Thetford road. The local constable at Winford had spotted it on his rounds. Young chap, Keith Okelbie. Just joined the force. They'd taken a look at it, yes, but it had seemed to be undamaged, so they'd rung up the owner, an old chap near Sheringham, and he'd picked it up the same day. They'd had him check the interior and he'd confirmed that nothing else had been stolen. Seemed glad to find it was still in one piece, and they'd been only too happy to get it off their hands. Fingerprints? No. They hadn't bothered with them. It was probably just some youngsters out on a spree. Oh, they wanted to see the Spinney? Then they'd best contact Okelbie. He lived down at Winford. Police house there. Easy enough to find.

But Constable Okelbie hadn't proved all that easy to find. He'd been out on a case, and it had taken them another half-hour to track him down. At Primrose Spinney they'd stood on the edge of a clump of trees and stared at the ground. Baked hard by the sun, it had revealed precisely nothing, not even a set of tyre marks, and they'd driven back to Norwich with all McKenzie's forebodings confirmed and with

Tench in deep suspicion that the case of Phoebe Marriott was, in some unaccountable way, slipping out of his grasp.

He wasn't therefore in the best of tempers when, back at the station, Gregg greeted him with the news that he'd inspected both bikes with inconclusive results. Moses Shelton's, in a shed at the back of his Craymere cottage, was black, rusted over in several places and had a flat front tyre, which had resisted all his strenuous efforts to pump it up. Looking at it more closely, he'd discovered that a nail had gone straight through the tread and punctured the inner tube. And old Aaron Shelton hadn't been much help. Didn't know exactly when it had happened. Said he hadn't set eyes on the machine for a week, and, according to Gregg, didn't seem to care if he never saw it again, or his son, for that matter.

To check on Giles Leening's he'd had to drive out to Holt, and there wasn't much to choose between his and Shelton's. It, too, was black and in need of a clean, and the wheel rims were rusty. The bike that Sam Curl had seen down at Cley could well have been either, or it might have belonged to someone else altogether.

Nor had Constable Ellison been able to throw much light on the problem. He'd seen Curl at Cley and taken a statement, but the man had only glanced at the bike, nothing more. The light had been fading and, thinking about it, he wasn't sure after all that the colour had been black. It might have been blue or even dark green.

'Great!' said Tench. 'We've a suspect car that some joker's wiped clean, and a suspect bike that could be black, blue or green or even bloody magenta. God give me strength!'

What God gave him at that precise moment was WDC Gradwell.

After fruitlessly phoning her chief from the dress shop and then from the lab, she'd arranged the release of Miss Marriott's car and then driven at speed straight back to headquarters. Now she tapped on the open door of his office.

Her reception wasn't entirely what she'd expected.

Tench eyed her with something akin to mistrust.

'Step inside, Sue,' he said, 'and tell us the worst. We've a driver-less car and a riderless bike. What's your contribution? A bath chair abandoned at Morston Creek?'

Sue Gradwell raised a delicately pencilled eyebrow.

'Sir?'

'Nothing missing?'

'Oh . . . Yes, sir. A bra.'

There was a moment of silence.

'A what?'

'Phoebe Marriott's bra, sir. It wasn't with her clothes.'

Tench cast his mind back.

'It wouldn't be,' he said. 'She wasn't wearing one.'

'Her sister says she must have been. She never went running on the beach without a bra.'

'Well, the crime squad searched the sands . . . Have you checked with the lab?'

'Yes, sir, and Sergeant Lester. No such item was found.'

'And you think her sister's right?'

'Very likely, sir, yes.'

There was another silent pause.

'What about you? Would you go running without one?'

Sue Gradwell seemed amused.

'No, sir, I wouldn't. Strains the pectoral muscles, if you know what I mean, sir.'

Tench apparently did.

'I can imagine,' he said drily. 'Did you get a description of this missing piece of lingerie? The make and the size?'

'Yes, sir.'

'Thousands like it, I suppose.'

'No, sir. I wouldn't think so. This one's a bit different.'

'Different?'

Sue Gradwell nodded her head very firmly.

'Unusual, sir.'

'How?'

'Well, sir,' she said. 'Let's put it this way. A bra's rather like a suspension bridge . . .'

Tench listened.

With patience.

He didn't interrupt.

At last he leaned back.

'And Giles Leening made sketches?'

'Yes, sir. That's what Miss Marriott says.'

'And you believe her?'

'Yes, sir. On this point, I do.'

Tench glanced at his watch. Then he picked up the phone.

'Get me the *Eastern Daily Press*,' he said. 'I want to speak to Dave Ransome.'

10

That was at three forty-five.

Five minutes later he put the phone down.

After that, things moved fast. Once Tench got a sniff of a worthwhile clue, he could be quick off the mark.

'Right,' he said. 'Ransome's making arrangements to hold the front page. Andy' – he turned to Gregg – 'get out to Upper Sheringham. There'll be a press photographer waiting outside the Red Lion. Your job's to make contact with Brigadier Crawley. You'll probably find him inside. He's manning the bar at a wedding reception. Ask for Colonel Dick. That's what they call him. If he isn't there, track him down. He lives at Repton Lodge on the edge of the park. I want his car – the Lagonda – photographed as it was at the time it went missing. Get him to take the ribbons off. And make sure the number-plate's clearly visible. Police appeal in tomorrow morning's *EDP*. Anyone who saw it between seven thirty Tuesday evening and six o'clock Wednesday morning to contact us here or at the incident room in Blakeney. Photographer has instructions to get the prints to Ransome as soon as possible. OK?'

'OK, sir,' said Gregg.

'Don't waste any time. Get cracking right away . . . George?'

'Sir?'

George was Detective Constable Rayner: solid, square-built, phlegmatic and dependable.

'Drive out to Wells. See the landlord of the Norfolk Wherry. His name's Bill Bastable. Check on three points. Was Moses Shelton there on Tuesday evening, and if so, what time? Did he offer Bastable anything? And is Bastable himself a reliable witness? For your information, we've interviewed Shelton. He claims he got to the Wherry about half-past nine, had a pint in the snug and then rode off to Morston. Says he called because he'd promised to let Bastable have a couple of rabbits. We don't know this chap Bastable, so give him a run-down. Make sure he isn't covering for Shelton. Don't let him pull the wool over your eyes.'

'Sir.'

'Right. Get on with it . . . Now, Mac . . .'

'Young Giles?'

'Young Giles. He should be back from school by the time you get to Craymere. If he's got any sketches of this wonder bra, we need them. Take Sue along with you. She knows what we're looking for. Once you get hold of them, whip them back to Ransome at the *EDP* office as fast as you can. Pictures'll be on the front page tomorrow morning. Anyone who's set eyes on it to get in touch with us. Ransome's got the number of the incident room.'

'You'll be here if we run into any kind of snag?'

'I'll be at this desk. Ledward's dragging his feet. It's time we had his report. And the one from the lab. I'll be phoning around. If the line's engaged, keep ringing. This may be the break we've been waiting for.' He frowned at McKenzie. 'What d'you mean by snags?'

The sergeant gave a shrug.

'He might say there are no sketches.'

'Diana Marriott said he made some.'

'Even if he did, he could say he'd destroyed them; torn 'em up, burnt them . . .'

'Then get him to make another.'

'And what if he refuses?'

'Why would he do that?'

'It is possible, sir.' Sue Gradwell intervened. 'If he still intends to market this new design of his, then he won't want it plastered across the morning papers for everyone to see.'

'You mean it's a priceless industrial secret?'

'I don't honestly know, sir . . .'

'But', said McKenzie, 'he may well think it is . . . So what are we to do? Tear the place apart?'

'You won't need to,' said Tench. 'He won't be any trouble. Goddammit, Mac, he's only a schoolboy. He's wept enough tears over Phoebe Marriott to flood Craymere Common. He wants her killer caught just as much as we do, and if he does have a sketch, it may be the one clue we need to lay hands on the man. He'll understand that. He's an intelligent lad.'

'He's a stubborn one, too.'

'Then hand him over to Sue. Let her exercise her charms. That's bound to do the trick.'

'And if it doesn't, ring you?'

'No,' said Tench. 'Bring him in, and bring his sketch pad and a couple of pencils with him. We can't afford to wait. I've promised Ransome a picture and he's going to get a picture, even if I have to sit down and draw one myself.'

11

McKenzie knocked on the door of Number One, Craymere Common.

When it opened, she stood there: the same fair-haired, freckled girl that he'd seen there before. She was wearing school uniform, and eyed him with what was clearly disappointment.

'Oh, it's you again,' she said.
'Who were you expecting?'
'The other one,' she said. 'The good-looking one.'
'We can't all claim to be love's young dream.'
'A detective shouldn't be fat. He should be suave and sophisticated.'
McKenzie patted his midriff.
'This isn't fat. It's substance. All the best detectives have to have substance.'
'That's rot,' she said. 'Look at Lord Peter Wimsey.'
'Never heard of him,' McKenzie told her. 'We've come to see Giles.'
The girl looked round him, as far as Sue Gradwell.
'Who's that? Your sidekick?'
'This', said McKenzie, 'is Woman Detective Constable Susan Gradwell.'
'She doesn't look like one either.'
'Like what?'
'A detective.'
'Well, she is. And she eats little girls. Where's Giles?'
'In his room. He's hibernating.' She turned towards the stairs. 'Giles!' she called. 'Visitors!'
She listened, then waved them in.
'Comatose,' she said. 'Best go up. He won't answer.'

She was wrong.

Giles wasn't exactly comatose, nor was he in a state of even semi-hibernation.

The bedroom door was open, and he was sitting at the table, working on a sketch.

'Remember me?' McKenzie asked him.
'Detective Sergeant . . . McKenzie?'
'That's right, and this is WDC Gradwell.'

Sue Gradwell was examining the pictures on the walls. McKenzie walked round the table and looked down at the drawing.

'Phoebe?' he said.

'Yes.' The boy nodded. 'I never had the chance to do a real portrait. I felt I had to have one. I wanted to remember her as she was when she was happy. I haven't quite got it right yet.' He added a smile line at the corner of the mouth. 'You wanted to ask me something?'

'We think you can help us.'

Giles looked up at him, uncertain.

'I've told you all I know.'

'Not to worry, lad.' McKenzie turned back the chintz cover and sat down on the bed. 'We're not here to ask questions. We're looking for something.'

Giles took off his glasses and laid them on the table.

'What is it?' he said.

'A sketch.'

'Oh.' The boy seemed relieved. He waved a hand round the room. 'Well, take what you want if you think it'll help.'

McKenzie glanced at Sue Gradwell.

'I'm afraid, Giles,' she said, 'the one we want isn't here. It's a sketch of something that Phoebe was wearing. An item that's missing. We need to know what it looked like.'

The boy frowned.

'She was running. She wouldn't have been wearing anything I'd sketched. Just a blouse and skirt. Things that she'd bought.'

Sue Gradwell shook her head.

'We weren't thinking of those ... You see, Giles, we know she was wearing something very special. A new kind of bra. One that you and she had worked on together.'

'Oh, that.' His eyes, for a moment, showed a flicker of apprehension. 'It's missing?'

'We haven't found it ... You helped to design it. You must have made sketches.'

'Yes ... There are some.'

'Can we see them, please?'

Giles got up from the table. He crossed to the chest of drawers and pulled one open. Then he suddenly slammed it shut, and turned back towards them.

'What are you going to do with them?'

'We want the newspapers to print them.' McKenzie had never been strong on diplomacy.

The boy tossed his head. He leaned back against the drawer. 'No. You can't do that.'

'We have to do it, lad.'

'No, you can't. It's a secret. Between her and me.'

Sue Gradwell moved across to the table. She sat down in his chair and studied the portrait.

'You were fond of Phoebe, Giles, weren't you?' she said.

'I loved her.' The words came out fiercely. 'Why don't any of you believe me?'

Sue Gradwell glanced up at him.

'I believe you, Giles. She's a very lovely girl.'

'She was. Now she's . . . No!' There were tears in his eyes.

'Someone killed her, Giles. You want us to find him, don't you?'

'Yes, of course I do.'

'And Phoebe would, too. She'd want you to help.'

'I don't know . . . I don't know.' He brushed at the tears. 'Can't you leave me alone?'

Sue Gradwell waited. When she spoke her voice was soft, the words almost whispered.

'You loved this girl, Giles. Whoever killed her was a beast. He could kill others like her. He may be trailing another such girl even now. Another beautiful girl that someone else loves. D'you want that to happen?'

Giles closed his eyes, shook his head.

'Then you have to give Sergeant McKenzie the sketches.'

The boy turned again, seemed to hesitate; then slowly, reluctantly he opened the drawer. He drew out something white that he bunched in his hand. He held it out to McKenzie.

'Here. Take it,' he said. 'That's what you're looking for. You don't need to put anything about it in the papers.'

Sue Gradwell took it. She spread it out on the desk. Then she passed it to McKenzie.

'Is it the one?' he asked.

She nodded.

'Yes, Sarge. As far as I can tell.'

They both looked at Giles.

'Sit down, lad,' McKenzie said.

Giles lowered himself on to the edge of the bed.

'Where did you find it?'

'Down on the beach.' The boy didn't look at him. He stared at the floor.

'Whereabouts on the beach?'

'Out at Blakeney Point.'

'When was this?'

'Tuesday night. It was lying on the shingle. I just picked it up.'

'You were out on Blakeney Point last Tuesday night?'
'Yes.' The word was barely audible.
He looked up at Sue Gradwell, and then at McKenzie.
'Don't you understand?' he said. 'I just wanted something that belonged to her. That's all.'
He looked at both of them again.
'It's clean,' he said. 'I washed it.'

5

THE NAKED DOLL

Men deal with life as children with their play,
Who first misuse, then cast their toys away.

William Cowper: *Hope*

1

'Where is he?' said Tench.

His tone was one of weary resignation.

'Waiting in the interview room with Sue Gradwell. His mother's there too.'

Tench made no comment, but his eyes asked a question.

'He didn't want her to come, but she insisted,' McKenzie said. 'Thought it best to humour her. He may be an adult in the eyes of the law, but, as you said, he's still only a schoolboy. We need to tread carefully with this one, Mike.'

Tench gave a sigh.

'You're probably right. Did he tell you why he was out at Blakeney Point?'

McKenzie shook his head.

'Didn't ask him. Just brought him straight here. He seems anxious to talk.'

'I bet he does,' said Tench. 'Well, let's go and see what he has to say for himself this time. It'll need to be good.'

Giles was sitting at the table in the interview room, with his mother beside him. Sue Gradwell stood behind them, close to the door.

He said nothing as Tench and McKenzie sat down; merely stared at the table. It was Mrs Leening who spoke. She was casually dressed and her hair was in some disorder. Wisps of it strayed across her face, and she brushed them back with her hand.

'Why have you brought him here?' she said. 'He hasn't done anything.'

'Mrs Leening' – Tench sounded at once both tired and sympathetic – 'you already know Detective Sergeant McKenzie. Let me introduce myself. My name is Tench. Detective Chief Inspector Tench. I'm inquiring into the murder of Phoebe Marriott.'

'Surely you don't think . . .'

'No, Mrs Leening, I don't.' Tench was swift to interrupt. 'Let me make two things clear. Your son isn't under arrest, and at the moment I see no reason to charge him with anything. But he has told us things which we know are not true, and we have to ask him more questions.'

Giles spoke.

'I'll explain, but I don't want her here.'

Tench looked at Mrs Leening. She gave a helpless shrug.

'I think, Giles,' he said, 'that your mother ought to stay.'

The boy kept his eyes lowered.

'No. I'll answer the questions, but not in front of her.'

She turned to him.

'Why not?'

'Just go,' he said. 'Please.'

'Perhaps . . .' Tench glanced at her again.

She breathed very deeply.

'I'll be waiting outside . . . He's a good boy,' she said to Tench.

'I'm sure he is, Mrs Leening.'

'He wouldn't do anything bad. But at his age it's sometimes difficult to understand them. They have strange ideas . . .'

'Mother. Just leave us.' Giles was tight-lipped.

'Sue,' said Tench. 'Take Mrs Leening to the staff canteen. See that she gets a cup of tea.'

He waited till they'd gone and the door had closed behind them.

'Mac,' he said.

McKenzie took Phoebe Marriott's bra from his pocket and laid it on the table.

'Now, Giles.' Tench was resolutely matter-of-fact. 'You say you found this out at Blakeney Point.'

For the first time Giles looked at him.

'Yes,' he said. 'On the shingle.'

'Whereabouts exactly?'

'Close to the terns. Between them and the sea.'

'And this was on Tuesday evening?'

The boy nodded.

'What time?'
'It must have been round about half-past nine.'
'Was it dark?'
'Getting dark.'
'But the sun had gone?'
'Yes.'
'What were you doing out at that time on Blakeney Point?'
'I was going to meet Phoebe.'
'Then you knew she'd gone running?'
'Yes.'
'How did you know that?'
The boy seemed to hesitate.
'You see, Giles,' Tench said, 'I'm at a bit of a loss. Yesterday, when Sergeant McKenzie first came to see you, you said you'd spoken to Phoebe on Monday evening and you hadn't seen her since then...'
'No.' Giles shook his head.
'How d'you mean? No.'
'I didn't say that.'
'Then what did you say?'
'I told him I'd seen Phoebe on Monday and she'd said that her sister was going up to London. He didn't ask me whether I'd seen her again.'
A pause.
'But you did?'
'Yes.'
'When?'
'On Tuesday, after she got back from the shop. I went across to see her.'
'Why did you do that?'
Giles took a deep breath.
'When we talked on Monday, she said she might go running. I said I'd go with her, so I went across to see if she'd made up her mind.'
'And what did she say?'
'She said it was too hot to go right away. She'd leave it till later. I told her that that'd be better for me, because I had a lot of homework and it'd give me the chance to get most of it done. She said no, I must finish. Homework came first. She'd go on her own, because she wanted to be back at the car before dark. She said she'd drive down about eight o'clock. If I'd finished, OK. If not, it didn't matter.'
He looked up at Tench.
'I never intended her to go on her own. I was going to break off just before eight o'clock, and leave the rest till I got back. But I was

struggling with a problem they'd set us in maths, and when I looked at my watch it was ten past eight.' Tears glistened in his eyes. 'It's my fault, isn't it? If I'd gone with her, this would never have happened.'

Tench was quiet, persuasive.

'I don't think you can blame yourself for that, Giles,' he said. 'You weren't to know.'

The boy bit his lip.

'I knew enough to know that she shouldn't have gone down there on her own.'

'She told you something?'

'Yes. On Monday.'

'What did she tell you?'

Giles brushed away the tears with the back of his hand.

'She thought there was someone watching her,' he said. 'Someone on the sands.'

2

'A man?' Tench was quick to seize on the point.

'She didn't know. She never saw whoever it was. It was just a feeling she had. That someone was watching her.'

'How often had this happened? Just once?'

'More than that. She said two or three times.'

'Recently?'

'Yes, in the last few weeks.'

'When she was on her own.'

'I think so. I asked her if she'd mentioned it to Di, and she said no, she hadn't.'

Tench rested both elbows on the table.

'Think carefully, Giles. Think back to what she said. This may be important. Where did she get this feeling? Was it at some particular point on the sands?'

'No, different places. Once when she was running below the sea bank, and then on the shingle at the edge of the dunes. She said she thought there was someone in one of the lows – the hollows in the sand.'

'Did she go and look?'

'Yes, she said she did once, but she couldn't see anyone.'

McKenzie had been silent for longer than normal. Now he shifted in his seat.

'So,' he said, 'this was just an impression. She never actually saw this alleged Peeping Tom.'

'No, she didn't.' Giles turned his head and looked straight at McKenzie. 'But she was usually right about things like that.'

'You mean she had a vivid imagination.'

'No, it wasn't imagination.' The boy fired up. 'It's hard to explain. You never knew Phoebe. If you'd known her, you'd understand.'

'I'm a simple soul,' McKenzie said, 'so try to explain.'

'She seemed to have an extra sense. She knew when things were happening.'

'We all know when things are happening, lad. We hear them. We see them.'

'Well, she didn't,' said Giles. 'She knew. That was all.'

'Was she frightened?'

'Not . . . frightened.'

'Apprehensive?'

'Perhaps.'

'Then why did she choose to go running on her own? It doesn't make sense.'

'It would . . .'

'If I'd known Phoebe. But I didn't and it doesn't.'

'She believed . . .'

'Believed what?'

'Well, that fear was something that had to be conquered. That you faced up to things. You didn't let them beat you.'

'You mean she was irresponsible.'

'No, just determined. She said she wasn't going to let anyone stop her running on the beach.'

McKenzie shook his head.

'That's way beyond me. Maybe the Chief Inspector can fathom it, but I can't.'

'Let's go back to Tuesday night.' Tench seemed anxious to get the questioning back on track. 'You looked at your watch. It was ten past eight. What did you do?'

'I ran downstairs and looked for the car. It had gone. So I fetched my bike from the shed and set off for Cley as fast as I could. I knew I'd meet up with her somewhere on the sands.'

'You rode down to Cley. Where did you leave the bike?'

'Close to the car. I just tossed it down.'

'Were there any other cars parked there at that time?'

Giles frowned.

'There was one. Some kind of sports car. I didn't take much notice.'

'Then you set off along the sands.'
'Yes. At a run.'
'But you didn't see Phoebe.'
'I didn't expect to see her. Not right away. She'd got a long start.'
'Go on.'
'Well, there wasn't any sign of her, and I began to get worried. Then just below the point where the birds were nesting, I saw that. Phoebe's bra.' He jerked a hand towards the table. 'It was lying on the shingle.'
'You recognized it as hers?'
'Of course I did, yes.'
'So what did you do?'
'I picked it up and looked at it.'
'And?'
'It was pretty clear that someone had torn it off.'
'How did you know that?'
'It fastens with a couple of hooks and eyes at the back. The eyes had been ripped out. The fabric was torn. You can see for yourself.' He reached out and pushed the bra towards Tench.

The Chief Inspector glanced at it and nodded.

'And after that?'
'I looked around, but there wasn't a sign of anyone. I was scared for Phoebe. I think I panicked a bit. I stuffed the bra in my pocket and started to search. I was desperate to find her. I must have run another hundred yards along the shingle, then I turned up the dunes and made for the lows. I looked in half a dozen, but all of them were empty. I remember I stood there, still, for a moment. I didn't know what to do. I walked back towards the terns, and then . . . I caught a glimpse of something.'

He stared at the bra.

'What was it, Giles?' The words were deliberately gentle. 'What did you see?'

'She was there,' he said. 'Phoebe. Stretched out among them.'

He bowed his head and turned away. His shoulders began to shake. 'I knew she was dead. It was the way she was lying. She had to be dead.'

3

Tench gave him time.
  'How was she lying, Giles?'
  'Not like Phoebe. She wouldn't . . .'

'Wouldn't what?'

'She wouldn't have done that, even for me.'

'Done what? Tell me, Giles.'

'She was . . .'

'Yes?'

'It was her clothes . . . her blouse and skirt . . . pulled away . . . just as if he'd . . .'

'What, Giles?'

'Touched her. Fondled her . . . She wouldn't have let him do that. She wouldn't ever. Not Phoebe.'

Tench watched the boy intently.

'Who was he, Giles?'

'I don't know. I don't know.'

'You never saw him?'

'No. I've told you. There was no one.'

'Did *you* touch her, Giles?'

'No.' He tossed his head savagely. 'I couldn't. I wanted to, but the birds wouldn't let me.'

'You tried to get closer?'

'Once. Only once. The birds all rose up. Like a beating black cloud. I could feel them all around me. Then one of them swooped down and landed on her face. And she never even moved.' He looked up. 'It was horrible.'

Tench saw his eyes. They stared not at him, but through him, away to the sand and the body on the sand. He'd seen eyes like those. A private soldier's eyes. At the end of the war in Germany. A boy of eighteen, describing what he'd seen when he'd driven into the concentration camp at Belsen.

Eyes tormented by memory.

He felt what he'd felt then: a pang of compassion.

'What did you do after that?'

Giles wrenched his gaze back again to the table.

'I don't know. I don't remember. I ran.'

'Ran where?'

'Back across the dunes and then down to the sea. I didn't look back. All the way along the beach I just looked at the sea.'

'You ran back to Cley.'

'I must have done, yes. I remember picking up my bike and riding back home. Everything was quiet, all the way to Blakeney. It was still, like a graveyard . . . I don't think I really believed what I'd seen.'

'And when you got home?'

'I locked myself in my room. No one saw me.'

There was silence, then McKenzie leaned forward.

'Why the devil didn't you tell us all this before?'

Giles closed his eyes. He shut McKenzie out.

'I suppose . . . I was afraid.'

'Afraid? Afraid of what?'

'Of how things would look.'

'And how did you think they'd look?'

'I'd arranged to be with her. I'd followed her on my bike. I'd found her on the sands . . . and . . .'

'Yes?'

'When I got home, I discovered I still had that in my pocket.'

McKenzie held up the bra.

'You mean this?'

Giles nodded.

'I thought my fingerprints might be on it. That's why I washed it.'

'Then all this tale about sitting in Breckmarsh Mill and communing with the sea was just a pack of lies.'

'Not really, no. Some nights I do go down to the mill.'

'But you didn't on Tuesday.'

'No. I've told you I didn't.' The boy fired up again.

'Then it *was* a pack of lies.' McKenzie was scathing. 'D'you realize what you've done? You've misled the police. You've wasted their time. You've withheld vital evidence, and not only that, you've destroyed some as well. If it hadn't been for you, we might already have been on the trail of this man.'

'I know.' There was a flash of anger. 'D'you think I don't know?' He looked up at Tench. 'I'm sorry. I didn't mean to make things difficult.'

'Sorry . . . ? Sorry . . . ?' McKenzie leaned back in his chair. 'Your witness,' he said to Tench in a tone of disgust. 'Charge the little bugger and let's get on with the case.'

Tench said nothing for fully five seconds. He just looked at the boy. Then he swept up the bra and thrust it down in his pocket.

'Go home, Giles,' he said. 'Take him away, Mac. Hand him over to Mrs Leening. Tell her we don't need him any more for the moment.'

McKenzie gave a shrug. He heaved himself up.

'Follow me, lad,' he said. 'And think yourself bloody lucky I'm not the one who gives the orders round here.'

4

'I think he's got the message.'

'Let's hope so.' McKenzie was still unrelenting. 'Left to me, I'd have charged him.'

'No point, Mac. He's just a mixed-up boy, and he's not going anywhere.'

'He could still have done it. He was there, on the spot, and he's a big enough lad.'

'I don't think so,' said Tench.

'There's something about him that's not quite right.'

'Why? Simply because he designs women's clothes?'

'Maybe.' McKenzie was guarded. 'I think we should keep an eye on him.'

'OK. We'll keep an eye on him, but at the moment we've other, more important things to do.'

'The Peeping Tom?'

'We've got to follow it up. It's the one solid clue we've been presented with so far.'

'If you believe Giles Leening.'

'Don't you?'

McKenzie threw out his hands.

'Who the hell knows? She may have said what he told us, or it could be just another tale he's concocted. Even if he was, for once, telling us the truth, it may have been all in the girl's imagination. We may be going on a goose chase.'

'Could be, yes, but we've still got to go.'

'Then we're back at Blakeney Point?'

'Looks very much like it.'

'And we're searching for a random killer. The one thing we didn't want.'

Tench was thoughtful.

'I don't think we've quite reached that point yet, Mac. We've got to work on the assumption that it wasn't wholly random.'

'You mean it was planned? It still could be random.'

'In one sense, yes. In another one, no. There could be some link. Let's hope there is. Our job's to try and find it.'

'So what do we do next?'

'First thing,' said Tench, 'talk to Lock and Ellison. They've been out today, interviewing the wardens. Let's see if they've come up with anything useful.'

Detective Constable Lock had taken a statement from the head warden, Langrick. Tench read it through. It contained little beyond what Langrick had told him the morning before. He'd been working on his own from midday on Tuesday because Bob Phelps, who should have taken over from Turner, had had an emergency dental appointment. In the evening he'd done the usual rounds of the Point, including a visit to the ternery, and checked that all visitors were clear of the area. He'd returned to the lifeboat house just after eight o'clock, written up his log, listened to a radio programme about the scheme to establish National Parks, and gone to bed about half-past ten. He'd slept soundly, heard nothing unusual and hadn't suspected that anything untoward had happened until John Lubbock had knocked on his door next morning. That was shortly after seven.

Tench pushed the report aside, and turned towards Lock.

'Did you ask him whether he'd ever seen the Marriott girls?'

'Yes, sir. Said no, not to his knowledge. If they normally went running early in the evening, he wouldn't have been up at that end of the Point.'

'And what about Turner?'

'Big fellow, sir. Six foot, broad-shouldered. Lives near the church at Wiveton. Went off duty at high tide on Tuesday, just after midday. Laid the boat up at Blakeney and cycled home. Spent the afternoon in his garden, and the rest of the day inside with his wife. Both in bed by ten. Early to bed and early to rise: that seems to be his motto. Said yes, he had seen two girls in shorts running along the beach. About a fortnight ago, when he'd been up at the tern colony. Pretty girls they were, very much alike. He'd wondered if they were twins. They'd sat down to rest on the edge of the dunes. He thought he'd better warn them to keep clear of the birds, but they set off back along the shore before he had the chance.'

'He didn't speak to them?'

'No, sir. That was what he said.'

'What did you make of him?'

'Sound enough chap, sir, as far as I could tell. Seemed keen on his job. I asked him whether he ever brought anyone else over with him in the boat. He said no, but his colleague, Bob Phelps, did from time to time. Gave a lift to some pal of his from Blakeney, a birdwatcher. Didn't know his name, but Bob called him Terry.'

Tench looked across at Ellison.

'You saw Phelps. Did he mention this?'

Detective Constable Ellison, young, fresh-faced and still feeling his way as a member of the team, seemed to be a trifle disconcerted by the question.

'Sorry, sir,' he said. 'Didn't ask him, I'm afraid.'

'And he didn't volunteer the information?'

'No, sir.'

'Never mind,' said Tench. 'What did he have to say?'

Ellison consulted his notebook.

'Said he was supposed to take over from Joe Turner at high tide on Tuesday, but he'd been awake most of Monday night with toothache. Knew he'd have to have it out, so he rang his dentist to try and make an appointment.'

'Did you get the name of the dentist?'

'Yes, sir. A Mr Hayhurst in Wells.'

'OK. Go on.'

'Well, the only time this Hayhurst could fit him in was at three o'clock on Tuesday afternoon, so he rang up the warden and told him he wouldn't be able to get out to the Point.'

'Did he keep the appointment?'

'Yes, sir, he did. I checked with the dentist. Extraction of an upper right incisor.'

'Good. Did Phelps say what he did after that?'

'Went back home, so he told me. When the freezing wore off, he began to feel more than a bit sorry for himself, so he dosed himself with a couple of neat whiskies and then went to bed. Said he was dead tired anyway after the night before. Slept till six the next morning.'

'He lives on his own?'

'No, sir. With his mother.'

'And she was in the house?'

'Yes, sir. Poured him the whisky.'

'What sort of a chap is he?'

'Slim, fair-haired, average height. Soft-spoken. Seemed to me to be an inoffensive type of bloke. Still a bit of a mother's boy, I'd imagine. She fussed around him quite a lot. "Are you sure you're all right, Bob? Don't you think you ought to have another day at home, dear?" Anyone would have thought he'd had his appendix out. She'd have driven me barmy in less than half an hour, sir, and that's a plain fact.'

'But he was going back to the Point today?'

'Intended to, yes, sir. High tide. Half-past two. Said he was going to meet Turner like he usually did, down at the quay.'

'And he hadn't seen either of the Marriott girls?'
'Said not, sir. No.'
'Right.' Tench nodded twice, slowly. 'Well, there's nothing much more to be done tonight. You'd better both get off home. Conference here first thing tomorrow. Pass the word around. We should have Ledward's report by then, and the one from the lab. And we may get some response to Ransome's press appeals. With a bit of luck they'll provide us with something more to work on.'

He waited till they'd gone.
'Mac,' he said. 'This bird-watcher . . .'
'Weird. Never trusted 'em,' McKenzie said sourly. 'Birds are all right. I've nothing against birds, but leave 'em to get on with it. That's what I say.'
'And there are birds and there are birds.'
'True. Very true.'
'And binoculars can spot them.'
'True again. So . . . ?'
Tench pulled the phone towards him and lifted the receiver.
'I want to speak to Langrick, the warden at Blakeney Point. See if you can get hold of him, will you?' he said.

5

It took ten minutes for the WPC on the switchboard to make contact with Langrick.
Tench heard his voice, brusque and businesslike.
'Hello.'
'Mr Langrick?'
'Yes. That's right.'
'This is Detective Chief Inspector Tench. I'm speaking from Norwich.'
'Yes, Chief Inspector?'
'Nothing to worry about, Mr Langrick. Just checking some information . . . Is Mr Phelps about?'
'Not at the moment, no.'
'Then perhaps you can help . . . I believe he sometimes takes a friend across to the Point. Someone called Terry.'
'That's right. Terry Jagger.'

'A bird-watcher.'

'Photographer, Chief Inspector. He takes pictures of birds.'

'D'you know where he lives?'

'There's nothing wrong, is there?' Langrick was clearly troubled.

'No, Mr Langrick. We're just anxious to speak to anyone who may have been on the Point. It's purely routine. We're seeking information, nothing more than that, and we'd like to have a word with Mr Jagger. He may possibly have seen something . . . I was told he lives in Blakeney. Is that right?'

'No, Chief Inspector. He did live in Blakeney, but I saw him this morning. He was taking pictures of the terns. He told me he'd just bought a cottage at Cley.'

'Cley? Whereabouts?'

'Somewhere on the coast road. The place is called Zitundo, or something like that. Peculiar name.'

'You're probably right, sir. There are a number of cottages with names like that in Cley. They're called after ships that once traded there. Mr Lubbock lives in one of them, Umzinto Cottage. Zitundo's likely to be one of the others . . . Well, thank you, Mr Langrick.'

'That's all?'

'Yes, sir, that's all. Sorry to have troubled you. We have to check with everyone, you understand that. They just might have seen something unusual, something that didn't conform to the normal pattern. You haven't remembered anything else yourself, sir, have you?'

'Not that I recall, Chief Inspector.'

'Well, if anything comes to mind, sir, you know where to find us.'

'Yes. Yes, of course . . . He's a good photographer, Jagger. We've used some of his bird prints in pamphlets about the Point. Spends quite a lot of his time over here.'

'Well, thank you very much. We'll get in touch with him, Mr Langrick.'

Tench put the phone down.

'You heard that?'

'Yes,' McKenzie said. 'Cley.'

'I wonder if Lubbock knows him.'

'It's a fair enough bet. He seems to know just about everyone in the village.'

'You think a word might be useful?'

'Can't do any harm. Give him a tinkle.'

Tench did. The bell buzzed. There was no reply.

'Out somewhere,' he said.

'Probably pounding the shore with the end of his stick.'
'Could be anywhere. Not worth bothering tonight.'
'You don't fancy a leisurely drive down to Cley in the evening sunshine?'
'Fifty miles there and back? No, we've chased enough shadows for one day, Mac. It can wait till the morning. Go home and hit the hay. It's going to be another of those long days tomorrow.'
McKenzie looked down his nose.
'I feel more like hitting the bottle. How about it?'
'Where at?'
'The Adam?'
Tench glanced at the files overflowing his in-tray.
'You go ahead. I'll follow. That is, if I've time. But I wouldn't bank on it if I were you.'
'The McKenzies have never been solitary drinkers. We come from a line of carousing clansmen. I get bleary-eyed if I'm staring at a pint.'
'Then be strong-minded. Sit back and think of Bannockburn.'
'No point. They were drunk.'
'Who?'
'The tartan hordes. Reeked of usquebaugh. It was that that did the trick. It laid the English low . . . I'll have 'em lined up and ready. What'll it be? Tonic water?'
Tench grinned at him wearily.
'Bugger off, Mac,' he said. 'I've some thinking to do.'

6

He needed to think. He was clear about that. But whether such thought would elucidate matters or make him feel one whit better than he did, that wasn't so clear.
He stared gloomily at the files. Then he dragged out the one that held Rayner's report, and began to read with the conviction that it wouldn't provide him with any spark of comfort.
It didn't. Rayner had driven down to Wells and sought out Bill Bastable at the Norfolk Wherry. His impression, conveyed mainly in flat monosyllables, was that Bastable was a plain, blunt man with a deal of good sense. His assessment of Moses Shelton had been bruisingly frank and much the same as Jim Thober's. He'd called him a bloody inebriate (the longest word in Rayner's report) and said he

wouldn't trust him as far as he could spit a cobble; but he had confirmed that at half-past nine, or near enough, on Tuesday, he'd served him with a pint of ale, Shelton had taken it into the snug and hadn't been there at quarter to ten. Yes, he'd been offered a couple of rabbits, but he'd turned them down. He knew Moses too well. Slip them under the bar and he'd be trying to cadge drinks on the slate until Christmas; and anyway, what use were two bloody rabbits?

So much for Moses Shelton.

Tench closed the file and tossed it back in the tray. Then he pushed back his sleeve and looked at his watch.

Quarter to eight.

In another hour and a half it would be forty-eight hours since two murderous hands had closed around Phoebe Marriott's neck.

But whose hands?

He still didn't know, and he seemed no closer to solving the problem than when he'd stood beside Lubbock and looked down at the body.

He'd been told more than once that, in a murder inquiry, the first forty-eight hours were the vital ones. After that the trail grew progressively fainter, more difficult to trace. And what had he got to show for the efforts of a team of trained detectives dashing round Norfolk? A Peeping Tom on the dunes who'd never been seen and might never have even existed at all, and a man armed with nothing more lethal than a camera taking snapshots of birds.

So far he'd been chasing shadows: shadows on the sand.

And these? Did they promise to be anything more?

It was like being lost at night in a gathering mist on the mud-flats at Blakeney, with no guide but the wandering fires of phosphorescence dancing on the marsh and winking into nothing.

Will-o'-the-wisps.

Like clues that led nowhere.

All he had were imponderables. Mights and might nots.

Phoebe Marriott might have seen a watcher on the dunes, and again she might not.

The boy, Giles Leening, might be telling the truth at last, or again he might not.

Whoever it was that stole the brigadier's car, drove it to Cley and then left it on the edge of that spinney at Bradenham might well have followed the girl along the sands. Or again, he might never have seen her at all.

The warden, Joe Turner, could have noticed the Marriotts on more than one occasion. He could have spoken to them, struck up an acquaintance.

And who could say that Bob Phelps had already come out with the whole of the truth?

He pushed himself up, took a turn round the room with his hands in his pockets and ended up at the window, gazing out across the roofs and church spires of Norwich.

Tomorrow might be different.

There might be some clue in the forensic reports that would lead them down an altogether different trail. Someone might pick up the *Eastern Daily Press* and remember seeing the car; might perhaps be able to describe the driver.

Or again they might not.

Phoebe Marriott's bra. He'd thought for a moment that that was the clue that might possibly help them to track down the killer. But that had gone, too. Another will-o'-the-wisp. He'd had to send word to Ransome to forget all about it.

Who did hold the key to this baffling conundrum?

Was it Diana Marriott?

He sat down again.

Think, he said. Think.

Another host of imponderables.

Twin sisters, wildly attractive, living together, who might or might not have had a lesbian attachment. Who might have shared secrets that neither would ever want to divulge. Bound together in a pledge to hide from the world the life that they led behind the walls of Downs House.

Two sisters, tight-lipped, protecting one another.

He remembered Lubbock's words when he'd handed back the diary. 'If I were you,' he'd said, 'I'd lock that away. Put it out of your mind. It could prove to be nothing but a dangerous distraction.'

But what if Lubbock were wrong?

And he couldn't help feeling that Lubbock might be wrong.

One thing was for sure. Diana Marriott must have known more about her sister than anyone else could possibly have done.

Must have known?

Did know.

He had a sudden quite irrational conviction that the answers he was seeking lay in Downs House.

Diana Marriott knew something: something that, for reasons that she'd kept to herself, she hadn't yet told.

He picked up the files and dropped them in a drawer.

Five minutes later he was on the road to Holt, and beyond Holt, Craymere.

7

When he drew to a halt at the gate of the bungalow, the sun had all but disappeared.

He walked up the path and jerked the metal chain. The bell rang, but that was all. It died away into silence.

He rang a second time, but there was still no response.

He tried the door. It was unlocked.

He pushed it open.

'Miss Marriott?' he called.

There was no sound from inside.

He took a step forward and called her name again.

Nothing.

The doors that led off the hallway were closed.

The one on the left opened on to the sitting-room. He turned the knob and let the door swing away from his hand.

Beyond was semi-darkness.

For a moment he was puzzled. The curtains were drawn across the windows: heavy damask curtains that shut out the light.

He felt for the switch on the wall, found it and pressed.

Then he moved forward swiftly, stopped and stared down.

Diana Marriott lay stretched on the rug in front of the fireplace. She lay on her back, her arms flung out from the sweep of dark hair that spread round her shoulders. Her lips were blue, there was blood round her mouth, and her tongue was clamped firmly between her teeth.

Her white silk blouse was drawn up to show her breasts, her long tan skirt was rucked round her ankles, and her pink lace-edged knickers girdled her knees.

There was bruising on her throat, and on top of her, face down, lay a doll: a large doll with dark, flowing hair. One of her hands was on the small of its back and the other clutched its buttocks.

The doll was naked, and the fingers of its right hand rested on the nipple of the girl's left breast.

6

PATTERNS

> There is no crime without a precedent.
>
> Seneca: *Hippolytus*

1

Three o'clock in the morning.

High water at Morston Creek.

Ripples lapped the mud. The black skeletons of planks and ladders that served as landings formed crazy patterns above the watery banks of purslane and samphire. Rowing-boats, yachts and small cabin cruisers lolled gently at anchor: shadows in the darkness that enveloped the creek. All was soundless save for a distant murmur that might have been the sea, breaking on the shingle where, two nights before, Phoebe Marriott had felt those unyielding hands close round her neck.

Nothing moved but the boats, rocking, swinging as the tide began to turn.

Morston was asleep.

A mile inland, there were those who still slept at Craymere Common, but fitfully, rising from time to time to peer through their cottage windows at the toings and froings outside Downs House.

There the lights still burned.

The Chief Super had come and gone, promising reinforcements by daylight. Reg Ledward, predictably fretful, had carried out his usual brief examination and driven back to Norwich, leaving Tench to digest the grudging information that the girl had died between six and eight o'clock; that, like her sister, she'd been manually strangled; and that the case bore all the marks of a duplicate killing. Diana Marriott's body was on its way to the mortuary, and the doll, tagged and sealed, had been taken to the lab for immediate analysis; but the rooms at Downs House were still alive with activity. Lights flashed as photographers turned their lenses on every object that might provide a clue; fingerprint experts dusted doors and windows, furniture and fittings with brushes that they hoped would reveal the killer; and men on their hands and knees, armed with tweezers, examined carpets and rugs and dropped minute findings into plastic bags.

Tench watched it all happen. He stretched and yawned.

'How much longer, Sergeant?' he said to Sergeant Lester.

'Reckon we'll be through in another half-hour, sir. Maybe less than that.'

'Anything you can tell me?'

'Not immediately, sir, no. Nothing much disturbed. Doesn't seem to have been a struggle. Probably seized her from behind. All over very quickly.'

'And no signs of forced entry?'

'No, sir. Nothing. The back door was unlocked.'

'And the front one, too.'

'Looks as if she let him in.'

'Or he followed her in. If she was killed soon after six, she'd probably only just have got home . . . Was she wearing a wrist-watch?'

'Yes, sir. Right wrist.'

'I suppose it hadn't stopped?'

'No, sir. No such luck. Still ticking away merrily.'

Tench stared at the rug.

'What makes you think it was a man?'

Lester looked puzzled.

'Sorry, sir. Don't get it.'

'You said she let him in. Why him? Why not her?'

The sergeant scratched his head.

'Hadn't thought about it, sir. Not the sort of thing you do think about, is it?'

'I suppose not,' said Tench. 'But the doll . . .'

'Little girls play with dolls, little boys with guns?'

Tench gave a shrug.

'Something like that. Just a thought, Sergeant. Maybe it's best to keep an open mind.'

He found McKenzie in the hall, inspecting an index pad by the phone.

'List of numbers. Could be useful.'

'Have the print men dealt with it?'

'Dusted it an hour ago. And it's on film.'

Tench took it from him.

'Go home, Mac,' he said. 'There's nothing more to be done here. Get a couple of hours' kip. Once Lester's finished, that's what I'm going to do . . . I want everyone back in the office at eight. We've got to start again.'

'Well, at least we know one thing.' McKenzie, for once, was obstinately cheerful. 'They weren't random killings. Someone had it in for our delectable twins. The question is, why?'

'And more to the point, who? You know what I think, Mac? I think we've been looking in all the wrong places. We've had all our spotlights turned on Phoebe Marriott. We should have taken a much closer look at her sister.'

'It's a bit late for that now.'

'Far too bloody late.'

'Perhaps that'll help.' McKenzie gestured to the pad.

Tench dropped it in his pocket.

'It might,' he said, 'but I reckon we've still got a long way to go. Let's hope we can make it before Rosie decides we'd better call in the Yard.'

2

Sergeant Lester had underestimated the work that remained. It was another full hour before he and his squad were ready to leave.

Tench watched the vans roll away towards Langham, and looked at his watch.

It was quarter past four. There was only half an hour to go before sunrise.

He debated whether to drive home to Norwich.

It seemed at that moment a waste of effort. Kath wouldn't be there. He'd be turning the key on an empty house.

They'd been married five years. He'd met her while he was still a student at Cambridge, and she a counter assistant at Heffer's bookshop in the town. During his first six months in the police, they'd rented a basement flat in Fakenham, and once he moved to Norwich to train for the CID under Lubbock, they'd set themselves up in a semi-detached at Costessey and she'd got herself a job in one of the city's bookshops. Now she had a small backstreet shop of her own near the Maddermarket Theatre, and with his recent promotion and the end of petrol rationing, they were thinking of making yet another move, this time to one of the outlying villages.

Theirs was a happy marriage. They'd always been close, even in the early days when he'd lingered in Heffer's buying books that he couldn't strictly afford, and she'd slip out and share a coffee down at the Copper Kettle on King's Parade. He always missed her when she wasn't around. And that was the trouble: she wasn't around. She was miles away, in Harrogate, at a booksellers' conference.

The night's events had made him restless. His mind was still alert. He didn't want to be on his own, mooning round an empty house. He needed to talk. And he couldn't talk to Kath.

He started up the car, did a swift three-point turn in front of Downs House and drove back to Morston. There he swung right on the coastal road, and headed east towards the fingers of light beyond Blakeney.

It was half-past four when he drew to a halt by the Green at Cley, opposite Lubbock's cottage.

There was no sign of life.

He switched off the car lights, leaned back in his seat and reluctantly closed his eyes.

They were going to need the reinforcements that Hastings had promised.

Even if, as Ledward had implied, it was Phoebe Marriott's killer who'd murdered her sister, all the witnesses questioned about that first death would have to be questioned all over again: Miss Medlicott, the Hollands, Aaron Shelton, the Leenings. Even the sullen, uncooperative Moses would have to be brought from his cell to face a further inquisition.

They'd have to pull out all the stops. House-to-house inquiries at Morston and Langham, and, if those yielded no results, at Cley and then Blakeney. Men with clipboards knocking on doors. Where were you last evening? Why were you there, and who can vouch for the fact that you were indeed there? Did you hear or see anything that might be suspicious? Was there anyone else you know who was out last night? Did you know either of the Marriott sisters or any of their friends? If you did, can you name them and give their addresses?

Questions to be repeated time and time again at house after house, and then posed a second time to cover Tuesday night as well.

And not only that. All the inquiries he'd already set in train would have to be doubled. He was going to need that speed-boat that Hastings had mentioned. The wardens at the Point – Langrick and Turner and Phelps. They'd have to be hauled in and questioned afresh. Boatmen, hoteliers, members of the local ornithological societies and wildlife groups. They'd have to be sounded out too. There was Downs House to be searched, and the Sheringham shop. Files, letters, bills, anything that might possibly yield up a clue would need to be sifted. Time-consuming work.

Then there was Jagger, the man with the camera. And they'd have to check out responses to Ransome's press appeals, follow up any clues in the autopsy reports and those from the lab, probe all the sisters' business connections.

And there was the inquest on Phoebe Marriott . . .

He was going to need literally dozens of men.

There were two murders now. That meant double the load.

And if they were dealing with two distinct killers, treble the load. But were they?

Surely not. The odds had to be against it. Whoever killed Phoebe Marriott must have murdered her sister. Both had been strangled, manually strangled, both the bodies laid out in the same precise way. Find the man who'd been stalking the sands on Tuesday night, and that would be the man who'd brought death to Downs House.

The man . . . or the woman.

Perhaps Lubbock was right. Perhaps it was a woman.

Would a man leave a doll behind at the scene?

The doll . . .

Yes . . . The doll . . .

He felt his thoughts begin to wander. They were slipping away.

What about the doll?

The doll was important.

If only . . .

If only what?

If only it could speak.

. . . But some dolls did speak.

Some dolls could tell secrets.

Secrets . . . He tried to keep a grip on the word.

Secrets . . .

What secrets?

Everyone had secrets.

Even dolls had secrets . . .

He was still thinking about the doll when he drifted off to sleep.

*

When he woke it was daylight. The clock on the dashboard showed quarter past five, and someone was trying to break through the window of the car.

He reached out and wound it down.

'Saw you when I drew back the curtains,' said Lubbock. 'Been up all night?' He was fully dressed, stick in hand, and immoderately cheerful.

Tench was far from cheerful. His shoulders were stiff, and his tongue felt like fur. He tried to sit up, and winced.

'How did you guess?'

'Simple deduction, laddie. You're a long way from home, you've denied yourself the joys of the marital couch, and you look as if you haven't had a wash and a shave since yesterday morning.'

'You sound to me just like that bloody man Holmes.'

'He was usually right.'

'More's the pity. At the moment my sympathies are all with Watson.'

'Self-commiseration's a waste of energy,' said Lubbock. 'It's another bright morning. How about taking a stroll along the beach? Breathe the salt air. It's a cure for all ills.'

Tench regarded him balefully.

'Forget it,' he said. 'We've two bodies already. The last thing we need is for you to find a third.'

'Did you say two?'

'That's right. Two.'

Lubbock leaned on his stick.

'I think, laddie,' he said, 'we'd better have a talk.'

'Coffee' – Tench swung himself out of the car – 'and you can lend me a razor. After that we'll talk.'

3

Lubbock speared a fried egg with his fork.

'A doll?' he said. 'What kind of a doll?'

'A large one.'

'Male or female?'

'Decidedly female. Long dark hair.'

'And where was it left?'

'On the body.'
'Whereabouts on the body?'
'Clutching one of her breasts.'
'And a naked doll, you say?'
'Very naked. So was she.'
'Interesting,' said Lubbock.
'Interesting enough to draw one or two conclusions?'
'You're the detective. I'd sooner hear yours.'
'Two murders, one murderer?'
'Looks very much like it.'
'Someone who knew the Marriott sisters?'
'I'd say so.'
'And knew what was going on between them, and disapproved?'
Lubbock cut a slice off his rasher of bacon.
'Not strong enough,' he said. 'Disapproval doesn't kill. Whoever strangled them felt more than mild disapproval.'
'Disgust?'
'Loathing, I'd say.'
'There weren't any signs that the house had been forced.'
'That fits,' Lubbock said.
'It was someone, then, that Diana Marriott knew and felt she could trust?'
'Maybe, maybe not. There could be other explanations. What time did Reg Ledward say that she died?'
'Between six o'clock and eight.'
'And when did she normally close up the shop?'
'Six, so she said.'
'Then he could have been waiting. Pushed his way in when she opened the door. Or perhaps she didn't lock it behind her straight away.'
'Yes, I had thought of that.'
'Or', said Lubbock, 'he might even have had a key.'
Tench poured himself a second cup of coffee.
'Not likely, is it?'
'Why shouldn't it be?'
'Well, suspecting what we do about the Marriott girls . . .'
'You mean if I'd said "*she* might have had a key", that would have been more feasible?'
'Why not? You said yourself that it could have been a woman.'
'So it could.' Lubbock mopped his mouth with a large white handkerchief. 'But I wasn't thinking of someone who'd been given a key.'
'Well, none's been stolen as far as we know.'

'Those, laddie, are the operative words. "As far as we know." The point is, we don't know.'

'Diana Marriott said nothing.'

'She may not have known.'

'You mean Phoebe could have known?'

'Not necessarily, no. Neither of them may have known.'

Tench frowned.

'But surely they'd know if a key was missing.'

'Would they?'

'I'd have thought so. I would. Wouldn't you?'

'Keys can be borrowed and then returned, and nobody need be any the wiser . . . Have you taken a look at this dress shop of theirs?'

'No, not yet. Mac and Sue Gradwell have been doing the leg work.'

'Well, I have,' said Lubbock. 'I was down in Sheringham yesterday afternoon. Went to stock up on tobacco. There's a fellow called Blake has a place by the clock tower. Keeps a lot of different brands and makes me up a mixture . . . Did you know they had an ironmonger's shop next door?'

'Yes, Mac said so.'

'I took a stroll round it. Bought a packet of screws. There's a key-cutting service. Keys cut while you wait. And they don't waste much time. Take a key in, and in less than five minutes you're out with a duplicate. Opens up all sorts of possibilities, doesn't it? Someone she knew, like you said, and felt she could trust. Someone who knew the shop. Knew what she normally did with her keys. Where she left her handbag . . . Has it struck you how careless some women are when it comes to their handbags?'

'OK,' said Tench, 'but it's all just conjecture.'

'Of course it's conjecture. But it's still a possibility. Let's do some conjecturing. What else can we do?'

'Right, then.' Tench drained his coffee and pushed aside the cup. 'Someone gets hold of a duplicate key, waits for Diana Marriott to get home from the shop, opens up the door, takes her by surprise, grabs her by the neck and chokes her to death. It's a remote possibility, but let's say it happened. What's your opinion? Are we looking for a man, or could a woman have done it?'

'Oh, there isn't any doubt that a woman could have done it, but if I were you I'd be looking for a man.'

'Why?'

Lubbock shrugged.

'No particular reason. Just an odd feeling. Call it my nose for a murder, if you like.'

'All right, then. What else does this nose of yours tell you? What kind of a man would he be, this killer?'

Lubbock took his time. He peered inside the teapot and poured himself another cup. Then he filled his pipe and lit it.

'When I was a sergeant down at Yarmouth,' he said, 'I worked with a chief inspector called Winch. He was better read than I was, far better read than I'll ever be. I suppose, in a way, he was rather like you: always quoting lines from some book or other. He was a damn good copper, too. Knew his job inside out . . . I remember once we were dealing with a case very like this one. A young woman stripped and sexually assaulted. Found dead on the beach. And we were asking ourselves much the same question: what kind of a man were we searching for? Well, Winch came out with a quote from some French bloke. I've forgotten his name. Wrote a hell of a long book all about his past life . . .'

'Proust?'

'That's the one. What he said stuck with me because, in the end, it proved to be so prophetic; and when the case was over I got Winch to write it down. I've got it filed away somewhere, but I can still remember it word for word. This chap Proust was a bit of a sensitive soul. At least, that's what I gathered. Had a layer of skin less than most other people, and what he said was this. "The magnificent and pitiful family of the hypersensitive is the salt of the earth. It's they, not the others, who've founded religions and created masterpieces . . ." Winch added a line, of course. "And it's they," he went on, "who murder and abuse unsuspecting young girls." '

'So,' said Tench, 'what exactly does that mean?'

'It simply means this. You're expecting me to say: look for a neurasthenic, a hypersensitive, a sexual inadequate, some man who's been conditioned to believe that young women are predatory beings . . .'

'A mother's boy?'

'Perhaps . . . But I'm not going to tell you that. Not in this case. That isn't the type I'd have in my sights. I'd be looking for somebody altogether different. A very ordinary man. One with nothing to mark him out from the general run. One who's lived, up to now, a completely blameless life. No record of violence. Nothing at all to indicate that he might, one day, go out and strangle a girl.'

Lubbock paused.

'And', he said, 'I wouldn't be looking to find him round here. I'd be looking in Bradenham.'

4

'Oh, that makes things easy.' Tench was ironic. 'All I have to do is find a grey man who wears a grey suit and lives among thousands of others in a town fifty miles from the scene of the crime... Anyway, why Bradenham rather than Blakeney? I know that was where the Lagonda turned up, but whoever stole it could have dumped it anywhere in Norfolk.'

'But he didn't,' said Lubbock. 'He dumped it a mile and a half out of Bradenham on the edge of that spinney.'

Tench looked at him shrewdly.

'That's not the only reason, is it?' he said. 'Mac and I were out there yesterday afternoon, checking with the locals. I told you that. And now you're suggesting we go back again and trawl through the place for this totally unremarkable man: one who may or may not have murdered a girl on the other side of Norfolk. You're making a connection, and it's based on something more than a wild assumption about a stolen car that could have nothing whatever to do with the crime... You know something, don't you? Something I don't. So what is it? Let's be hearing.'

Lubbock drew hard on his pipe.

'What d'you know about Bradenham?'

'Small market town on the Suffolk border, a few miles from Thetford. Mainly brick and flint, but some timber-frame houses, relics of the wool trade. Ruins of a twelfth-century Cluniac priory. A sleepy little place, full of antique shops and tea-rooms.'

'Anything else?'

'Mac says when he goes there it rains cats and dogs, and he once got an Irish penny in change.'

'Did you know that some taxi-drivers won't take you there? No, laddie, you didn't. How long have you been in Norfolk? Four years, is it?'

'Four years last February. 1946.'

'You're still a foreigner, Mike. And Mac wouldn't know what I'm talking about. He was up at Catterick, training army recruits.'

'You're talking about something that happened during the war?'

'That's right. Round about the time you were swatting a few scorpions on the edge of the desert.'

'Go on then. What about the taxi-drivers?'

'Next time you're in Thetford, ask them whether they'll take you to Bradenham. You'll find that some may be willing to do it. Others'll just shake their heads and drive on.'

'Why would they do that?'

'They don't like the place, laddie. It gives them the creeps.'

'You mean they're afraid?'

'To put it bluntly, yes.'

'Because of what happened?'

'Because of what they think may possibly have happened.'

'And what did happen?'

'Between 1941 and 1944, in the course of three years, there were six separate murders, all within a radius of a couple of miles. Four of them were in Bradenham, the other two at isolated farms just outside, but there weren't many people beyond Norfolk and Suffolk who heard much about them. It was wartime, there was censorship and newsprint was scarce. A couple of the national dailies gave them a fleeting mention, but folk had other things to worry about at that time. We were the ones who were worried, but not for the usual reasons. In each case it was clear, almost from the outset, who the murderers were. They were all of them men, and the victims were women. All but one were caught and hanged. The odd one out killed himself.'

Lubbock paused long enough to tamp down his pipe.

'What troubled us', he said, 'was the incidence of all these violent crimes within such a restricted area. They began when a farmer at Trusford Heath, a fellow named Walsh, blasted his wife with a shotgun. That was in April 1941. Five months later a butcher from Bradenham, Alfred Wensley, split his fiancée's skull with a cleaver; and the following summer there were two more killings in quick succession, both within the town. An accountant, David Devereux, battered his wife to death with a hammer, and a soldier on leave stabbed a barmaid outside one of the pubs. Then there was a lull till the autumn of '43, when another farmer, called Jacques, cut the throats of his wife and daughter while they were asleep, and then threw himself in front of a train at Melton Constable station; and six months after that a language teacher at the local grammar school, Anthony Marsden, strangled his wife with a towel as she stepped from the bath.'

'Coincidence?' said Tench.

'On the face of things, that was the logical explanation, but back in Norwich we were investigating a series of capital crimes, and we had to probe a bit deeper. We uncovered strange parallels between the cases that we couldn't logically account for. You see, laddie, all these men had lived thoroughly unimpeachable lives. They were ordinary men. They had no records of violence. They'd never done anything to indicate that one day they might, perhaps, murder somebody else; but in each case there were signs that, in the weeks immediately prior to the killings, their characters had, for some reason, altered. They'd suffered what we could only describe as a personality change, and one that was not merely abrupt, but also profound. From being very conventional men, whose conduct up to that time had been blameless, they'd turned, almost overnight so it seemed, into potential killers.

'And it was at that point,' said Lubbock, 'that Matthew Hopkins emerged from the shadows.'

5

'And who was Matthew Hopkins?'

'Tut-tut, laddie. Don't say you've never heard of him. I thought you read History at that college of yours in Cambridge.'

'I did, but there's a lot of it,' Tench said drily.

'True. Very true. And after all he was just an East Anglian aberration. Easily missed among all those kings who beheaded their queens.'

'So who was he?'

'He was a lawyer from Manningtree in Essex.'

'How long ago?'

'Mid-seventeenth century.'

'Then what's he got to do with all this Bradenham business?'

'I don't know,' Lubbock said, 'nor do those taxi-drivers in Thetford. Nobody knows for sure. That's the whole point . . . But let's get back to the man himself. Matthew Hopkins was a witchfinder general, anointed by Cromwell. And the most notorious. He was a man who repeatedly saw the Devil in others, and remained unaware of the Devil in himself. You might say he was possessed.'

'I'm a sceptic. You know that. You'll need to convince me.'

'Sceptic you may be, but hear the facts first before you make up your mind.'

'OK.' Tench resigned himself. 'Let's hear the facts.'

'Well, the whole sorry story began in Manningtree, when a local tailor complained that a one-legged woman called Clarke had bewitched his wife. Hopkins heard about this and took up his case. He had Mistress Clarke arrested and searched for witches' marks. You know what they were. Anything mildly abnormal: supernumerary nipples, extra fingers and toes, even commonplace blemishes such as moles and warts. Predictably, such a mark was found on Mistress Clarke, and after Hopkins had starved her of sleep for three or four nights, she confessed to having had carnal intercourse with the Devil and implicated a number of other women in the town. All of them went to the gallows.'

'And there's a link with Bradenham?'

'Yes, laddie, there is. Be patient and listen. Hopkins seems to have been infected by this early success, and decided pretty swiftly that his mission in life was to extirpate witches. So, given a free hand by the local magistrates, he recruited two assistants and made his way round Essex, using all the refinements of torture known to the Gestapo, and a few more besides. At one stage of his travels, nineteen unfortunates he happened to pick on were hanged in a single day... Then he moved into Suffolk, producing an even higher mortality rate, and once he thought he'd cleansed that county of witches, he crossed the border into Norfolk and set up base at Bradenham. There he hanged six women without delay, and then went on to Yarmouth where he hanged another five.'

'But he didn't get away with it?'

'He did for two years. Two years when he terrorized the whole of East Anglia. Then justice caught up with him. Someone with more courage than the rest informed against him. He was thrown into a river and, happily, floated: a sign that he'd made a pact with the Devil. So they took him out and hanged him.'

'Serve the bugger right.'

'As you put it so succinctly, laddie, serve the bugger right. If ever there was a man who was evil personified, it was Matthew Hopkins. But explain him if you can. I can't, except to say that if he wasn't possessed of the Devil, he was Old Nick himself.'

Tench furrowed his brow.

'I'm trying to see the link,' he said. 'This man worked from Bradenham and hanged six of the town's women. Are you trying to tell me that, just because of that, you've got some wild idea that these wartime murders were all committed by men who were suddenly gripped by some malevolent spirit?'

'No, Mike, I'm not. I keep an open mind, and so should you till you've heard all the evidence. What I'm saying is this. These Bradenham killings followed a very peculiar pattern. If you can explain them, then you're more of a sceptic than I imagine you to be. You see, laddie, it wasn't simply the connection between Hopkins and Bradenham that made us stop and think. It was because of what we found when we came to investigate the last of the murders. That of Valerie Marsden.'

6

'She was the teacher's wife?'

Lubbock nodded his head.

'Marsden was on the staff of Queen Mary's Grammar School. He taught French and German.'

'And he strangled her.'

'Right. But before we get on to Anthony Marsden, let me mention one or two of the things that seemed odd. There'd been a sequence of murders, all in one place and all within a relatively short space of time. In each of the cases the victim was a woman. There'd already been five before Mrs Marsden. She was the sixth, and she was also the last. And Matthew Hopkins was responsible for six deaths in Bradenham, all of them women.'

'That has to be a coincidence.'

'It could be coincidence. Yes, of course it could. But there is another point that's worth a little thought. The medieval witchfinders always looked to find the Devil in a woman, rather than a man. All women, they believed, were lustful by nature, and that made them more susceptible to the blandishments of Satan... Now, about this spate of murders. The strange thing was that each of these men seemed to have convinced himself, rightly or wrongly, that the woman in the case had committed a carnal sin. The two farmers, Walsh and Jacques, and Devereux, the accountant, believed that their wives had committed adultery. Wensley, the butcher, thought his fiancée had betrayed him with a friend; and the soldier, a sergeant in the Commandos, suspected that his girlfriend had been sharing a bed with somebody else while he'd been risking his life at Dieppe.'

'And Marsden?'

'He had other suspicions: suspicions more relevant to your present problems. He got it into his head that his wife was going to leave him to live with another woman.'

'A lesbian relationship?'

'Precisely that, laddie. And all the evidence pointed to the fact that every one of these men felt that what had happened reflected on their manhood. They felt, to use a phrase that the witchfinders used, that they'd each been unmanned: deprived of their virility. Especially Marsden. To be rejected for another man – that was bad enough; but to be cast aside in favour of a woman – that compounded the sin.'

Tench scratched his head.

'Aren't you reading things into this?' he said. 'Sexual jealousy's a common motive for murder. Perhaps the most common. I'm ready to admit that all these cases follow a pattern, but it's one that leads to a killing somewhere in England every day of the week.'

'I'm not denying that.' Lubbock examined his pipe with some dissatisfaction, and then knocked it out in his battered tin ashtray. 'But what gave these killings a whole new dimension were the books we turned up.'

'Books?'

'That's right. You know what they are, Mike, don't you? Printed leaves bound together and enclosed in a cover. We found one at Walsh's farm at Trusford Heath, and thought little of it. It was only when we came across another in the Marsdens' house at Bradenham that we put two and two together and made something that closely resembled a four . . . Have you heard of the *Malleus Maleficarum*?'

'No,' said Tench. 'What is it?'

'In Germany it's known as the *Hexenhammer*. In English it's called *The Hammer of Witchcraft*. It's a treatise written by two Dominicans at the end of the fifteenth century: probably the most terrible work on demonology ever compiled: a procedural handbook: a blueprint, if you like, for rooting out witches. It's the book that Hopkins, and all those who followed his miserable trade, took as their text.' He paused. 'D'you want to hear the rest? Or does your scepticism rule all this out as nothing but gibberish?'

'Go on,' said Tench. 'I'm listening.'

'There was no English translation till twenty years ago. Then a cleric, the Reverend Montague Summers, produced his own version. It was published in a limited edition of some twelve hundred copies, each of them numbered. There's one in the County Library in Norwich. The reference section. If you want to see it, ask them to fish it out.'

He reached for his tobacco jar.

'The copy we found when we searched Trusford Farm was numbered 697.'

7

He filled his pipe slowly, methodically, rubbing the loose tobacco between his palms.

'I ought to make it clear', he went on, 'that Lionel Walsh, the husband, was no semi-literate smallholder. He was the younger son of a landed family, educated at Harrow and Oxford, and his farm covered several thousand acres. How he came by that copy of the *Malleus* we never knew. He and his wife had no children, and none of their relatives remembered having seen it. We found it on a bedside table and impounded it, along with other items that we hoped would provide a clue. But it seemed, at that time, to have little bearing on what had occurred, so we eventually returned it. No reference was made to it when Walsh came to trial, and no mention of it ever appeared in the press. Six months later it was sold at auction as part of a job lot. It went to a second-hand bookseller from Framlingham, but three years after that, when we tried to trace it, he couldn't remember when it had been sold or who might have bought it.'

'But then, when Marsden strangled his wife, you found another copy.'

'Yes, but this wasn't the English translation. It was a German edition. We found it in his desk – he taught German, don't forget – and one of our sergeants, a young chap called Lennox, had done German at school. He fathomed out what it was. That was when we connected it with what we'd found years before at the Trusford farm. But, unlike the first time, there seemed to be a clear connection with the murder. Inside this copy, as we found it in the desk, were two handwritten sheets. They were in Marsden's handwriting, and from what we could tell, he'd made his own translation of two particular passages from the book. We called in the Head of Modern Languages at Gresham's, and he confirmed it, pointing out for us the relevant sections.'

Lubbock heaved himself up, and ambled across the parlour to a glass-fronted bookcase. He opened one of the doors, and pulled out a folder that he'd lodged between his copies of *Notable British Trials*. He laid it on the table.

'We had the two sheets photographed for evidence,' he said, 'and I got the lab to make a couple of extra copies. They're in there. Read them, and remember that when Marsden strangled his wife, he did it with a towel.'

Tench flicked open the folder. Inside were two prints. The writing was crabbed, the lines close together, and it took him some time to bring his eyes into focus, but at length he began to make sense of what he saw.

The top sheet was headed: 'MM' (obviously *Malleus Maleficarum*), 'Part One, Question Six. Concerning Witches who have Carnal Intercourse with Devils. Why do Women yield more easily to Evil than Men?'

Underneath this, Marsden had written: 'All witchcraft proceeds out of carnal lust, and such lust in women can never be appeased. Witness Proverbs, Chapter 30: There are three things that are never satisfied, and a fourth that can never say Enough. That fourth, the mouth of the womb, is in women. That is the reason why, to fulfil their lust, they open it to the Devil.'

Tench slid the print aside, and turned to the second.

This had a similar kind of heading: 'MM, Part Two, Question One, Chapter Seven. How Witches can deprive a Man of his Virility.'

He read on.

'There was once a young man who lived in Ratisbon. He had an affair with a girl, but when he threatened to leave her, he lost his virility. Brooding over this, he sought solace in a tavern where, drinking wine, he fell into talk with a woman nearby. She saw that he was troubled and asked him why. He told her the whole story, revealing to her touch that his virility had somehow been spirited away. She was wise, asked him who he suspected, and when he named the girl she said: "You must see her again and persuade her to restore to you what is yours. But if that has no effect, you will have to use force." That same evening the young man followed the girl, stopped her and pleaded with her to give him back his health. "You accuse me wrongly," she said. "I know nothing about it." Whereupon he seized her, wound a towel round her neck and drew it tight till she choked. "Give it back to me," he cried. "If you don't, I shall kill you." Her face was already suffused and turning black. "If you want me to heal you," she gasped, "let me go." He loosened the towel, and she laid a hand between his thighs. "You have your wish," she said. "Feel. It is there." '

Tench shuffled the prints together, and slipped them back in the folder.

'Well?' Lubbock asked.

'I'm surprised Marsden's counsel didn't plead he was insane.'

'Oh, he did. That was what we expected. But the judge wouldn't wear it. Said the man knew exactly what he was doing. The jury agreed.'

Tench looked at the prints again.

'I'll grant you one thing. It's a peculiar business. But that's as far as I'm willing to go. What do *you* think about it?'

'I don't know, laddie. I never did know. I'm merely giving you the facts. You'll have to make your own assessment. Let's hope that, as far as the Marriotts are concerned, it means nothing at all. There've already been two deaths. You don't want to find yourself landed with six.'

'Too bloody true.' The words were spoken with feeling.

'I can only repeat what a local shopkeeper told me, when I questioned him over the Marsden case. He was a chap I knew well: sensible, down-to-earth, very much the agnostic, but he put into words what those taxi-drivers felt. "I don't know what it is," he said, "but there must be something here that makes men go berserk." So, unless you can prove that whoever stole that Lagonda dumped it there by sheer chance, I'd keep the Bradenham murders in mind.'

'Don't worry,' said Tench. 'You've made certain of that ... Any other, more down-to-earth tips to offer?'

Lubbock ignored the irony. He struck a match, stoked up his pipe and gave his opinion from behind a screen of smoke.

'If I were you, laddie, I'd take a much closer look at that naked doll. It was clearly intended to carry a message, but it's the first valid clue that's turned up in this case. Dolls can often be traced back to their owners. Parents have bought them somewhere. Children have treasured them. And some are quite distinctive. So why leave a clue like that lying around?'

'As you said, to make a point.'

'A pretty expensive point, if it leads you to the killer. It seems to me, Mike, that he's made you a present. That means one of three things. He's either getting careless or arrogant or he wants to be caught. All hopeful signs ... You know what I'd do? As soon as that doll's returned from the lab – and the sooner the better – hand a couple of prints of it over to Ransome. Then take it to Gilbert Franks at the Castle Museum. Assistant Curator. He's an expert on dolls. One look at it and he'll tell you not only what it's made of, but who made it and when. He's very precise. Talks like a pansy, but don't be deceived. He's as tough as old boots. Flew a Spitfire in the Battle of Britain. Clicked for a DFC ... That reminds me. You mentioned a mother's boy. Is there one in the frame?'

'Not really. At the moment all we're doing is thinking possibilities. He seems to have an alibi.'

'Who is he?'

'One of the wardens. A chap called Phelps.'

'Must have seen him,' said Lubbock. 'Can't call him to mind. What does Langrick say about him?'

'Swears that he's harmless... By the way, d'you know Terry Jagger?'

'Who?'

'Terry Jagger. He's a photographer. Takes pictures of birds. Lives at Zitundo Cottage.'

Lubbock shook his head.

'Can't have been there long. The place has been empty since Dan Merrick died. It was still empty last week. He must have moved in in the last few days. Is he in the frame, too?'

'No, but Phelps ferries him out to the Point. If he's been taking shots of the terns, he could have seen something.'

'Well, I can't say I've met him, but I'll take a stroll down to the village later on. It's about time I paid old Isaac a visit.'

'Who's Isaac?'

Lubbock seemed to find the question mildly amusing.

'Isaac Bone,' he said blandly. 'Coastguard. Retired. Eyes like a hawk. Lives next door to Zitundo. He's bound to know something. Leave it to me.'

7

NAMES AND NUMBERS

> Why, sir, you know no house nor no such maid,
> Nor no such men as you have reckoned up.

William Shakespeare: *The Taming of the Shrew*

1

Tench sat at his desk in Norwich, and stared at the autopsy report on Phoebe Marriott. He read it through a second time, and concluded that it left him more confused than before.

According to Ledward, death had occurred not earlier than nine o'clock on Tuesday evening and not later than ten. All the signs pointed to manual strangulation. Cyanosis was present in the lips and the ears, there was bloodstaining round the mouth and a protrusion of the tongue, which had been partially bitten through. In addition there were petechiae, minute haemorrhages, on the face and in the whites of the eyes, and these were also visible in the lungs, the back of the throat and the lining of the nose. Even more significant, there was extensive bruising to the throat, and one wing of the hyoid cartilage had been fractured and part of it driven inwards towards the windpipe.

The body, the report went on, was that of a normal healthy young woman. She was not virgo intacta, but there were no signs of recent sexual intercourse or of sexual molestation. There were no apparent scars, nor were there any traces of blood beneath the nails. That meant that she hadn't scratched her attacker. The only solid clue that Ledward could offer was his discovery, under the middle fingernail of the girl's right hand, of a single maroon-coloured animal fibre, probably wool, such as might have come from a sweater. This had been passed to the lab for analysis.

He turned to the lab reports. The car had yielded nothing of any consequence. The only fingerprints found, apart from those of Phoebe Marriott and her sister, had been his own, on the purse and the handle of the door. Casts of the footprints found on the shore suggested they were those of a man who, had he been wearing shoes, would have taken size seven. No prints had been found on any of the clothes the girl had been wearing, apart from some blurred and blood-stained ones of her own, but there were salt-water stains on her blouse, skirt and knickers; and the fibre that Ledward had found beneath her fingernail was confirmed as being wool. It had no particular characteristic that marked it out as being of any distinctive type. It could have come from any of a thousand woollen garments on sale in the shops.

Typical, Tench thought. They'd found a bit of fluff that meant nothing at all.

It could have come, not from anything her killer had been wearing, but from something of her own. Only one thing about it was certain: it hadn't come from the cardigan she'd left in the car. That had been navy blue.

He pushed the reports to one side, and found his mind wandering backwards to Lubbock.

All this business about Bradenham. Was it possible that there could be a connection with the case? No. He shook his head. All his instincts denied it. It wasn't the first time that his old chief had flown off at a tangent about witchcraft. He remembered one particular occasion in the winter of '47. They'd been investigating the murders at Elsdon Hall, and he'd brought up all that rigmarole about the curse that Old Mother Craske was supposed to have laid on the Wilder family. He'd made it clear to him then that, as far as he was concerned, it was nothing but a load of superstitious nonsense, and he was still of the same opinion.

And yet . . .

And yet what?

The old boy had been persuasive . . .

Could there, after all, be something strange about the place? Were there more things in heaven and earth than he, Mike Tench, was prepared to accept?

No, there damned well weren't.

He pulled himself up sharply.

Hadn't the Chief Super warned him? 'Don't, for God's sake,' he'd said, 'let him catch you off balance. If you do, you could find yourself chasing a hare.'

That was sound advice. He couldn't afford to spend time chasing hares. He'd already chased enough geese.

Forget about Bradenham.

Lock it away, like Phoebe Marriott's diary. Put it out of mind. It was nothing but another dangerous distraction.

He glanced at his watch. Nine forty-five. At least things were moving. The house-to-house squads were already at work, rapping on doors at Morston and Langham. Two more teams under Darricot were doing the rounds from the incident room at Blakeney, making inquiries at local hotels and questioning boatmen. McKenzie was taking statements from the cottagers at Craymere; Sue Gradwell and Rayner were searching Downs House; Ellison was out at Wiveton, with instructions to bring in the warden, Joe Turner; Spurgeon had gone to Cley to track down Terry Jagger; Gregg was in Sheringham, sifting through the Marriotts' business files; and Lock was standing by to take the incoming calls, and running his finger down telephone directories to identify names and numbers on the index pad that they'd found the night before.

It was time that he asked a few questions himself. Chased up the lab. He had to know about that doll and get his hands on it, fast.

He reached for the phone, but it rang before he could lift the receiver.

It was Charlesworth, the sergeant on duty at the desk. He was mildly apologetic.

'Sorry to bother you, sir,' he said, 'but there's a young lady down here. Says she has to speak to the Detective Chief Inspector. Won't take no for an answer.'

'Who is she?'

'Says her name's Barbara Leening, sir. Claims she knows something about this Craymere affair.'

Tench took a deep breath.

'Send her up,' he said.

2

She was wearing her dark green blazer and skirt, and she looked at him wistfully.

'Cor,' she said. 'You really are something. Are you happily married?'

'Sublimely,' Tench told her. 'Shouldn't you be at school?'

'Call me Babs,' she said. 'Yes.'

'Then what are you doing here?'

'You don't sound very pleased.'
'Why should I be pleased? You're truanting from school.'
'Not really,' she said. 'I'll be back this afternoon.'
'Does your mother know you're here?'
Her eyes opened wide.
'Course not. Why should she?'
Tench felt that he was somehow losing his grip.
'Sit down,' he said.
'You ought to say please. It's polite to say please.'
'Please sit down, Miss Leening.'
'Babs.'
Tench walked round the desk and pulled up a chair.
'If you want to speak to me, Babs' – he emphasized the word – 'then do as I say and sit down.'
She sat on the edge and gazed at him fondly.
'I knew you'd be masterful,' she said. 'All of them are.'
'Who?'
'The best detectives.'
Tench shrugged off the compliment.
'How did you get here?'
'Bike as far as Holt,' she said. 'Then I caught a train.'
'Have you had any breakfast?'
She shook her head.
'Didn't have time.'
'Would you like some?'
'Aren't you going to ask me what I know about the murder?'
'No. D'you want some breakfast?'
She thought for a moment.
'What have you got?'
'Egg, bacon, sausage . . .'
'Chips?' she said hopefully.
Hunger stared him in the face.
'I think we might rustle up a plateful,' he told her. 'I suppose you'll be wanting tomato sauce too?'

They sat on either side of a canteen table, and he waited till she'd finished the last of the chips.
'Well? Were they good?'
She wiped her mouth on the back of her hand.
'Absolutely super.'
'You feel better?'
'Yes, heaps.'

'Then perhaps you've learnt something more about detectives. They aren't just masterful. They have their soft spots. Even the very best of them.'

'Lord Peter Wimsey?'

'I was thinking of Sherlock Holmes.'

'Oh, him,' she said witheringly. 'He wasn't a detective. He knew all the answers. The best detectives don't. They need to be helped.'

Tench eyed her with some amusement.

'So you think I'm a good detective. I don't know all the answers, and you've come to help.'

'Well, you don't,' she said, 'do you? You don't know about the car.'

'Which car was this?'

'The one by the barn.'

'Which barn?'

'Starling's barn.'

'Let's start at the beginning, shall we?' said Tench. 'You know what happened last night at Downs House?'

'Course I do,' she said. 'It was Phoebe's sister. She got it in the neck. Everybody knows. All that racket going on. You weren't exactly pussyfooting round the place, were you?'

'You mean Lord Peter would have gone about on tiptoe?'

'That isn't funny.' She was stern, unforgiving.

'I apologize,' said Tench. 'So tell me about this car.'

'It was last night. I went to play tennis at Langham.'

'I didn't know they had any tennis-courts at Langham.'

'They don't. It's a friend's house. They've one at the back.'

Tench nodded.

'OK. You went on your bike?'

'Only way to go. There aren't any buses after six o'clock.'

'So what time did you go?'

'Just before seven.'

'And you saw this car, and it was by Starling's barn?'

'Yes, he's a farmer. Lives between us and Langham. It's on the edge of his field.'

'Where exactly?'

'Just above Downs House. There's a track to it from the road, and when you get to the barn there's this path runs all the way down to Garret Hill.'

'At the back of the house?'

'Yes.'

'And where was the car?'

'Parked on the track. I saw it as I passed, and it was still there when I came back. I couldn't see any driver.'

'What time was that?'

163

'About half-past eight. So I went and had a look at it.'
'Go on,' said Tench.
'It was like this blazer, dark green. Long and very low, with one of those canvas hoods. It had big goggle lamps and the wheels had wire spokes.'
'Did you get the make?'
'I took a peek at the licence. Is there a car called an Alvis?'
'Yes, there is.'
'Then that's what it was.'
'And of course,' said Tench, 'you made a note of the number-plate.'
'Had to, hadn't I? That's the very first thing a good detective does.'
'So what was it?'
She took a small piece of paper from her top blazer pocket, two more from the side pockets, and another from an inner one; then she laid them out in a line on the desk. The same number was scrawled in pencil on each. It was a Norwich registration.
'I wrote it down four separate times,' she explained. 'Didn't want to lose it.'
Tench looked at her with something close to approval.
'You know,' he said, 'I think you might make a detective. Woman Detective Constable Barbara Leening.'
'Babs.'
Then she blushed.
'You're kidding. D'you mean it?'
'Every single word.'
'You know what?' she said. 'That's positively, positively super. I could hug you to death. You really are an angel.'
Tench raised a hand.
'Don't think of it,' he told her. 'Detectives just can't afford to be angels. Sometimes they have to be really, truly brutal.'
'They do?'
'Oh, yes. Even Lord Peter. Right now he'd do exactly what I'm going to do.'
'What's that?'
'Put you on a train back to Holt,' said Tench. 'You need to be at school. If you want to be a detective, you've got to learn the four Rs.'
She frowned.
'You mean three.'
'Four,' said Tench firmly. 'Reading, Riting, Rithmetic and Rules.'

He handed one of the scraps of paper to Lock.

'Alvis, dark green,' he said. 'Seen near Downs House. Owner needs tracing. Get on to it right away . . . I'm driving Miss Leening down to the station. Afterwards I'll be at the lab and the Castle Museum. Once you get an answer, give me a ring.'

He turned at the door.

'And for God's sake don't tell me that this one's been nicked.'

3

Kenton, the young analyst who worked at the lab, lifted up the bag containing the doll and placed it on his desk.

'Sorry,' he said. 'No fingerprints worth recording. Whoever handled it last must have worn gloves.'

Tench murmured that he hadn't expected him to find any.

'What about the doll itself?'

Kenton pulled it out of the bag.

'Cloth body,' he said. 'Head and limbs made of wax. It's a mixture of beeswax, East Indian wax and spermaceti – that's a white substance found in the heads of sperm whales. There's also ground safflower and talc. Rouge, if you like. It's been used as an agent to colour the wax. Eyes are made of glass. Eyebrows, eyelashes and hair are natural: human hair. Each strand's been inserted separately, probably with something like a blunt needle. The limbs are attached to the body by stitching through a series of eyelet holes. Limbs and head are wax shells. My guess is that they haven't been sculpted. The wax has been poured into pre-cast moulds and stiffened with muslin. I don't know very much at all about dolls, but this one appears to be competently made, and it must be fairly old because the wax has begun to fade.'

'What d'you mean by fairly old?'

'Oh, fifty years. If it's been kept under glass or hidden away in a box, it could be older than that. You really need someone who's a specialist in dolls to put a date to it.'

'It's not stamped with a maker's name?'

'No, nothing like that, but someone's written a name and address on the back. Probably one of its owners. That might help you to trace its history.'

'Show me,' said Tench.

Kenton laid the doll face down on the desk, and swept aside the hair from the nape of the neck.

'There,' he said. 'It's written in Indian ink. You wouldn't normally see it. It's hidden by the hair.'

Tench leaned forward. Across the top of the shoulders someone had inscribed in a flowing hand what looked like 'Montanari 12 Oxford St.'.

He peered at it more closely.

'Montanari?'

'That's what I thought.'

'Sounds Italian to me. If it's Oxford Street, London, it could be a shop.'

'It could,' Kenton said, 'but I wouldn't have thought a shop would have had its name written in ink like that. I'd be willing to wager it's someone who owned it at one time or other. Someone from a family called Montanari.'

Tench stared at the doll.

'We don't even know that it's London, do we? It could be Oxford Street, Manchester for all we can tell. Or an Oxford Street, for that matter, anywhere in England. I know Manchester like a book. And the places round about. I was born and brought up there. Show me a map and I'll point to at least a dozen Oxford Streets within a dozen miles. There's one in Bolton, one in Oldham, one in Ashton, one in Eccles. They're all over the place. Take the whole country, and there must be literally hundreds of them.'

'London's still the best bet. I'd start looking there first.'

'It's a matter of time,' said Tench. 'Time and resources. I've already got the Chief Super breathing down my neck. In another twenty-four hours it may be the Met. . . . This doll. Are you sure about its age?'

Kenton scratched his head.

'I can't claim to be an expert. All I have to go on is the state of the wax. It shows signs of ageing. That indicates to me that, unless it's been very carefully preserved – in a glazed wooden case or under a glass dome – it must have been poured at least fifty years ago. What you really need on the job is a specialist: someone who's made a lifetime's study of dolls . . . What about the bods at the Castle Museum? Or you could try the Strangers' Hall. That's probably a better bet. They've got a toy collection there. Up at the Castle it's all Cromes and Cotmans and Greater Spotted Cuckoos.'

'And Terns and Gannets and even Spitfires.'

Kenton blinked.

'Spitfires?'

'Spitfires,' said Tench. 'One of the curators there flew them, I'm told. Fellow called Franks. Stationed at Biggin Hill during the war. Knows a lot about them, and about dolls. Quite an expert on dolls. I think I'll toddle round with this naked nymph of ours, and let him take a look at her. You know what these fighter pilots are for the women. There's always a chance he may have met her before.'

4

Mr Gilbert Franks hadn't met her before, but he was none the less entranced.

He held her at arm's length and purred with approval.

'My, my!' he said. 'And where did you find this one?'

'Left on the body of a murder victim, sir. Why? Is she special?'

'Yes, indeed, I'd say so. I'd definitely say so.'

'How can you tell?'

'The technique that's been used in making her, Chief Inspector, and also her shape.'

'I gather that she must be getting on in years.'

Franks nodded his head, not once but several times.

'If she's what I think she is, then she's older than both our ages put together.'

'We need to trace whoever left her at the murder scene,' said Tench, 'and we thought you might be able to give us one or two clues. It's possible she's passed through a number of hands, but someone – we think maybe one of the owners – has written a name and address on her back.' He brushed the hair aside. 'Here, sir. Take a look.'

Mr Franks did more than take a look. He examined the inscription through a magnifying glass, and then nodded again in even greater excitement.

'Montanari,' he said. 'Yes, I knew it was. It had to be.'

'The name means something to you?'

'Oh, yes, Chief Inspector. It means a great deal.'

'Then you may be able to help us. The address is Oxford Street. Is that Oxford Street in London?'

'It most certainly is.' Mr Franks seemed amused. 'Don't tell me you've had the police out in London searching for Montanari.'

'Not yet, sir, but we thought . . .'

'Waste of time, Chief Inspector. Complete waste of time. He left Oxford Street – let me see, when was it? 1874, or possibly '75. That's exactly three-quarters of a century ago.'

Tench was, understandably, at something of a loss.

'Then who was he, this Montanari?'

'Who was he? Dear me!' Franks assumed disbelief. 'Surely you must have heard of him!'

'Never, sir,' said Tench.

'He was Richard Napoleon Montanari, the son of Madame Augusta Montanari. And she' – he paused as if on the verge of some shattering revelation – 'she was the most famous of all the Victorian makers of dolls. She won a prize for her dolls at the Great Exhibition. Died in 1864. That was when her son took over the business.'

'Richard Napoleon.'

'Exactly, Chief Inspector. He was named after his father, another Napoleon, and he's the Montanari on the back of this doll.'

Tench looked at the inscription, and then at Mr Franks.

'I think, sir,' he said, 'you'd better give me every bit of information you can about this naked young lady.'

They sat at a table with the doll reared up between them.

'Yes, she is naked, isn't she?' said Franks. 'It's a pity she's not wearing her petticoats and dress. If I'd been able to see them, I'd have placed her right away. The Montanari trousseaus were works of art: all of pure silk, and all hand-stitched; though once he'd taken over, Richard tended to make them less lavish.'

'Tell me about the Montanaris.'

'Well, before Madame Montanari arrived on the scene, dolls' bodies were always moulded like adults'. The fashions of the time decreed narrow waists. She produced and marketed the first real baby dolls made of poured wax, and then went on to extend her range till it covered all ages from infants to fully matured young women. She was the doyenne of the nineteenth-century world of wax dolls. Famous world-wide.'

'So the dolls she made can be easily identified?'

'No, I wouldn't say that. Dolls of a similar type were subsequently made by a number of other firms, notably the Pierottis, and so few were marked with the maker's name – even the Montanaris – that it's often quite difficult to link them to any particular maker. Let's take this one, for instance. If it hadn't been inscribed with the Montanari name, and lacking as it does the clothes that go with it, I could have hazarded a guess that it was probably their work. But I wouldn't have had proof. I could perhaps have dated it to within twenty years. Having seen the inscription, I can narrow that down to two.'

'How would you have put a date to it?'

'Mainly, Chief Inspector, by the shape of the body. It's an adult female, and you can see that the hips are excessively wide. That points to the middle of the nineteenth century, when the crinoline was in fashion. A doll would need wide hips to support the dress she was wearing, and that indicates to me that this one was made between the mid-eighteen-fifties and the mid-eighteen-seventies. Once the crinoline went out and the bustle came in, dolls had much slimmer hips.'

'And how does the inscription help?'

'Simple,' said Franks. 'Richard Montanari took over the firm in 1864. At that time he was working in Fitzroy Square. In 1872 he moved into premises at 12 Oxford Street, but by 1875 he wasn't there any longer. He'd switched to Rathbone Place. So, if this doll was made in Oxford Street, the most probable dates are either 1873 or 1874.'

'Nearly eighty years ago.'

'That's right. And let me add that it's almost unique. I've been lucky enough to see a number of Montanaris, but I've only seen one that was inscribed in this way. They're comparatively rare.'

Tench pondered.

'Does that mean they're valuable?'

'Yes, as dolls go. Even when they were first sold in Victorian times, the price was very high. For an undressed Montanari you'd have had to fork out five guineas at least. That meant that only wealthy parents could afford them. They were treasured possessions. Nowadays it's a matter of scarcity value. A doll like this sold at auction could well fetch two or three hundred pounds. With a trousseau, much more. That's not to say that someone couldn't have picked it up cheap, if the vendor didn't know precisely what he was selling.'

'And someone could have bought it, and not known its value.'

'Unless he was an expert, he'd have had no idea.'

Tench was silent for a moment. He stared at the doll.

'If you wanted to trace its recent history,' he said, 'what would you do?'

'You've photographed it?'

'Yes.'

'And the inscription?'

'On its own.'

Franks pulled a tape-measure out of his pocket, and measured the doll.

'Twenty inches,' he said. 'That's tall for a Montanari. It was probably made in response to an order . . . You've got prints. Get them out to the newspapers, local and national. Circulate them to museums and auction houses. Take them round and show them to antique dealers and the owners of shops that sell second-hand goods. It may have come from a country house, or some wealthy family that's hit a financial rock and had to sell up. That would make tracing it a fairly simple matter. On the other hand, it may have been stowed away in an attic for years, and tossed out to a rag-and-bone man by someone who thought it just wasn't worth keeping.'

'And in that case, we might never track down the last owner.'

'That's possible,' said Franks, 'but I wouldn't give up too easily. If it isn't unique, it's practically so. And the clothes must be somewhere. Unless, of course, your murderer's had himself a bonfire. If he has, then he's not just a killer, he's an ignorant vandal. That should at least help you to single him out.'

5

Single him out?

That was simple.

You did it just like that, with a snap of the fingers.

It wasn't often that Tench yielded to a sense of futility, still less to a cynical appraisal of his job; but, climbing the stairs to his office, he found himself swearing and pounding the handrail.

To hear people talk, it was all so bloody simple.

All he had to do was find an ordinary man with a blameless record somewhere in Norfolk: an inconspicuous someone who took size seven shoes, probably wore a maroon-coloured sweater, went around strangling attractive young women, and might or might not be an ignorant vandal.

Oh yes, utterly bloody simple.

Simplicity itself.

He swore a little too loudly as he opened the door.

Nor was he cheered by Lock's words of greeting.

'The Alvis, sir. Nicked.'

He groaned.

'Where from this time?'

'The Feathers, sir, at Holt. Reported missing by its owner, a Henry Venables, at half-past seven last night. He's an accountant, lives at Kelling. Seems he took his girlfriend out to dinner at the Feathers, and parked the Alvis in the courtyard at the back. They were having a drink when she found she'd left her handbag on the back seat. He went to collect it. Car had disappeared.'

'Has it been found?'

'Not yet. They're still searching.'

'Let me know as soon as you get any news.'

'Right, sir.'

'And keep your fingers crossed that it doesn't turn up at Bradenham . . . Anything else?'

'Mr Lubbock rang up.'

'What did he have to say?'

'Left a message, sir.' Lock pulled out his notebook. 'Said there was no sign of Mr Jagger at his cottage. Place was locked up. But he had a word with someone called Isaac Bone. He gave him a description. Apparently Jagger's in his mid-twenties, about five foot nine, with hair that looks as if it's been permed. According to Mr Bone he's an arty-crafty type. Wanders around in a roll-neck and flannels. Drops in at the George for a pint now and then. Mr Lubbock said he spoke to the landlord at the George. Doesn't think much of Jagger. Calls him flashy. Says he thinks too much of himself by far.'

'Did Lubbock see Spurgeon anywhere around?'

'Waiting outside the cottage, sir. Said he'd hang on a while in case Jagger showed up.'

'Right . . . No response to the press appeals?'

'A couple of vague sightings of the brigadier's car, sir. You know the kind of thing. Might have been the one. Didn't see it too clearly. Thought I'd better report it.'

'Whereabouts were they?'

'One at Caister and the other at Snettisham. They both sound way off the target to me, but we're following them up.'

'Nothing more?'

'Yes, sir. Ellison's brought in the warden, Joe Turner.'

'Where is he?'

'Down in the interview room, sir, or was. Not in the best of tempers, so Ellison says. Watering his tomato plants. Didn't take kindly to being dragged away.'

'Too bad,' said Tench. 'I'm not exactly full of summer sunshine myself.'

Mr Turner was certainly not in the best of tempers.

A tall, square-shouldered man in an open-necked shirt, grey jacket and trousers, he sat with his elbows on the table and glowered at Tench.

'Is this really necessary, Inspector?' he said. 'I've already made a statement to that young detective. What's his name? Lock?'

'Lock, sir, yes, and yes, it is necessary.'

'It's very inconvenient.'

'I'm sorry, sir, but we are investigating a murder. In fact, two murders. You've heard about the one at Craymere last night?'

'Yes, of course I've heard, but I don't see that it's anything to do with me. I was nowhere near Craymere.'

'That may be so, sir . . .'

'No maybe about it. Never stirred from Wiveton.'

'None the less, sir, the two murders are connected. The victims were sisters . . . Where were you last night?'

Turner showed a flash of exasperation. He gripped the edge of the table.

'I've already said. Wiveton.'

'Whereabouts in Wiveton? You came off duty when? Half-past two?'

'Nearer three o'clock.'

'And what did you do for the rest of the day?'

'Picked up my bike . . .'

'Where from?'

'Keep it chained to the rails at the side of the quay.'

'And then?'

'Rode it home.'

'And after that?'

'Stayed there.'

'You didn't leave the house?'

Turner's lips tightened.

'Look, Inspector. If I tell you I stayed there, that means I stayed there. Ask the wife. She was with me. What d'you want? A minute-by-minute report?'

'What time did you go to bed, sir?'

'Ten o'clock. Always do.'

'Thank you,' said Tench.

'Is that it? Can I go?'

'Not yet, sir. Let's go back to what you said in your previous statement.'

Turner glanced up at the clock on the wall.

'Inspector,' he said. 'I'm due to go over to the Point at high tide. Can't this wait till later? There are jobs I have to do.'

'We all have jobs to do, sir,' said Tench. 'Mine, at the moment, is to track down a murderer, and you may be able to offer some help. In fact, you and your colleague, Mr Phelps, may be the only two people who can possibly help.'

Turner breathed deeply.

'I've told you all I know.'

'Perhaps not quite all, sir.'

'You think I've been holding back part of the truth?'

'I think, sir, we may not have asked the right questions. You told Constable Lock that you'd seen the Marriott sisters on the beach at Blakeney Point.'

'I said I'd seen two girls. I don't know who they were. They may have been the Marriotts.'

'Point taken, sir,' said Tench. 'You didn't speak to them?'

'No. I was going to warn them to keep away from the terns, but they set off back towards Cley.'

'Was that the only time you saw them?'

'I hadn't seen them before, and I haven't seen them since.'

'This occasion when you saw them. Were there any other people around at the time?'

'Quite a few, yes. The weather was good, and high water was late on that particular day.'

'Anyone you recognized?'

'Only Bob Phelps's friend. The one who goes bird-watching. He was down in one of the lows with a pair of binoculars, watching the terns. I think he had a camera.'

'Did you speak to him?'

'No.' Turner shook his head. 'I don't really know him. Just seen him around at odd times with Bob.'

'And there was no one else you knew?'

'Not that I remember. Trippers in the main, out from Blakeney and Morston. We get them every day . . . Could have been one of them, couldn't it? Most likely was.'

'You mean . . .?'

'The chap who killed the girl . . . Came out in a boat, hid in one of the lows, walked back along the beach . . . Girl's dead, he's away, no one's any the wiser . . . Simple, I'd say.'

Tench gave him the withering glance that Lubbock had once reserved for trainee detectives.

'I wish to God it were, Mr Turner,' he said.

6

Back in his office, he asked himself what he'd learnt.

The answer was nothing, apart from the fact that Phelps's pal, Terry Jagger, had been hanging around the dunes with a pair of binoculars and might or might not have had them trained on the Marriotts.

Well, he needed to see Jagger. He had to speak to him; make his own assessment of the man. He could only hope that Spurgeon managed to find him.

He rang the lab and told Kenton that he was going to need prints of the doll for circulation, and was just about to dial Ransome at the *Eastern Daily Press* when McKenzie rang through from the phone box at Morston. He sounded short of breath.

'Did you ever have to run the gauntlet at school?' He was wheezing like a long-decrepit donkey-engine.

'No,' said Tench. 'Why?'

'Because to get here, I've had to. The whole damn place is swarming with pressmen: packs of them, every one avid for blood. They've been snapping at my heels all the way down from Craymere. I've even had to turf one out of this box, and there's half a dozen more of them queuing up outside.'

'Let them wait.'

'Oh, I've fended them off, but they're going to need some kind of statement, and fast.'

'Tell them they'll get one as soon as I've anything useful to report . . . Is Ransome among them?'

'I think he's somewhere at the back of the queue.'

'Tell him not to waste his time. Get him to ring me from the incident room at Blakeney . . . Have you finished down there?'

'Just about.'

'Any joy?'

'Not a bloody lot. Whoever got into that house last night was a second Claude Rains. The Invisible Man. No one in Craymere so much as set eyes on him.'

'Not even our panel of curtain-twitchers?'

'Grace Medlicott never looked out all evening. She was busy in the kitchen, baking cakes for some all-women's bun-fight at Binham. Mrs Leening had a cold and hit the hay early; and the fat one, Mrs Holland

– she wouldn't have seen him if he'd walked in by the front door waving a flag. Her bed faces the wrong way. She's looking down to Morston. I didn't see the girl, the one who's always on about Lord Peter Wimsey. She'd already gone to school. But her mother says she was out playing tennis at Langham, and Giles was stuck in that study of his, toiling away at quadratic equations . . . Anything at your end?'

'Another stolen car, but that's about all . . . Gradwell and Rayner? Have they finished too?'

'On their way back,' McKenzie said. 'Should be with you any minute. From what I heard them say, they've drawn a blank as well . . . Have the boffins persuaded that doll to confess?'

'It's opened its mouth and whispered its name, but nothing that looks like a worthwhile lead.'

'Then we're still stuck in limbo.'

'Floating around between heaven and hell, and still without a paddle.'

'Goddammit,' McKenzie said, 'there must be one around somewhere . . .'

The rest of his words were lost in a crackling noise like machine-gun fire.

Tench waited till it stopped.

'What the hell was that?'

'Just the wolves getting restive. Don't worry. They're only whetting their fangs on the door.'

'You'd better get back here before they lynch you,' Tench told him. 'We need to talk, Mac. If we don't crack this case pretty soon, there'll be another pack of wolves on the way from the Yard, and you know what that'll mean.'

McKenzie had no doubts.

'A loitering death,' he said. 'Right. I'm on my way.'

If Tench had been addicted to keeping a diary, his record of the next half-hour might well have run as follows:

12.58 Took call from Ransome. Gave him known details of DM's murder and told him about doll. Said we needed front-page exposure and appeal to all readers. Anyone with any knowledge of a doll with this inscription to contact us here. Also mentioned the Alvis. Requested information. Might get something on the car, but the doll's just a long shot.
1.05 WDC Gradwell and DC Rayner reported back from Downs House. Gradwell said the search had revealed nothing that was

overtly suspicious. Handed over three manilla envelopes – one containing letters, another holding bills, and the third half a dozen cheque books and numerous stubs. Also single copy of a monthly magazine, *East Anglian Life*. Said there was an article about the Marriott sisters. Thought I might find it interesting. She'd marked it by turning back the corner of the page. Asked her, hadn't she found Diana Marriott's diary? She said sorry to disappoint me, but no, no sign.

1.18 Saw DC Lock. Still no trace of the stolen Alvis, and no reports of anyone having seen the Lagonda on Tuesday night. Maybe not surprising. Whoever drove it to Primrose Spinney from Cley would probably have taken the secondary roads. And it was dark. Farmer from Winford phoned in to say he hadn't seen the Lagonda, but had noticed another car parked at Primrose Spinney, ten o'clock Tuesday night. A black Austin Seven. Hadn't bothered to check the registration. Most likely a courting couple. Seems the Spinney's well known as a trysting place.

1.27 DC Spurgeon brought in Terry Jagger. Questioned him down in the interview room. Seemed willing enough to help. Candid. Quite unruffled ...

7

Mr Jagger was more than merely unruffled. He was, so it seemed, entirely at ease. Wearing a yellow roll-neck sweater, brown twill trousers and a flat tweed cap, he was lounging in a chair chatting to Spurgeon. His hands were in his pockets, his legs were stretched out, and his ankles in brown and yellow checked socks were negligently crossed.

He stood up when Tench came in, and held out his hand.

'Chief Inspector Tench?'

'Mr Jagger?'

The handshake was firm, the eyes bright and unflinching. Terry Jagger was well-built, undeniably handsome and apparently self-possessed. He sat down, removed his cap and tossed it on the table. His hair, Tench noted, fair, almost golden, was naturally wavy rather than permed.

'I'm sorry to have to bring you all this way, sir,' he said, 'but we've been trying to make contact with you all morning.'

The young man smiled.

'Yes, I'm sorry about that. I was out on the marshes, dodging about to get some shots of the redshanks . . . I gather it's about this murder at Blakeney Point.'

'That's right, sir. We need to talk to anyone who might give us a clue. I believe you go out to the Point quite frequently.'

'Once or twice a week, apart from the winter.'

'You're a photographer.'

'Yes. Freelance.'

'You take shots of birds, and sell them for publication.'

'That's the general idea. There are plenty of magazines that deal with ornithology. *Country Life*, *British Birds*, *The Countryman*, *Country-Side*. Enough to keep me busy.'

'And to make a living?'

'A modest one at least. I do some portrait photography, and I'm getting to be quite a dab hand at landscapes.'

Tench pulled out a chair and sat down.

'Tell me, Mr Jagger. How do you normally get out to the Point?'

'Depends on how long I intend to stay. If I know what I want to do and it won't take too much time, I go and come back on one of the pleasure boats. Or I go with Bob Phelps – he's one of the wardens – and travel back with the trippers.'

'And if you want to stay longer?'

'If I think the weather's likely to last all day, and I want to rove about or spot the birds from the lows, I park the car at Cley and walk there and back along the beach.'

'I understand you've recently moved down to Cley.'

'Yes, a week ago.'

'From Blakeney.'

'That's right. I used to live near to Phelps. That's how I got to know him.'

'Why did you move to Cley?'

'It's the best place for birds. The marshes there were the first Local Nature Reserve. I can walk to them from the cottage.'

Tench nodded.

'You said you had a car. What make is it?'

'An old Sunbeam Talbot. Pre-war vintage. Handed down from my father.'

'When did you last use it to get to the Point?'

'Yesterday. I needed some shots of nesting terns.'

'Morning? Afternoon?'

'Morning. I was out there early and back by midday.'

'Were you there last Tuesday?'

'The day of the murder? No. The last time I was out there before yesterday was a week ago. Friday. I don't go at weekends. Too many visitors.'

'Did you know the Marriott sisters?'

Jagger shook his head.

'No. Never met them.'

'D'you think you've ever seen them out at the Point?'

'I may have done. I see hundreds of people out there.'

'Pretty girls. Two of them, running on the sands.'

'I have seen a couple of girls running together, but I wouldn't know whether or not they were the Marriotts. In any case, I only saw them from a distance.'

'When was this?'

Jagger scratched his head.

'Can't remember exactly. A fortnight ago?'

'Please think, sir,' said Tench. 'Was there anyone near them?'

'You mean a possible murderer?' Jagger seemed amused. 'No, Inspector, not that I could see.'

'We have to check every possibility, Mr Jagger.'

'Yes, of course. I understand that.'

'In the last three weeks, how many times have you been out to the Point?'

'Oh, roughly half a dozen.'

'Have you ever seen anyone acting suspiciously?'

'In what way, Inspector?'

'Hanging around, hiding in the lows.'

'You mean a Peeping Tom? No. Can't say I have.'

Tench felt the old familiar sense of frustration. It swept across him, engulfed him. Was there any logic in what he was doing? He'd got little enough from Turner, and now he was getting even less from Jagger. The whole bloody rigmarole was just a waste of effort.

Let them talk, Lubbock said. Something at some time'll drop into place.

Well, maybe. But it was taking a devil of a long time to drop.

He drew a deep breath and tried another tack.

'You said you'd been practising landscape photography.'

'That's right. At odd moments.'

'Have you taken any landscapes out at the Point?'

'A few.'

'In the last three weeks?'

'Yes, I took some a week ago.'

'Can you possibly let us have prints, Mr Jagger?'

'I should think so. Why not?'

'How soon can you let us have them?'

Jagger shrugged his shoulders.

'Later on this afternoon?'

'You've got your own dark-room?'

'Yes, at the cottage. At the moment it's very much a makeshift affair, but it serves its purpose.'

'Then you can drop them in at Blakeney? The incident room?'

'Willingly, Inspector, if you think they're likely to be of any help.'

'We can't say yet, sir, can we? There just might be someone on them that we happen to recognize.' He looked up at Jagger. 'I have to ask you this, sir, but it's purely routine. Where were you last Tuesday evening between seven o'clock and ten?'

There was a flicker of a smile.

'You mean I need an alibi?'

'Simply for the record. We have to work on a process of elimination, Mr Jagger.'

'I think you can eliminate me, Inspector. I was at home.'

'At Zitundo Cottage?'

'Yes, I was fitting up the dark-room. I'd spent the afternoon here in Norwich, buying what I needed.'

'And last night, where were you?'

'Still at home, Inspector. Developing the shots I'd taken of the terns and running off some prints. In fact, I've been at home every evening this week.'

Tench resigned himself to another fruitless session.

'I had a strange idea that you might have been, sir,' he said. 'Everyone I speak to seems to have been at home.'

'Not very helpful, eh?'

'No, sir. Not very . . . By the way, did you know that there'd been another murder?'

Jagger stared at him.

'Another?'

'Yes, sir. Last night. Miss Marriott's sister.'

'Out at the Point?'

'No, not this time. At Craymere. You hadn't heard?'

'Not a whisper. I've been out on the marshes since just after dawn.' Jagger frowned. 'Two sisters? Why on earth would anyone want to kill them both?'

'I don't know, sir,' said Tench. 'Can *you* suggest a motive?'

Jagger gave a laugh.

'I wouldn't attempt to, Inspector. I'm just a simple sort of chap. I never had any pretensions to your line of business.'

8

It was Lubbock's contention, expressed more than once to a captive Tench, that every murder investigation, like a flowering plant, had its own season.

Solving a murder was, he maintained, like tending a rosarium. You needed to prune the evidence you'd gathered, tossing most of it aside as quite immaterial; you scratched yourself from time to time following clues that led absolutely nowhere; and then one day, after weeks or perhaps even months of waiting, the case would open out, all at once, like a flower.

Looking back, much later, on the Craymere affair, Tench always said that that moment arrived when Detective Constable Desmond Lock tapped on his door.

Not that, as he shook Jagger's hand and watched him walk out of the interview room, he had any idea that such a moment was close. He seemed indeed, even then, to be repeatedly scratching himself on the thorns.

By two o'clock he was back at his desk, and facing a predictably windswept McKenzie.

'Mac,' he said, 'let's do some thinking. Two heads are allegedly better than one.'

'What have we got so far?'

'Not a great deal. Nothing that gives us a really firm lead. Let's start from scratch. Two murders. First question. Two killers, or one?'

'One,' said McKenzie. 'All the signs point that way.'

'So we're looking for a single killer. Second question. What do we know about him?'

'He strangles women with his hands.'

'And leaves no fingerprints. There were none on the doll.'

'Then he must be wearing gloves.'

'Rubber gloves?'

'I'd say so. And he pads around on bare feet.'

'Even on the shingle, according to Lester.'

'Well, Lester's the expert, but if he took off his shoes to strangle the girl, then the soles of his feet must be made of concrete. That shingle's got bits of shell sticking up like razors.'

'Sounds crazy, doesn't it?'

'Just about as crazy as dumping her body in a colony of terns.'
Tench pursed his lips.

'He may be crazy in one sense, but he's not a man who does things without good reason. Both these murders were planned, and when it comes to killing he's clinically efficient. He doesn't give the victim a chance to draw blood.'

'OK. So we're dealing with a man who plans his method of killing in advance. Who knows what he's going to do, and what he's not going to do. That leads us on to something else that's strange.'

'What's that?'

'The sex angle, Mike. We've got a man here who half-strips a girl. He tears off her bra, pulls up her blouse, yanks her skirt and knickers down to her ankles, and does nothing else. He doesn't rape her or mutilate her. He doesn't even stick his fingers up her crotch. He just leaves her lying there, and calmly walks off.'

'And the second time he kills, he leaves behind a doll.'

'I've a feeling', McKenzie said, 'that that doll holds the key to the whole damn business. In the end it's going to talk, and when it does it's going to whisper a hell of a lot more than merely its name.'

'Then let's take a closer look. This killer of ours strangles two women. He partially strips them to reveal their breasts and genitals, but he goes no further. On the body of the second he places a doll, a naked female doll. He deliberately arranges the dead woman's arms to make it appear that, in an access of passion, she's torn off her clothes and embraced its nakedness. And he sets the doll's fingers so that the tips of them seem to be stroking her nipple. It's a tableau, a set piece. So what does our killer intend us to see?'

'A lesbian love scene, that's all too obvious.'

'And that means?'

'That he knew what the sisters were up to.'

'So we're looking for someone who knew both the Marriotts. Third question, then. Did they know him?'

'The probable answer's yes. There's just a chance it might be no.'

'Then let's take the probability. Someone who knew and was known to the Marriotts. Who've we got who fills the bill?'

'Moses Shelton, but he's out. He could hardly have strangled a girl from his cell . . . What about the wardens?'

'None of them knew either of the girls, so they say. Langrick and Phelps claim they never even saw them. Turner admits he may have done, but before he could speak to them they were well out of range. And there's no evidence that the sisters had anything to do with them, or that they knew Jagger, though he thinks he may possibly have seen them from a distance. So who does that leave?'

'You know damn well who it leaves, Mike,' McKenzie said grimly. 'It leaves us with Giles, our innocent schoolboy. He's still the prime suspect. On the evidence we've collected so far he has to be. They knew him, he knew them. He's told us he was somewhere close to the terns at exactly the time Phoebe Marriott was murdered, and last night he was close enough to Downs House to have taken a break from quadratic equations.'

'You mean he ran across the road with a twenty-inch doll? All in broad daylight?'

'Perhaps he didn't need to. That doll could well have belonged to the Marriotts. It may have already been in the house. He could have known it was there.'

Tench shook his head.

'No, it's not Giles.'

'You said that before. What makes you so sure? Logic, or instinct?'

'A bit of both, Mac. He just isn't the type, and he doesn't know how to drive.'

'You're certain of that?'

'Well, his sister should know, and she says he doesn't. I asked her this morning.'

McKenzie ran a hand through his tangle of hair.

'These cars may have nothing to do with the killings.'

'They must have,' said Tench. 'Look at the pattern. The brigadier's Lagonda was stolen from Blakeney and driven to Cley. That's the nearest point of access to the place where Phoebe Marriott was murdered. Then this other chap's Alvis disappears from Holt, and where does it turn up? A couple of hundred yards from Downs House, and it's there at the very time her sister gets strangled.'

'Coincidence?'

'No.'

'Then if we're looking for someone who knew both the girls – and it's someone they knew – there's only one answer. This murderer's a man that we haven't yet met.'

'I'm beginning to wonder all over again if it could be a woman. Remember, Mac, neither of the victims was raped.'

'A woman who had links with this dressmaking business?'

'It could be. Why not?'

'Then we need to know more about the people they dealt with.'

'That means waiting for Gregg. He's sorting out the shop . . . Sue Gradwell brought in some letters and cheque books. We could take a look at them.'

'What about that telephone pad I picked up?'

'Lock's been tracking down the numbers all morning,' said Tench. 'He should have finished by now. He's had long enough. I'll get him to bring it in.'

He reached for the phone.

9

In one hand Lock held the index pad and a typewritten list; in the other, a map.

'Have you traced them all?' Tench asked him.

'All except one, sir. That's a bit of a problem.'

'Which one is it?'

Lock passed him the list and the pad.

'It's under the letter S, sir. The name's given as Snitterly, and the number's 28, but there's no Snitterly in any of the Norfolk directories.'

'Perhaps it's ex-directory.'

'I checked with the exchange, sir. There's no Snitterly recorded anywhere in Norfolk.'

'Could it be a place?'

'I checked that too, sir. No Snitterly exchange. There isn't one in the country.'

'Strange,' said Tench. He flicked open the pad and examined the entry. 'No first name or initials. Just the surname and number. Well, wherever this person called Snitterly lives, it must be a small place. It's a two-figure number. That means it's a village. If I were you I'd ring the supervisor. Tell him it's urgent, a murder inquiry. Ask him for a list of all exchanges in Norfolk that carry that number. There can't be that many.'

'It may take some time, sir.'

'Give him the details and let him get on with it . . . Anything more on the Alvis?'

'Yes. It's been found, sir. Report's just come through.'

'Where?'

'It's turned up at a place called Mickle Covert.'

'Where's that?'

'It's at Sapwell.'
'And where the devil's Sapwell?'
Lock made a face.
'D'you really want to know, sir?'
'Don't tell me it's Bradenham.'
'A mile and a half out, sir, on the road to Diss.'
Tench swore. Then he seemed to be thinking.
'Diss. That's the opposite side to Primrose Spinney.'
'That's right, sir, yes . . . But there's something else, too.'
'Go on,' said Tench. 'Give me all the gory details.'

'Actually, sir, it could be a bit of a breakthrough. It was the village constable at Sapwell who came across the car. He thought he'd take a look at this place, Mickle Covert. Not to find the Alvis – that wasn't in his mind; but it seems that last night, about half-past ten, he was passing there on his bike and he noticed another car parked at the same spot. Apparently it's way off the beaten track, and he thought it a bit suspicious, so he had a nose around and made a note of the number. Then he went back this morning to see if it had gone, and discovered the Alvis parked in its place. And this is the point, sir. The one that was there last night was a black Austin Seven, the same type that that farmer reported he'd seen on Tuesday at Primrose Spinney. I spoke to Inspector Cartwright at Bradenham. They've traced it. It's registered to a Dorothy Rodway. She lives at Delph Cottage, Bridgham.'

'And where's that?'

Lock unfolded the map and spread it out on the desk.

'Look at this, sir,' he said. 'The whole set-up's quite interesting. This is Bradenham.' He pointed it out. 'Here's Winford and Primrose Spinney. And this is Sapwell and Mickle Covert. One's about a mile and a half west of the town; the other's a mile and a half to the east.'

'And where's this place Bridgham?'

'Here, sir,' said Lock. 'Roughly a mile and a half to the north.'

McKenzie leaned across the desk.

'It's a triangle,' he said, 'and Bradenham's right in the middle of the base.'

Tench looked up at Lock.

'Did you tell them to hold the Alvis till the lab wallahs get there?'

'Yes, sir. They've already had it towed into Bradenham.'

'Do they know anything at all about this – what did you say her name was? Dorothy Rodway?'

'No, sir. Not yet. Inspector Cartwright was going out to Bridgham to make inquiries.'

Tench glimpsed a speck of light. He pushed back his chair and picked up the map.

'Good work, Desmond,' he said to Lock. 'Come on, Mac. Bridgham. Let's take a look at this Rodway woman.'

'She's probably ninety-two and blind as a bat,' McKenzie said gloomily, 'and from what I know of Bradenham and the luck we've had so far, that wouldn't surprise me.'

8

LITTLE THINGS

It has long been an axiom of mine that the little things are infinitely the most important.

Sir Arthur Conan Doyle: *A Case of Identity*

1

Delph Cottage, Tench decided, was a gross misnomer. It was too big for a cottage and looked indeed more like a sizeable farm house, though if it had ever had any ancillary buildings, these had long disappeared. Nor was there any sign of what Moses Shelton, or others steeped like him in local lore, would have known as a delph or a drainage ditch. Probably the stream it served had long since dried out.

Isolated was the word to describe Delph Cottage. It stood on its own amid a treeless expanse of flat Norfolk fields, and the only other dwellings anywhere in sight were the clustered cottages that made up the tiny village of Bridgham, a good three-quarters of a mile to the west.

It was a curious house: something of a hybrid. The gable ends with stepped gables were built of brick, but the side walls were clearly framed out of timber, and the dominant feature was a peculiar three-tiered black-and-white porch with a gable at the first floor and another above it, set back into the tiles to form an attic window. At one end there was an open lean-to, roofed in tarred felt, and underneath it was parked a black Austin Seven.

There was a police car on the drive, and Cartwright and one of the sergeants from Bradenham were peering in at the windows of the house.

The inspector was a tall, lean, thin-lipped man with a hair-line that was rapidly receding into baldness. He turned as Tench and McKenzie drew up, and came forward to meet them.

'Strange business, this,' he said.

'You can say that again,' said Tench.

Cartwright pointed to the Austin.

'Your lads'll need to run the rule over that, as well as the Alvis. It's been driven by someone, but not Mrs Rodway. She's been away for a fortnight.'

'Where is she now?'

'God only knows, Mike. Somewhere in Scotland, touring around. She didn't leave an address.'

'Who is she?'

Cartwright raised a couple of pencil-thin eyebrows.

'That's a bit of a mystery, too. You can see what this place is like. Out on the lone prairie. No immediate neighbours. So we did the next best thing. Went into Bridgham and asked some questions there. There's a general store-cum-post office, so we popped in and spoke to the bloke that runs it. He didn't know much either, even though he delivers her papers every day. Described her as good-looking, dark-haired, round about thirty. Calls herself Mrs, but he said he'd never seen a man about the house. Thought she must be either a widow or divorced. He'd heard she ran a hairdressing business in Thetford. Anyway, she called in the shop the week before last and cancelled her papers. He asked her when she wanted them started again, and she said she'd be back on the sixteenth, Friday. That's today. Didn't say where she was going. Told him to hold her post. She'd pick it up when she got back.'

'But she hasn't turned up yet?'

'Not while we've been here, and the house is locked up. We did trace the hairdresser's shop in Thetford, but that's been closed for a fortnight too. Notice on the door says it's due to reopen again on Monday. There's a small haberdashery shop that adjoins it, and the woman there said she employed an assistant. Gave us her name and address. Council estate in Thetford. We found the girl and she told us a bit more. Mrs Rodway's a divorcee. Took over the business five years ago. Couldn't help us to trace her, but said she was touring Scotland with a friend of hers, a woman. Using the friend's car. So all we can do, it seems, is to leave Sergeant Bennett – this is Sergeant Bennett – to sit here and wait for her.'

Tench walked round the Austin.

'Let me know as soon as she gets back,' he said, 'and no one's to move the car.'

'Don't worry. They won't. We'll have someone on guard till the boffins arrive.'

'We'll need to have a talk with the lady,' McKenzie said.

Cartwright looked towards Tench.

187

'Here, or in Norwich?'

'Norwich'd be better.'

'Leave it with me. I'll have someone drive her down. If she's been on the road from Scotland, she won't be too happy, but better that than sitting around waiting in Bradenham. I'll give you a warning buzz, though God only knows what time she'll turn up. It's a case of watch and wait.'

Tench frowned at the car.

'An Austin Seven,' he said. 'Looks in pretty good nick, but it must be pre-war. They haven't made them since then. Who the devil could have pinched it twice in three nights?'

'Anyone.' Cartwright waved a hand at the fields. 'Look at the place, Mike. Miles away from anywhere. Nobody around. Pick the lock, simple. Change the wiring, easy. But it must have been someone who knew she was away, and he must have known she wouldn't be back till today.'

'Then let's hope she can give us a clue,' McKenzie said.

'I wouldn't bet on it,' said Cartwright. 'You know these village stores. Gossip shops, most of them. It wouldn't surprise me if three parts of Bridgham know she's away, and half of Thetford too. And I don't reckon anyone's going to step forward and put up his hand.' He slapped the bonnet of the Austin. 'That reminds me. I've got a little present in the car. We gift-wrapped it specially.'

He walked back to the police car, and took out a plastic bag and a sheet of paper.

'There's always the chance of a fingerprint,' he said. 'One missing handbag. We found it stuffed underneath a seat in the Alvis. That's a list of the contents. We used a pair of tweezers. Doesn't look to be much missing, if anything at all. He even left the money. Two five-pound notes and a handful of silver. Whoever he was, he wasn't short of cash. Not that he bothered to fill up with juice. The tank's almost dry.'

2

Back in Norwich, Tench dropped the bag on Lock's desk.

'Get that across to the lab,' he said, 'and check the list against ours. See if anything's missing . . . Any news yet on Snitterly?'

'No, sir. The supervisor's working on it . . . Gregg's arrived with a whole lot of files from the shop.'

'Any messages?'

'Yes, sir. A Mr Franks rang through from the Castle Museum. Said would you phone him as soon as you were back ... And the Chief Super wants a word.'

'I thought he might,' said Tench. 'Well, he comes before Franks. I'd better see him first.'

Hastings was unexpectedly cheerful.

'Lock tells me you may have got a breakthrough,' he said.

'Too early to say, sir, but yes, it is possible.'

'Who's this Dorothy Rodway?'

Tench explained.

'So someone's used her car while she's been gallivanting round Scotland?'

'Looks like it, sir.'

'But the likelihood is she won't know who it was.'

'It must be someone who knew she was away, and knew the Marriott sisters well enough to realize what was going on at Downs House.'

'But so far the vital connection's missing?'

'It's missing, sir, yes, but there must be one somewhere ... I've been thinking about what Mr Lubbock said.'

'The lesbian triangle?'

Tench gave a nod.

'There could be a link with this Rodway woman. We're told she's been in Scotland, but as yet we've no proof. We only know what she went around telling other people.'

'You think she may have been deliberately spreading a lie?'

'I don't really know, sir. We're still waiting to see her, but it wouldn't be the first time that someone's contrived to fake an alibi, would it?'

'No, it wouldn't,' said Hastings, 'but surely, Mike, the odds are all against it. You're suggesting she spread this tale about a holiday, and then stayed at home?'

'Well, maybe not at home, sir.'

'But somewhere close by.'

'That could be a possibility.'

'And used her own car? Seems to me it's a much more plausible explanation that she knew nothing at all about what was going on.'

'Unless there's some connection we've still to unearth.'

'With the Marriotts?'

'Yes, sir.'

'An infatuation with one of them?'

'Could be, but there must be something else too. Something that originally brought them together.'

'A business connection?'

'That's what I've been thinking, and there's only one way to uncover it, sir. Gregg's been down at the Sheringham shop, and he's brought in a load of files. We need a team to comb through them.'

Hastings shifted in his seat.

'Where's Darricot?'

'He's in charge of the squads at Blakeney. They've been down there all day. They're questioning local boatmen and staff at the hotels.'

'How many of them are there?'

'A dozen, sir. Two squads of six.'

'They'll be finished by this evening?'

'Hopefully, yes.'

'Then they're the ones to use. You take them over. Let Darricot get back to his patch in the city. But you're going to need space. They can't work in that poky little pub room at Blakeney.'

'It is a bit cramped, sir.'

'Far too cramped for a major murder investigation, and that's what this Craymere affair's turning into. Let me make a suggestion. Keep the Blakeney place open for local contact – someone like Rayner or Spurgeon can man it – but relocate all the essential work here. How does that sound?'

'It's a good idea, sir. We're a bit dispersed at the moment. We seem to be chasing about all over Norfolk.'

'That's unavoidable, I'm afraid, in a case like this, but we do need to concentrate as much as we can. Agreed?'

'Agreed, sir, yes.'

'Good. There's a couple of rooms you can use in the annexe. I'll get them rigged up ... Keep me up to date, and remember I'm here to help. If you do get a breakthrough and need my backing for a warrant to search this place at Bridgham, don't hesitate to call me. Any time, day or night. Let's crack this on our own, Mike. We don't want a team of whizz-kids from the Yard sniffing round.'

'No, sir, we don't.'

Hastings looked down his nose.

'You mean God forbid? Well, let's hope he does. Keep your fingers crossed and pray.'

3

Keep your fingers crossed and pray?

Well at least, Tench thought, it was a subtle variation. It enlisted the help of both sovereign powers: God and the Devil.

Not that he expected much assistance from either. Salvation, if it came, was far more likely to come from Mike Tench.

He checked the time: ten to six; then he dragged the phone towards him and dialled Franks's number.

The line buzzed twice, then he heard the curator's voice.

'Castle Museum, Gilbert Franks.'

'Detective Chief Inspector Tench.'

'Ah, good evening, Chief Inspector. I was hoping you'd ring. I've some news, for what it's worth.'

'You have, sir?'

'Yes, indeed. I've been making some inquiries since you were here this morning. Ringing round friends who might have seen the Montanari. Well, perhaps not friends; more business acquaintances. I made a number of calls, all to no avail, but at last I came up with a positive response. There's a second-hand dealer in Swaffham. Name of Trevaskis. Cornish I'd imagine, though precisely how he came to end up in Norfolk I wouldn't care to say. He has a shop in the Market Place. Deals in bric-à-brac: most of it, in my recollection, quite worthless; but I asked him about the doll and he remembered it distinctly. I was very much surprised. I'd almost given up hope.'

'He sold it, sir?' said Tench.

'He both bought it and sold it. It seems he attended an auction, Chief Inspector. It was earlier this year, at a country house in Cambridgeshire. A place called Wentworth Court. I believe it's close to Ely. He bought a number of job lots and the Montanari was amongst them. He clearly had no idea of its value, nor had those who sold it, and I must admit that it gave me a great deal of pleasure to make him a little wiser than he'd any right to be. But to come to the point. He displayed it in the shop along with all his other miscellaneous jumble, and then a couple of days later sold it for next to nothing.'

'Who did he sell it to, Mr Franks?'

'A young lady who gave him five pounds in cash. He thought he'd made a good sale.'

'Was he able to describe her?'

'Not with much accuracy, I'm sorry to say. He said she was slim, she had a good figure and her hair was quite dark. That was all he remembered.'

'Well, that's something,' said Tench. 'At least we know it was a woman. I'm very grateful for the help, sir. Can we perhaps reimburse you for the calls?'

Franks sounded amused.

'I wouldn't really worry, Chief Inspector,' he said. 'You'll pay for them on the rates.'

Tench sat for a moment, biting his lip. Then he called in McKenzie.

'The doll. Bought in Swaffham by a young, dark-haired woman.'

'Our friend Mrs Rodway?'

'Could be. Who knows? We'll have to see what she's like. According to all accounts this woman was slim. It could just as well have been one of the Marriott sisters, or any one of a thousand other slim, dark-haired women. They're not exactly scarce.'

'Swaffham's close enough to Thetford. It's closer than either Craymere or Sheringham.'

'Yes, that's true, but it doesn't mean much. All we can do at the moment, Mac, is hazard a few guesses.'

'We don't seem to be doing much else,' McKenzie said. 'And we're missing the point. There must be a connection that we haven't yet spotted. Some scrap of evidence that's lying hidden away somewhere in one of the files.'

'But which of them?'

'God knows ... Let's go through them again.'

Tench slid back his chair and reached down to open a drawer in the desk. As he did so, the phone rang. He straightened up again and lifted the receiver.

'Chief Inspector Tench?'

It was the WPC who was manning the switchboard.

'Speaking,' said Tench.

'I've a PC Harris on the line, sir, from Blakeney. He says it's urgent.'

'Then I've no doubt it is,' said Tench. 'Put him through.'

Steve Harris was the resident constable at Blakeney. He'd done the first check on the local hotels, and he'd been working all day with Darricot. Now he sounded worried.

'Thought I'd better ring you right away, sir,' he said. 'I've been glancing through the files in the incident room.'

'Something wrong?'

'Looks like it, sir, yes. It's Bob Phelps, the warden. He made a statement to one of your detective constables.'

'Yes, it was Ellison.'

There was a rustle on the phone as if a page had been turned.

'That's right, sir. DC Ellison.'

'You're not happy about something?'

'Well, sir. Phelps says that on Tuesday he paid a visit to the dentist and had a tooth out. Then he went back home, and began to feel a bit rough when the freezing wore off. Says he was dead tired because he'd had a bad night with the pain the night before, so he drank two neat whiskies, went to bed early – half-past six so he says – and slept solidly through until six the next morning.'

'So,' said Tench, 'what's the trouble?'

Harris didn't mince his words.

'Well, he's lying, sir, isn't he? He was down on the quayside at eight o'clock. I saw him.'

4

That was when the Marriott case, all at once, seemed to gather its own unstoppable momentum.

McKenzie was privy to only half the conversation.

He heard Tench say, 'What was he doing?', then 'Where's Inspector Darricot? Get him for me, will you?' and when Darricot himself picked up the phone, 'Yes, I want him here. Bring the bugger in.' After that he slammed the receiver back on its hook.

McKenzie was intrigued.

'And who's the latest for the thumbscrews?' he asked.

'Phelps. Our pal the warden. Looks like he spun Ellison a whole pack of lies. He was hanging around outside the Blakeney Hotel at eight o'clock on Tuesday. That's just about the time when somebody nicked the brigadier's car. Hell's bells, Mac! Does anyone in Norfolk ever tell the truth?'

'There must be one or two somewhere. Perhaps we haven't met them.'

'Well, young Mr Phelps is due for a grilling. He needs to be taught a lesson. We'll get the truth out of him if it takes us all evening. Not that it's likely to do us any good. He couldn't have been anywhere near Craymere last night. He was out at the Point.'

McKenzie mused for a moment.

'Do we know that? For sure? He wasn't around when you rang up Langrick.'

'Well, it was his turn for duty. And he did tell Ellison he intended to go.'

'He told Ellison a lot of things.'

'And Turner said nothing. He was due to hand over to Phelps at the quay.'

'Perhaps they're all spinning lies.'

'Well, it's easy enough to check. I'll give Langrick a ring.' Tench reached for the phone. 'Where's Ellison?'

'Down in the CID room with Lock.'

'Let's have him up here. See what he really thinks about Phelps. You go and collect him. I'll get through to the Point.'

It took McKenzie longer than he'd expected to track down Ellison. He discovered him at last in the staff canteen, drinking a cup of coffee and munching a rock bun.

'Forget the banquet, lad,' he said. 'The DCI wants to see you.'

They tramped up the stairs and back to the office.

Tench was staring at the phone.

'You were right, Mac,' he said.

'He didn't go?'

'Oh, he went. On the dot. But then he came back. Met Turner at the quay and set out for the Point, but while he was still on the way, Langrick got a telephone call from his mother. Seems that Mrs Phelps has been waiting for months for a cataract operation, and as soon as her darling boy left her to go on duty, she had a telegram from the Cottage Hospital at Holt. They'd had a cancellation and wanted her in right away. She needed her son to drive her, so Langrick packed him off back as soon as he arrived. Had to do that because of the tide.'

'So he wasn't out at the Point last night?'

'No,' said Tench, 'he bloody well wasn't.' He looked up at Ellison. 'Sit down, Bob,' he said. 'You took his original statement. The one about Tuesday night.'

'That's right, sir. It's in the file.'

'His mother backed him up?'

'Confirmed every word, sir. Said his mouth was playing up, so she dosed him with whisky and sent him to bed.'

'What time was that?'

'Half-past six, so she said. Then she checked his room when she went to bed herself. That was round about quarter to ten. He was fast asleep, so she didn't wake him up. She had to pay a visit in the middle of the night, but there wasn't any sound, and it was six o'clock next morning before she heard him stirring.'

'The middle of the night? Did you ask her when exactly?'

'She didn't know, sir. It was dark, and she didn't look at the clock.'

Tench seemed to be thinking.

'Phelps. Any brothers or sisters?'

'Had a sister, sir. She's dead. Probably explains why his mother's so protective.'

'Did she tell you that, or was it Phelps himself?'

'He told me, sir, but I did have a word with Mrs Phelps on her own.'

'And she corroborated it?'

'Yes, sir . . . In her own way.'

Tench looked at him sharply.

'How d'you mean? Her own way.'

Ellison furrowed his brow.

'It's difficult to describe, sir.'

'Something didn't ring true?'

'I can't really be sure, sir. It wasn't what she said. It was the way that she said it.'

'You mean she was evasive?'

'No, sir. Far from it. The opposite, I'd say. I was trying to get some idea of what went on between her and Phelps, and I said it must be hard, losing an only daughter. And . . . well, she turned on me, sir.'

'What did she say exactly?'

'She said, "My daughter's dead. I don't want to discuss her." Very short, sir. Dismissive.'

'And?'

'I wouldn't swear to it, sir. I could well be wrong, but it was more like she was trying to persuade herself.'

There was silence in the room. Ellison waited.

'Will that be all, sir?'

'What? Oh, yes, Bob.' Tench came out of his reverie. 'That's the lot for now.'

'Right, sir.' Ellison made to go, and then halted at the door.

'By the way, sir,' he said. 'Snitterly.'

'What about it?'

'Lock said you'd want to know. It's the old name for Blakeney. Comes from the Domesday Book. At that time the village was known as Esnuterle.'

For a second Tench looked blank.

'How did he find that out?'

'I just happened to hear him asking around, sir,' said Ellison, 'and I said I'd heard it mentioned once when I was in Cley. Quite a time ago now. You remember, sir, don't you? I did part of my National Service down there. Out on the marsh with the ack-ack battery.'

McKenzie waited till the door closed behind him. Then he looked across at Tench.

'Are you thinking what I am?'

Tench took a deep breath.

'I don't know what you're thinking, Mac, and to be honest about it, I don't even know what I'm thinking myself.'

'Phelps lives in Blakeney.'

'So what? He's hardly unique in that, is he? His name isn't Snitterly, and where's his link with the Marriotts? It's all wild conjecture. The whole damned affair's still as much of a riddle as ever it was. There's only one thing I do know.'

'What's that?'

Tench swept the files aside.

'I've had just about enough of these mindless Norfolk oafs who think they can lie to the police and get away with it. We can't very well string Phelps up by his thumbs, but if he doesn't come clean, then by God he's going to squirm.'

5

Robert Phelps had no intention of squirming. He was only too ready, so it seemed, to come clean.

A thin young man, with a mop of fair hair and an over-large nose, he was quite unconcerned when Tench pointed out with considerable candour that the statement he'd made to Detective Constable Ellison left much to be desired.

'You were lying, Mr Phelps.'

There was a smile and a shrug.

'Yes, I'm sorry about that.'
'You admit it?'
'Oh, yes.'
'You weren't in bed on Tuesday evening?'
'Not all the time, no.'
'You went out?'
'Yes, I did.'
'Where did you go?'
'Down to the quay and then out along the Carnser.'
'How far along the Carnser?'
'Not very far. I sat down and watched the tide. It was beginning to turn. Then I walked back home.'
'You were seen at eight o'clock by the Blakeney Hotel.'
Phelps was unperturbed.
'Yes, that's about right. I was checking the boat to see if the mooring lines were secure.'
'You were close to the hotel. Did you go into the car park?'
'No, I checked the boat, walked along the Carnser and then went back home.'
'You did nothing but take a stroll?'
'No, nothing at all.'
'Then why did you lie to Constable Ellison?'
'I had to, hadn't I?'
McKenzie glowered at him.
'What d'you mean? You had to? People don't have to lie to the police. Not unless they've got something to hide.'
'Oh, I know that,' said Phelps. 'That's what I had.'
'What?'
'Something to hide.'
'Then what the devil was it?'
'That I'd gone for a walk.'
McKenzie closed his eyes.
'Your turn,' he said to Tench. 'If you can work it out, you're a better man than I am.'
Tench wrestled with the logic.
'You needed to hide from Constable Ellison the simple fact that you'd gone for a walk?'
Phelps shook his head firmly.
'No, not from him.'
'Who then?'
The youth hesitated.
'Well, to tell you the truth . . .'
'That'll be a change.' This from McKenzie.

Phelps ignored him. He simply gave a sigh.

'As a matter of fact,' he said, 'I just didn't want my mother to know.'

It was a familiar enough tale when at last it came out, and one that Tench, for all his scepticism, found himself reluctantly inclined to accept.

Mrs Phelps, it appeared, was both a widow and an over-possessive mother. She was consumed by the fear that her only boy would one day marry and leave her on her own; and like many of her kind, she indulged in the type of emotional blackmail which merely breeds subterfuge in its victim. The knowledge that her son had taken a shine to a local girl had produced in her, at first angry protest, then accusations of disloyalty, and finally hysterics. She'd become suspicious of his every move. 'I suppose', she'd say, 'you're going out again to meet that scheming little trollop.'

There'd been trouble on the Monday when, in spite of an aching tooth, he'd taken the girl out to the pictures at Holt – 'Demanding little hussy,' she'd said. 'She's no heart.' – and, still in pain on the Tuesday, the last thing he'd wanted was to have to face a repeat performance. When he'd found that, even with two whiskies inside him, he couldn't get to sleep, he'd stuck a bolster in his bed and sneaked out of the back door. He'd been out for an hour, and when he'd got back he'd discovered her fast asleep in a chair, blissfully unaware that he'd set foot outside.

'She wouldn't have believed I'd just gone for a walk,' he said. 'Even though Mollie was in Wells with a girlfriend, she wouldn't have let it rest.'

'All right,' said Tench. 'I can understand that. But why did you have to lie to Constable Ellison?'

Phelps looked at him almost in disbelief.

'I couldn't very well do anything else, could I? She was there all the time he was asking the questions.'

'Couldn't you have spoken to the constable on his own?'

'You don't know my mother. She clings like a leech.'

'You could have come to the incident room and explained. It would have saved us all a great deal of trouble.'

'Yes, I should have done, shouldn't I? It was stupid of me not to.'

The answer was disarming, but McKenzie still glowered. He seemed to be following a different line of thought.

'While you were out,' he said, 'did you speak to anyone?'

Phelps nodded.

'Yes, I had a word with Jake Scott. He runs the craft shop on High Street. He was out on the Carnser, walking his dog.'
'What time was that?'
'It must have been just after eight o'clock.'
'Will Mr Scott confirm it?'
'I suppose so. If you ask him.'
'Oh, we'll ask him,' McKenzie said. 'You had a sister.'
'That's right.'
'Older than you?'
'Yes, five years older.'
'But she died. Is that correct?'
Phelps seemed to hesitate.
'I'm not sure,' he said at last. 'I think she's still alive.'
McKenzie scowled.
'You told Detective Constable Ellison she was dead. That was another lie, was it?'
'Perhaps half a lie.'
'Half a lie? How can a lie be just half a lie?'
'She's dead to my mother. She's been dead for ten years.'
Tench raised a hand before McKenzie could speak.
'I think you'd better explain that statement, Mr Phelps.'
The young man looked at Tench, then he looked at McKenzie.
'She got herself into trouble,' he said. 'Mother turned her out.'
'Ten years ago.'
'Yes.'
'D'you know where she went?'
'No. I tried to find out. At one time, I think, she was living near Diss. Someone told me they'd seen her.'
'But they didn't tell you her address?'
'No, they didn't know it. Anyway, it's six or seven years ago now.'
'And you've never heard from her at all?'
'No, not a word. There were rumours from time to time, but I never told mother.'
'What kind of rumours?'
'I heard she got married, and then she lost the baby.'
'Did she marry the father?'
'No. Someone else.'
'And you don't know his name?'
'I've no idea where she lives, or what her married name is.'
'But you do know her first name,' McKenzie said, 'don't you? What is it? Dorothy?'
Phelps looked baffled.

'No,' he said. 'It's Jean.'

6

'Hell and damnation!'

McKenzie flung himself down on a chair in Tench's office.

'For a moment there,' he said, 'I thought we might have a link.'

'Too easy,' said Tench. 'Links have to be forged. It's bloody hard work.'

'Well, I still don't trust that smooth little bugger. Even if two people saw him at eight o'clock, he'd still have had time to pinch that car and drive it down to Cley.'

'We haven't a single scrap of evidence to show that he did, Mac. Unless we can prove some connection with the Marriotts, we're no further advanced than we were last Wednesday morning.'

'Then we're left with Mrs Rodway.'

'Looks like it,' said Tench. 'And we haven't had a call from Cartwright, so that means she still hasn't turned up at Bridgham. It's quarter to eight now, and it'll take them an hour to get here from Bradenham. You'd better hop out and get something to eat. God knows how long we're going to have to wait . . . I suppose Lock's off duty.'

'Went off at six-thirty.'

'Who's still down there?'

'Ellison and Gregg. Gregg's going through the files that he brought from the shop.'

'Tell them both to hang on till we know where we stand. You shuffle off. Be back here at nine. Hopefully by that time we'll have had word from Bradenham.'

'If we haven't,' McKenzie said, 'I'll start to wonder if this Bridgham wench isn't young Phelps in some sort of disguise.'

Tench stripped off his jacket and draped it over the back of a chair. Then he crossed to the window and threw it wide open.

There was a change on the way. The hot, dry spell was coming to an end. The sun was already hidden by a layer of cloud, there was hardly a breath of air, and away to the south he thought he could detect the low rumble of thunder.

He sat down at his desk and took from his in-tray the three manilla envelopes that Sue Gradwell had brought from Downs

House. Underneath was the copy of *East Anglian Life*. He picked it up and began to flick through the pages.

It was the usual compendium of articles with a regional slant, and she'd turned back the corner of one of the leaves to mark the piece about the Marriott sisters.

As far as he could see, it contained little that he didn't already know. There was a paragraph about the family, describing how, five years before, both their parents had died when the Perth to Euston sleeping-car express had jumped the points at Bourne End; and this was followed by a further lengthy section on how the two orphans had battled against fate to set up and make a success of their business. There was a photograph of the two of them, arms round each other, smiling happily at the camera; and at the bottom of the page, set side by side, were reproductions of a couple of Giles's sketches, one of them showing Phoebe in a very short skirt. Underneath was the caption: Is this the future?

Sue Gradwell had said he might find it interesting. Well, he supposed it was, but in a sterile sort of way. It told him nothing fresh, revealed no clue to the riddle that had plagued him now for three whole days. Three days of searching, and he was still no closer to finding an answer.

He straightened the fold at the corner of the page, running his finger across it to smooth out the crease. It was a simple, almost a reflex action – he never had cared to see leaves turned back – but in the course of it his eyes lit on something they'd missed.

A single line of very fine print.

He peered at it closely, then he carried the magazine to the window and held it to the light.

No, he hadn't been mistaken. The name was quite clear.

He stared at it, hardly believing what he saw.

So that was the link.

He stood for a moment absolutely still, trying to grasp all the disparate thoughts that were racing through his mind.

Then he moved. He all but ran to the desk, tossed the magazine down, and snatched at the envelope that Sue Gradwell had tagged as holding the Marriott cheque books and stubs.

He emptied them out in a pile and began to riffle through them. In a matter of seconds he found the name again.

He tore a strip off a sheet of paper and used it as a marker, moving on without pause to another book of stubs.

He worked through six books and found the name repeated on eight separate stubs.

Marking each of them in turn, he made a list of the dates.

It appeared that the Marriotts had made regular payments at the end of each quarter. The amounts varied from cheque to cheque, but there was clearly some kind of long-term arrangement.

He picked up the envelope holding the bills. They were clipped together with a bulldog clip, and Sue Gradwell had grouped them, month by month, in chronological order.

The last payment had been made on 31 March. He searched for the bill. When he found it, he hadn't any need to look further.

He read the business heading and the signature scrawled in receipt at the bottom.

That was enough.

He gazed at it. Just a flimsy piece of paper, hidden among dozens of others in a clip, but it told him more than all the questions he'd asked.

What had Lubbock said? 'It's the little things that count. Something at some time'll drop into place.'

Well, one little thing had certainly dropped into place with a vengeance.

Was it, he wondered, asking too much of Chance to hope for another?

He shrugged. Perhaps it was, but then Chance, by her very nature, was unpredictable.

He seemed to hear Lubbock's voice. 'You can never tell, laddie. Keep an open mind. The incredible can always happen.'

He slipped the bill into an empty box-file, along with the magazine and the stubs that he'd marked. The rest he swept up and returned to the envelopes.

Then he sat back and waited for Cartwright to ring, as the light began to fade and the thunder continued to rumble in the distance.

7

He didn't have to wait long. Not more than ten minutes.

Then the phone rang, stridently, cutting through the silence.

He picked up the receiver.

It wasn't Cartwright on the line, but the sergeant at the desk.

'There's a Sergeant Bennett down here, sir, with a lady. They've come from Bradenham.'

'Let me speak to him, Sergeant, will you?'

Bennett had clearly been told what to say.

'Inspector Cartwright's apologies, sir,' he said. 'He's sorry he couldn't ring you, but we've had a cloudburst in Bradenham. It's flooded the exchange, and the phones are out of order. He said I was to drive Mrs Rodway straight here.'

'That's fine, Sergeant. Can't be helped. Tell him not to worry. What time did she get back?'

'About an hour and a half ago, sir. We had to give her time to have a wash and change and make herself presentable.'

'She's tired, I suppose.'

'Bewildered, sir, I think. She's at a bit of a loss to know what's been happening.'

'How much has she been told?'

'Not much, sir,' said Bennett. 'The inspector thought we'd better let you do the talking. He simply told her there'd been some trouble around Bridgham, and we'd been asking a lot of people to help. He said he hoped she'd be willing to speak to you right away, since inquiries had reached a very critical stage.'

'And she didn't make any fuss?'

'I don't think she's the type, sir. Very quiet and ladylike. She did ask one or two questions on the way, but I told her I didn't know any more than she did. Said it was all being dealt with in Norwich.'

'Good. Are you taking her back?'

'Inspector Cartwright said to wait till you'd finished with her, sir.'

'Right.' Tench nodded briefly at the phone. 'I'm not expecting it'll take too long. Go and get yourself a cup of tea somewhere, Sergeant. I'll find someone to show her up.'

One glance at her was all that he needed.

He knew who she was.

It was Ellison who showed her in.

'Mrs Rodway, sir,' he said.

She wore a short grey jacket with a minute brown fleck, and a long, full skirt. The jacket was unbuttoned and swung open as she walked to show a deep red lining and a white silk blouse. Her hair was cut short and waved at the sides beneath a close-fitting hat that was also white with a narrow red band. She had black high-heeled court shoes, white elbow-length gloves and carried a black leather handbag. Round her neck was a single string of pearls, and a pearl droplet hung from the lobe of each ear. She was slim and elegant and, to Tench's way of thinking, extremely attractive.

He held out his hand.

'Chief Inspector Tench,' he said. 'Please sit down, Mrs Rodway. I'm sorry to have to bring you all the way from Bridgham, especially after you've been travelling all day. You must be very tired.'

'No,' she said, 'not really.' Her voice was soft, but each word she spoke was cut like a diamond. 'We stayed the night in Stamford, so we haven't driven far, but I would like to know what this is all about.'

'You went away when, Mrs Rodway? A fortnight ago?'

'Yes, Friday the 2nd.'

'And you haven't been home since?'

'No, Inspector. The nearest I've been was at Stamford last night.'

'Did you tell many people you were going away?'

'Around Bridgham? Only the post office. Of course, I do have a shop in Thetford. All my customers would know.'

'And you live on your own?'

'Yes, Inspector. Why do you need to ask?'

'We think that someone's been using your car, Mrs Rodway.'

She didn't seem surprised.

'Well, of course they have,' she said.

'You know about it?'

'Naturally. It was with my consent. Why should the police be so concerned about that?'

'We're investigating two serious crimes, Mrs Rodway. We believe them to be linked, and we've more than a suspicion that on each occasion your car was involved.'

'But that's ridiculous,' she said. 'What kind of crimes?'

'Two young women have been murdered . . .'

'No.' She shook her head. 'You must have got things wrong. There can't possibly be any connection with my car.'

'You sound very sure.'

'I'm positive, Inspector.'

'Why?'

'Because my brother had the keys.'

'Your brother?'

'That's right. When I go away, he always looks after the house and the car. I leave the keys with him. He drives over to Bridgham from time to time to check that everything's safe.'

Tench looked at her. The eyes that looked back at him were genuinely perplexed. And quite ingenuous. As Bennett had said, she wasn't the type to make a fuss. Nor was she the type to lie.

He didn't like what he had to do next.

'You're divorced, Mrs Rodway?'

'Yes, two years ago.'

'What was your maiden name?'

She told him.

'And what's your brother's name?'

She told him that too, but he knew it already. He'd known it from the moment she'd entered his office.

Her brother was younger, but the facial resemblance was too acute to be missed.

He did his best to treat her gently; said he could only hope that there'd been a mistake, but they'd have to check out the Austin just to make sure.

Then, once Bennett had left to drive her back to Bridgham, he rang the Chief Super.

'That warrant, sir,' he said. 'We're going to need it tonight.'

8

The single-storey cottage was built of brick and flint with a pantile roof, but they couldn't see that as they climbed the path to the door. It was just a black shape against a moonlit sky, and all the windows were dark.

Tench turned to Gregg.

'Round the back, Andy. Mac and I'll take the front.'

'Looks as if there's no one at home,' McKenzie said.

Tench searched the door. There was no bell or knocker. He hammered on the wood.

Inside, all was still. He stepped back and waited. No light appeared.

'There's no sign of his car.'

'Reckon he must have skipped it.' McKenzie had already made up his mind.

Tench walked round the side of the cottage.

'Any sign of life, Andy?'

'None, sir,' said Gregg.

Back again at the front, he tried the door. It was locked.

'Break it down, Mac,' he said.

McKenzie planted a heavy boot in the region of the lock. There was a splintering sound, and the door swung open.

Tench flashed a torch. There was a long, narrow lobby, with two doors on each side and another at the end. He swung the beam round, found a light switch and pressed it.

Above, a dim forty-watt bulb without a shade.

He took the right-hand door and McKenzie the left.

'Bedroom,' McKenzie said.

'Sitting-room,' said Tench.

They moved down the lobby. McKenzie threw open the door on the left.

'Kitchen.'

Tench was at his shoulder, the door at the end of the lobby at his elbow.

'That's the back door,' he said.

He twisted to the right.

'This must be the one.'

He gripped the knob, turned it and pushed the door open.

Blackness.

He could see a stone floor, but nothing beyond.

He fumbled for a switch and found it. Light flooded the room.

The place had clearly once been a washhouse. Set into the outer wall was a solid stone hearth and, above it, a copper. There was a deep sink in one corner, with a wide draining-board worn white from years of scrubbing, and pushed away in another were an old cast-iron mangle and a wooden dolly for stirring clothes; but these relics of the past shared what space there was with more recent additions. A table in the centre was stacked with processing dishes, transfer trays, bottles of chemicals, measuring cylinders and an upturned funnel. A bench at one end held an enlarger, still to be wired and connected to the mains, half a dozen cameras and a clear-faced clock that showed minutes and seconds. The whole room had been whitewashed, apart from the wall area round the enlarger; that had been painted black. Heavy black velvet curtains were drawn across the window, and a safelight with a cord-switch had been fitted in the ceiling, while another cord at head height had been strung from end to end. Clipped to it were a set of photographic prints.

There were roughly two dozen. Tench glanced at them, then he frowned and took a step closer.

'Mac!' he said. 'Over here. Take a look at these.'

McKenzie looked.

He gave a low whistle.

'So that's what they were up to!'

'Revealing?'

'Well, they're certainly not hiding much, are they?'

'Erotic, artistic or just plain pornographic?'

McKenzie walked down the line, examining the prints.

'Depends on your point of view. Titillating, I'd say.'

'There must be more of them somewhere.' Tench looked around. Next to the bench was a shabby chest of drawers.

'Look in there, Mac,' he said. 'I'll take these down.'

McKenzie slid the top drawer back and rummaged inside.

'Nothing here but printing paper and films.'

He slammed it shut and pulled out the one at the bottom. Then he stood for a moment, staring.

It was crammed with prints, tossed around at random. He picked up a handful and spread them out on the chest.

'Good God!' he said softly.

'Found something?'

'These. I think you'd better hang on to them.' He shuffled the prints together and handed them over. 'I've worked on murders for twenty years,' he said, 'but it's the first time I've ever seen anything like that.'

Tench studied the top one. Then he flicked through the rest.

'The man must be mad,' he said. 'How on earth . . .?'

He broke off. He was suddenly tense.

McKenzie was listening, too.

They looked at one another.

'There's someone at the door.'

Tench was there in three strides, but not soon enough. A key turned in the lock.

He rattled the door. It stayed shut.

He pounded it with his fists.

'Hell's bells, Mac!' he said. 'Where was he hiding? We looked in all the rooms.'

'There was a wardrobe in the bedroom . . . Or he could have been in the garden.'

'Quick!' said Tench. 'The window!'

McKenzie wrenched back the curtains. Behind them, in the recess, was a wooden black-out frame, a survival from wartime. Tearing it down, he threw it on the floor.

The window was a sash. He struggled to raise it, but years of neglect had jammed it firmly in place.

Gregg was outside, trying to pull down the top.

Tench waved him aside.

'Get out of the way, Andy,' he shouted. 'We're going to have to break it.'

He seized one of the processing dishes from the table and slung it at the glass. The pane cracked into pieces.

McKenzie grabbed another dish and knocked out the splinters. In a moment he and Tench were out in the garden.

'Seen anyone?' he said to Gregg.

The sergeant shook his head.

'There's been no one at the back.'

Tench wasted no time. Lights were springing up in the nearby cottages.

'Stop here, Andy,' he said. 'Tell the locals to stay inside . . . Round the front, Mac!'

As he spoke, there was the sound of a car being started; then, away to the right, headlights flashed on and began to move down the slope to the coastal road.

They dashed to the front. McKenzie was yelling.

'There's a lane up to Newgate. He must have parked there.'

They reached the top of the path. Below them, the car, its engine revving fiercely, roared away towards Cley.

Then, as they watched, the lights swung towards the sea, and like some flaring jack-o'-lantern began to trace a shimmering path across the marsh.

9

As soon as the police car turned on to the causeway, Tench rammed his foot down hard. He could still see the lights of the Talbot ahead of him, the beam sweeping right as the car neared the sea. Then abruptly it died.

'He's parked under the bank.' McKenzie was shouting above the roar of the engine. 'Where the hell does he think he's going?'

'God knows,' said Tench, 'but he won't get away.'

He swung the car into the bend, racing down the narrow tarmac strip towards the sea. Rounding the old battery observation post, the tyres hit the gravel, and he wrenched on the wheel and slewed to a halt.

In a second he and McKenzie had flung open the doors, and were sprinting across the gravel towards Jagger's car.

Tench peered inside.

'It's no good. He's gone.' He thumped the bonnet with his fist. The sound was echoed by a rumble of thunder over Cley.

They scrambled up the bank and stood on the top.

Clouds had covered the moon. In the darkness all they could see was the shingle and the waves lapping gently on the pebble-ridden shore.

'Which way's he gone?' Tench looked from left to right.

'It's a gamble,' McKenzie said. 'Perhaps we ought to split up.'

'No.' Tench was firm. 'We'll just have to risk it. Which way, Mac? The Point?'

'That's the place he knows.'

'Come on, then. Let's go.'

Tench made as if to plunge down the bank, but before he could move there was a sudden flash of lightning that lit up the marshes. The sails of the windmill stood out for an instant taut against the sky, and the string of cottages on the edge of the marsh sprang into vision, then vanished again as a wild clap of thunder seemed to rive the world apart, leaving darkness even more intense than before.

But in that moment of light Tench had seen all that he needed to see.

He stumbled down the bank and turned towards the Point.

'This way, Mac!' he yelled.

McKenzie was breathing hard at his heels.

'Did you see him?' he panted.

Tench was already running.

'Caught a glimpse of him, yes. He was carrying something. Looked like a bag.'

'How far ahead?'

'Far enough. Save your breath. If we don't catch him before he reaches the Marrams, we could easily lose him.'

They ploughed ahead along the shingle, hearing nothing but their footfalls, their own pounding breath and the low, pervasive grumble of the thunder as it rolled across the coast.

There was another flash of lightning, but it was too faint and transient to show anything but the lengthening hump of the bank.

Tench was settling into a regular stride, pacing himself – he didn't know just how far he'd have to run – but he was conscious that McKenzie was already dropping behind. He didn't look round. Somewhere in front was the man he'd been seeking for far too long, and he was determined to catch him, even if he had to roam the dunes of Blakeney Point till the dawn came up.

He ran on into darkness, the climbing ridge of the bank to his left and the sea to his right, seeing nothing ahead but the endless stretch of shingle unrolling in the gloom, feeling nothing but the stones and sand beneath his feet.

It wasn't till he heard the strident cries of the terns that he saw the man again, but by that time the doubts were crowding in on him fast.

Had Jagger climbed up the bank in the darkness, dropped down the other side and dodged back to the car? Had he already passed him? Was he chasing a shadow, something he merely thought he might have seen in that brief flash of light?

He stopped and listened, but all he could hear was the sound of the wavelets breaking on the shore, and somewhere ahead the screeching of the terns.

Then, as he stood there, a fresh fork of lightning split open the sky, the sand seemed to tremble under his feet as the thunder rolled out, and in that semi-blinding instant when the whole scene was thrown into brilliant relief, he saw the dark figure turning up on to the dunes.

In the aftermath, all was black as a dungeon, the terns screamed like demented spirits out on the lonely waste, but he was running, lengthening his stride, rasping through the marram grass, stumbling across the drifted ridges of sand.

He stopped again, crouching, searching the darkness, but the thunder clouds had blacked out all trace of the moon, and the pinpricks of light that were Blakeney or Morston away in the distance merely told him he was facing the land, not the sea. There was no sign of Jagger. The man had vanished like some wraith among the constantly shifting lows and blow-outs that pitted the Point.

He stretched himself, silently, flat on the sand, trying to make out the line where the dunes met the sky, but all he could see was a pitch-black veil that never varied in colour. Black merging into black, and then again into black.

He swore under his breath. It was all so futile. The night had made him blind. The terns, with their incessant tumult, had made him deaf to everything else. He had no more chance of tracking down his quarry on this empty, clamorous, blacked-out desert than a man robbed of all five senses at once.

True, he had a torch, but what use was that? It would illuminate nothing, merely warn Jagger to keep well clear.

He lay there, still searching the gloom, seeing nothing. He swore again softly. He'd be better off at Cley, raising the alarm, getting men out to the Point, ready to keep their eyes skinned once the dawn broke.

When was high water?

He reckoned up swiftly . . . Around four o'clock.

And sunrise?

At a guess, about quarter to five.

If the squads were warned, they could be out here by then. They could use Cotterill's boat, the one Hastings had promised.

He dug his fingers in the sand; tried to gather his thoughts.

There was a telephone down at the old lifeboat house.
How far away was that? A mile? No. More. Perhaps a mile and a half. The old lifeboat house. But then . . .

He reached back in his mind, remembering. It was painted black and set low, half hidden by the marram. The chance of finding it was slim on a night as dark as this.

Doubts crowded in again. Even if he tried, it could all be wasted effort. Jagger might just have been leading him on. Once on the dunes, he could well have doubled back, could be anywhere by now. What the devil had the man been thinking of to make a run for this desolate claw-spit of sand? And what had he been carrying? A bag? A box? And, if so, what was in it?

And where the hell was McKenzie?

The thunder still rumbled, but further away, towards Wells. There was lightning, but too faint and distant to help.

Then, all of a sudden, another thought struck him.

Turner's boat.

It must be beached on the Blakeney side of the Point. And Jagger would know where. He'd travelled out with Phelps.

Was that what he'd had in mind? To lie low till first light, then make for the boat and get away at high water?

There wouldn't be anyone around at that time. He'd have a clear run. He could strike out for Wells. Or somewhere even further. Brancaster . . . Burnham Overy Staithe . . .

That settled it. He had to get to a phone.

But which one?

The old lifeboat house was nearer. Cley was easier to find.

He pushed himself up from the sand, and stood hesitating, wondering which way to go.

Then, without warning, the whole pattern of the night erupted into change.

There was a dull explosive sound and a burst of flame high up on the dunes, and something writhing and screaming, fighting against the fire.

And Tench was running, flashing his torch, shouting wildly for help.

When at last McKenzie reached him, he was standing with the beam angled down.

In the circle of light lay a naked form, blackened, grotesquely twisted, coiled as if shielding itself from the glare.

He played the torch around. Clothes were scattered, haphazard. A pair of twill trousers, a maroon-coloured sweater, two yellow-checked socks and, apart from the rest, flung away it seemed in a last desperate gesture, a flat tweed cap.

Tossed down amid the scorched and still-smouldering marram was an empty can. The smell of petrol still mingled with the reek of burnt flesh.

Tench could find no words. He simply stared at the body.

McKenzie, though, had seen it all before. Long inured to the tragic absurdities of death, he was predictably laconic.

'Saves rope, Mike,' he said.

Even as he spoke, another jagged shaft of lightning cut a zigzag trail across the sky, the thunder rattled overhead, and for an instant the dunes were cast into brilliance before darkness closed down once again like a shutter.

Then, as if in irony, the rain began to fall, heavy, relentless, beating on the sand.

EPILOGUE

TIME FOR COFFEE

It is not given to men to know everything.

Horace: *Odes*

Outside Umzinto Cottage the sun was sinking, red as fire, into Blakeney.

Inside, in the parlour, the day had already declined into twilight.

'The trouble is', said Tench, 'that we'll never really know the whole of the truth.'

Lubbock picked up his tobacco jar, placed it between his thighs, took off the lid, and slowly, methodically, began to fill his pipe.

'It happens,' he said. 'Two murders, then a suicide, and everyone's left wondering ... I suppose there's no doubt it was Jagger who killed the girls.'

'No doubt at all. What we found in the dark-room was more than sufficient proof. All the rest was simply corroborative evidence.'

'The rest being what?'

'We found hair from both the girls on his sweaters, and fibres, too, from the clothes they'd been wearing. The scrap of wool that Ledward discovered under Phoebe's fingernail: that matched as well. We made a cast of his right foot – it was badly scorched, but it had somehow escaped the worst of the fire – and it fitted the prints Lester found on the sand. In the cottage there were two pairs of rubber gloves, both of them unwashed. They told the lab quite a bit. And in a drawer in his bedroom we turned up a Yale key, recently cut. It fitted Downs House. You were right about that. He must have had it made at that ironmonger's shop. We couldn't prove that he did, because they don't keep any records, but it didn't really matter. The photographs in the dark-room had already told us most of what we needed to know.'

Lubbock stoked up his pipe. It flared into life.

'From what I've been hearing, they must have been worth more than just a casual glance.'

'Oh, they were,' said Tench. 'Young Ellison spent a whole morning sorting them out. A good hour longer than he needed to take.'

'Pure pornography, were they?'

'I think it might be fairer to call them erotica. But erotica with a difference.'

'A difference?'

'Yes, they weren't deliberately posed.'

Lubbock removed the pipe from between his teeth.

'Are you telling me', he said, 'that he photographed those women in the act of making love?'

'He must have done. All the evidence pointed that way. There were too many frames that followed in sequence. We reckoned he must have taken one every other second. If we'd bound them in one of those flick-through folders, they'd have made an action film.'

Lubbock seemed to find this hard to believe.

'Are you sure they weren't posed?'

'All but positive about it. The expressions on the faces were far too authentic. A sound-track was the only thing that was missing.'

'And he'd done this more than once?'

'I think Ellison listed ten complete sequences. Must have been shot on different occasions.'

'Where?'

'Most at Downs House. There were a couple where we couldn't identify the setting.'

'Must have been quite a profitable sideline. At least for him.'

'For all three of them, I think. The Marriotts had made regular bank deposits that we couldn't account for.'

Lubbock seemed to muse.

'But the fact that all three of them were linked in some illegal pornography ring doesn't prove that he killed them. So what else did you find?'

'Another set of photographs. Mac said he'd never seen anything like them. He didn't mean that, of course, in the strictest sense. He'd seen plenty. So have I, and you must have seen thousands. But only in case files.'

'Go on.'

'Well, to put it simply, if we'd known about them on the night that Diana Marriott was murdered, we could have spared our own photographers a good deal of work.'

'He'd photographed the body?'

'From every possible angle. There were so many prints, he must have used a whole film . . . And there was more to it than that.'

'How d'you mean? More.'

'Spurgeon brought him in to see me on Friday afternoon. We knew he'd been spending some time on the Point, and we thought there was a chance that he might have seen something. He was one of those we'd listed as a possible witness. He'd been doing some landscape photography out there, so I asked him whether he could let us have some prints. He said he didn't see why not, and he'd drop them in later at the interview room in Blakeney. Well, he did. He put them in an envelope and addressed it to me, but I didn't get it till the following morning, and the prints weren't exactly landscapes. They were duplicate prints of the scene at Downs House. He must have spent the afternoon running them off.'

'He sent you prints of Diana Marriott's body?'

'Sounds crazy, doesn't it? But that's what he did.'

'And when you got them, he was dead?'

'A good twelve hours dead.'

'Well, laddie, there's only one rational explanation. He must have known you were on to him.'

'He never gave any indication. Seemed perfectly normal. And if he thought I suspected him at that time, he was wrong. I didn't know enough then.'

'Just what did put you on to him?'

Tench all but smiled.

'One of those little things that you're always telling me drop into place. It was so minute I could easily have missed it . . . We had a range of suspects, and we were looking for some kind of link with the Marriotts. Lock was working on the phone index pad that we took from Downs House. He was checking the names and numbers, and there was one he couldn't trace. The name was Snitterly, and the number 28. The exchange was missing.'

'Snitterly?' said Lubbock. 'That's the old name for Blakeney.'

'So Ellison told us, and that should have been enough. Craymere's on the Blakeney exchange, and we should have realized that. Whichever of the girls had written down the name – it was probably Diana – she hadn't bothered to add the word Blakeney to the number. Understandable, of course. What was the point? All she needed to do was pick up the phone and dial 28. If we'd checked on that number – Blakeney 28 – we'd have been at least half-way to solving the problem, but what foxed us was the fact that, in every other case, Blakeney numbers on the pad were preceded by a letter B. So we wasted time trying to find someone called Snitterly, and searching in vain for a Snitterly exchange. As we found out later, Blakeney 28 was Jagger's old cottage, the one he'd moved from to Cley. It was listed under Jagger, T. in the directory.'

'Ah, well,' said Lubbock, 'we all miss the odd clue. I've missed a few myself.'

'We certainly missed that. It was lucky for us that we had a second chance.'

Lubbock struck another match and relit his pipe.

'And who presented you with this one? Young Ellison again?'

'No. As a matter of fact, it was our Woman Detective Constable, WDC Gradwell. She found a copy of *East Anglian Life* while she and Rayner were searching Downs House. It had an article about the Marriott twins and their dress shop, so she brought it back for me to see. I read it: it was good publicity for them, but it didn't tell me anything more than I knew. At least I thought it didn't; then I noticed a line of very fine print running down the side of one of the photographs. There were three on the page: the top one was the two girls taken together, and underneath were reproductions of a couple of Giles Leening's sketches: fashion designs. The print ran down the side of the outer one of these, close to the edge of the sheet. You know how magazine editors seem reluctant to acknowledge the source of their pictures: they try to use the smallest possible type. This was so fine I had to take the magazine to the window to read it, but once there it was clear enough. It said "Photographs by Snitterly".'

'And that started you thinking.'

'It did more than that. It started me searching. Jagger was a commercial photographer. He'd been living in Blakeney, and Snitterly was Blakeney. I even began to hope that there might be some connection. If the girls had employed Jagger to photograph their fashions, they must have paid him to do it. Sue Gradwell had brought some bills and cheque stubs from Craymere, and I began to rake through them. It didn't take long. I found a series of cheque stubs, payments to "Snitterly", so I chose the latest of them and looked for a bill. It was among a lot of others in a clip: a formally printed sheet with a heading at the top, "Snitterly Studios". The telephone number was Blakeney 28, and it had been receipted at the bottom with a date and a signature: "T. Jagger, 5.4.50" . . . That was when I knew he'd been lying. He'd denied all knowledge of the Marriott twins. Never met them, he'd said.'

'Then seeing the Rodway woman and linking up the stolen cars settled it for you.'

'Yes, she had to be Jagger's sister. The resemblance was too great to be merely coincidence. It was clear she knew nothing about what had been going on. She told me quite freely who her brother was, and that gave us enough evidence to get a warrant to search the cottage.'

'And you found the photographs.' Lubbock pulled up a stool and stretched out his legs. 'Well, laddie, they say that murder will out.'

Tench gave a wry smile.

'They say that truth will out, too, but there are still a devil of a lot of things we don't know: things perhaps we'll never know.'

'That brings us', Lubbock said, 'to the nub of the problem. Just how much *do* you know?'

'We know the murders were planned. On the Monday we got Ransome to give us a front-page spread in the *EDP*. You must have seen it. Descriptions of all four cars and their registration numbers, together with pictures and a photograph of Jagger that we got from Mrs Rodway. Ransome wrote up an appeal for any sightings, and we had enough replies to make a pretty accurate stab at his movements. He used two locations: his own cottage at Cley and his sister's house at Bridgham. The fact that he had the keys to his sister's house and her car gave him a bolt-hole fifty miles from the scene of the murders, so that when the news broke he was well away from both Blakeney and Craymere and out of the picture. We think he'd been watching the two girls for weeks, using the lows out on Blakeney Point, and he waited till he knew that Phoebe would be running on her own. He was, in a sense, a business partner, and he must have been aware that on the Tuesday night Diana would be in London. We know he called in at the shop on Tuesday morning, and Phoebe told him she intended to go running that evening, but later than usual because of the heat. He must have already made plans, knew what he was going to do, because he had a delicate juggling act to perform.'

'Juggling?'

'With cars. Three of them,' said Tench. 'It seems he drove to Bridgham in his own, the Talbot, parked it and took the Austin to Primrose Spinney. From there we think he walked back to Delph Cottage – he could have done it in half an hour – travelled in his own car to Blakeney and left it outside his old cottage. The place was still empty, people were used to seeing the Talbot parked outside and it wouldn't have caused any comment. After that he waited, and some time just before eight o'clock he took the Lagonda from the Blakeney Hotel and drove it to Cley. He'd probably worked out two options. If there was no sign of Phoebe's car, he'd lie low till she arrived; if it was there already, he'd follow her. He'd use the landward side of the bank to keep out of sight. Then, after he'd killed her, he'd walk back to Cley, drive the Lagonda to Primrose Spinney, leave it there and take the Austin back to his sister's house. He'd sleep the night at Bridgham, and make a leisurely trip back to Blakeney next morning, probably using the train and a bus. Then he'd pick up his own car and drive it back to Cley.'

Lubbock shifted in his chair.

'A complicated business.'

'But cleverly planned. At a stroke, it removed him two steps from the murder.'

'And the same on Thursday?'

'Much the same, yes. We reckon he drove the Talbot to Delph Cottage as before; took the Austin to Mickle Covert, and then walked back to his sister's house. Went to Holt in the Talbot, and left it at some place where, parked all night, it wouldn't be conspicious. Maybe the Cottage Hospital. Spent the rest of the day in Holt, stole the Alvis from the Feathers, drove it to Craymere and parked by Starling's barn, close to Downs House. Walked from there down the path, round the back of the house, let himself in with the duplicate key and took Diana by surprise. After that he'd have driven the Alvis to Mickle Covert, picked up the Austin, made his way to Delph Cottage and slept there overnight. Collected his own car from Holt the next morning.'

Lubbock knocked out his pipe, refilled it and struck another match. It flared in the gloom.

'So you know how he did it, but you still don't know why.'

'You mean what was his motive for killing the girls?' Tench shook his head. 'We still don't know for sure.'

'But you must have some idea.'

'We've got a few clues, but that's about all.'

'What are they?' Lubbock said.

'Well, at first we seemed to be getting nowhere at all. We spoke to his sister. She knew him better than anyone else, and she told us quite a lot. The trouble was that, apart from an unsettled childhood, there seemed little that was relevant to his later state of mind . . . D'you want me to give you a run-down on what she said?'

'Why not? We've all night. I need to get the whole picture.'

'OK.' Tench shrugged. 'If that's what you want . . . They lost both parents early on in life. Like the Marriott twins, they were still in their teens. The father was land agent to Lord Desborough near Thetford. The mother was French, the daughter of a Paris advocate. They were both of them drowned in a boating accident in 1937. There were no paternal grandparents, so the children went to live with the mother's family in Paris. One of her sisters had married a farmer with a holding near Carentan in Normandy, and they spent the summer holidays there on the farm. They stayed in France till the Germans came, when they were shipped back to England. He was sixteen, she was twenty-one. There wasn't much money, so she went to work for a hair-stylist in Thetford, and did her best to steer him through adolescence. He went back to school, the local grammar, but never settled down. His exam results were no more than mediocre, and he was in and out of a number of jobs till the army called him up in 1942.'

'Best thing that could have happened,' said Lubbock, 'though it doesn't appear to have done him much good.'

'I think it did, for a time. Might have been better if he'd made it a career... He worked himself a commission and commanded a tank in the Western Desert; then, close to the time of the Normandy invasion, he was posted back to England. He was fluent in French and knew Normandy well, so they pulled him in to work with the SOE – Special Operations Executive – and dropped him in France just before D-Day to liaise with the Resistance. It wasn't his fault, but the circuit was betrayed, and the Germans whipped him off to a POW camp near Melun. He got away by posing as one of the French prisoners out on a working party, made his way to Paris, found refuge with some loyal friends of the family, and lay low there till the Allies moved in...'

'And I suppose he was one of those who, after the war, found it hard to adjust.'

'Yes. His sister had served in the Nursing Yeomanry, driving an ambulance. She'd married a Major Rodway, but was separated from him. Jagger came to live with her at Bridgham, but there the old restlessness reasserted itself. He found it hard to adapt to civilian life, and drifted from job to job till he somehow developed this passion for photography. She encouraged him, set him up with a couple of cameras, and helped him to rent a small shop in Bradenham that he used as a studio. He seems to have had flair for camera work, and made quite a name for himself in the town as a portrait photographer; but he wanted to concentrate on wildlife, so he moved down to Blakeney. She was happy about that. She hoped he'd settled down at last and found his own niche.'

'So he had,' said Lubbock drily. 'A pornographic niche.'

'She knew nothing about it, even though they were still very close. He used to drive over from Blakeney every Friday evening and spend the weekend with her at Bridgham. She was, after all, his only living relative and she'd always been something of a surrogate mother. But the fact that he'd been dabbling in murky waters came as a complete shock. She just didn't believe it till we showed her the evidence.'

Lubbock was thoughtful.

'D'you know how he came to get mixed up in this racket?'

'No. We can only guess, but it probably had something to do with his Parisian connections. We know Paris was his market and it was clear from his passport that he'd visited France at least half a dozen times in the last two years.'

The old man tapped his teeth with the stem of his pipe.

'Then what about the Marriotts? How did they become involved? From what you've said of them, they hardly seem the type to pose for pornographic pictures.'

'We think it must have been blackmail,' said Tench. 'It all began as a simple business connection. He was a local photographer with a good reputation, and a couple of years back they hired him to take publicity pictures of their fashions. Young Giles confirmed that: they used a number of his sketches. From then on, once again, it's a case of guesswork, and the obvious explanation seems the most credible. We can only think he uncovered what was going on between the two girls at Downs House, and threatened to make it public. They couldn't afford to let him do that. The scandal would have ruined them ... For him it was a chance to make some easy money. For them it was the only way to keep things secret. They had to go along with him.'

'Interesting,' said Lubbock, 'but it still doesn't explain to me why he killed them. The opposite, I'd say. They weren't exactly an expendable asset.'

Tench nodded in the half-light.

'That's true, but we turned up one significant piece of evidence. We questioned some of the Marriotts' regular customers in the hope that one of them might give us a lead. We spoke to a Mrs Marshall who lives at Beeston Regis, about a mile out of Sheringham. She's the wife of a solicitor, and she bought a lot of her clothes from the girls. She told us that about three weeks before they were murdered, she went into Sheringham to buy a new dress. When she got to the shop there was no one to serve her, but she heard raised voices from behind the curtained doorway at the back of the counter. Then, all of a sudden, Jagger pushed his way out. She knew him: she'd seen him there more than once. He was in a terrible temper, so she said. He shouted, "Right, you little whores! We'll see about that!", and he stormed past her and slammed the shop door so hard that the glass panel cracked. Then Diana came out. She was flushed and angry, and seemed rattled to find a customer waiting in the shop; but she apologized profusely and said it was just an argument over business. These things happened from time to time.'

'Sounds to me', said Lubbock, 'as if the girls had come to their senses at last. Threats of exposure can cut both ways.'

'That was what we thought. They wanted out, and they knew he was just as vulnerable as they were. What could he do if they ended the connection? Exposing them meant exposing himself.'

Lubbock laid down his pipe.

'It's a possible explanation.'

'More than possible. Probable. They'd never even think that he'd contemplate murder ... But it still leaves a lot of questions unanswered. If they were putting the screws on him, why didn't he just walk away and leave it at that? And why, when he'd planned both the killings so precisely – why did he act in such an utterly illogical manner? You'd have thought that once he'd strangled the girls – and he must have killed them quickly and silently: his special army training came in useful there – he'd have made himself scarce just as fast as he could. But he didn't. He hung around, laid them out neatly as much as to say, if you want exposure, I'll show you what it means. Once he'd strangled Diana, he set up that elaborate charade with the doll, and then calmly dallied around with a camera taking pictures of the scene from here, there and everywhere ... And added to that, he lied to me when he needn't have done. He could have admitted he knew the girls. He had a perfectly legal business relationship with them: he photographed their fashions. If he'd said so, it would have been no more than the truth. Anyway, I was bound to find out before long ... And why did he take off his shoes on the shingle? Why did he lay Phoebe out among the terns?' Tench slapped the table. 'It all seems irrational. The man must have been mad.'

'I take it I was right about the doll,' said Lubbock. 'It was somewhere in the house.'

'Yes.' Tench sighed. 'You were right, as usual. Phoebe bought it in Swaffham. Giles remembered seeing it. She kept it in an airing cupboard in the bathroom. Had some idea of dressing it up and using it as part of a window display. She probably talked it over with Jagger. Anyway, he must have known where it was ...'

Night was closing in fast. It was dark in the parlour, but Lubbock made no move to switch on the light.

'One thing puzzles me', he said, 'in this brave reconstruction. If Jagger had this set-to with the girls in the shop, why would Phoebe tell him she intended to go running on her own on the beach? You say he called in at the shop on the Tuesday morning, and that was when she told him. D'you know that for certain, or is it just another piece of wild speculation?'

'It's evidence. Volunteered by a sales rep from Norwich. He paid them a visit that morning. Jagger was there. He was talking to Phoebe. A friendly conversation, so the rep said. He heard her say she was going for a run on the sands.'

'Sounds strange to me. Three weeks before he was calling them whores.'

'Oh, I've no doubt he got round them. The last thing he'd want to do would be to put them on their guard. He probably used his charm: he had plenty of that. Smiled on them and told them how sorry he was that he'd lost his temper. Said if they'd made up their minds, that was good enough for him. He'd be sweet as sugar . . . But the fact remains that he didn't walk away. He killed them. Both of them. And even then he must have been planning to kill them.'

Lubbock took a deep breath.

'Well, you make a fair case. Flawed, of course, but fair. And it's possible to think of all kinds of explanations. Perhaps he always went about barefoot on the dunes when he was photographing birds. Bare feet make less noise. If he did it often enough and long enough, his soles would be hardened . . . Perhaps he laid Phoebe down among the terns because to him a dead body was nothing but carrion: food for the scavengers . . . Perhaps he killed the girls because he wanted one of them, and she didn't want him. Can you imagine what he might have felt, repeatedly watching two beautiful young women, naked, passionate, making love to one another? And knowing that neither had the slightest desire to do the same with him? As I said once before, it's bad enough to be rejected for another, a lesser man, but to be rejected for a woman, that's a hundred times worse. Think how frustration could have built up inside him. No wonder he called them a couple of whores.'

He tapped the arm of his chair.

'If I racked my brains,' he said, 'I could think up a dozen different theories, all of them just as feasible as yours. But why go to the trouble? It's guesswork, laddie, that's all it is, guesswork, and all of it fruitless. If I tried to work out what was in the man's mind, I'd be wasting my time, just as you're wasting yours. You're asking yourself a series of rational questions, and expecting to find a series of rational answers. But in this case there aren't any. You've been reading too many detective stories where everything comes to a neat and tidy end. But life isn't like that. It's uncontrolled, imprecise, and it leaves the ends ragged. In most murder cases, there are questions left behind that no amount of wild speculation can resolve . . . Am I right in thinking that Jagger didn't write any suicide note?'

'We haven't found one . . . yet.'

'And you won't,' said Lubbock, 'but there's no doubt he intended to kill himself, is there?'

'None, I should think. He chose the right place. We got a helicopter out to pick him up from the dunes, but I'm pretty sure he was already dead when we found him.'

'When was the last time his sister saw him?'

'The night before she went on holiday. He drove over from Cley to collect the keys.'

'Did she notice anything unusual about him?'

'Not really. She did say he seemed a bit preoccupied.'

'Preoccupied? That was the word she used?'

'As far as I remember.'

His old chief seemed to nod his head very slowly.

'Let me tell you a story, laddie,' he said. 'Some years ago we had to deal with a particularly nasty case of murder. A middle-aged man got out of his bed in the night, stripped himself naked, fetched a knife from the kitchen, and stabbed his wife in the throat as she slept. After that, he went into his daughter's room – she was just seventeen – and did the same to her. He ran a bath, washed the blood off himself, cleaned the knife and put it back in the kitchen drawer. Then he lay down on a sofa, covered himself with a raincoat, and probably, for all we could tell, went to sleep.

'The house was an isolated one, at least half a mile from the next nearest dwelling. The only early morning visitor was the postman. He came, delivered two letters, and left suspecting nothing.

'We never knew the actual sequence of events, but at some time the killer opened his roll-top desk, took out a copy of his will, and struck out the names of his wife and daughter. He left the desk open and the will on the table.

'Soon after it was light – the pathologist reckoned it must have been about five hours after the murders – he went upstairs again, apparently still naked. By that time the bodies had begun to stiffen. Rigor mortis had spread as far as the shoulders and upper arms, but not to the legs. He turned his wife over, and there on the bed he set up his own very pointed charade, implying that she was, as he quite wrongly suspected, an indiscriminate whore. Then he carried his daughter downstairs in his arms, and locked her away in the boot of his car.

'After that, he dressed, ignoring the bloodstains still on his body, swabbed his hands and face with a kitchen towel, opened all the curtains, phoned for a taxi and, leaving the house unlocked, told the driver to take him into town. Once in the High Street, he walked to a snack-bar, ordered a breakfast, ate it, drank a cup of tea, and went from there to a florist's where he bought a bunch of flowers, telling the girl who served him that they were a present for his wife. He then visited his bank, drew from his account five hundred pounds in notes, took another taxi home, went straight to the garage, started up his car and drove north to East Dereham and then towards Holt. At Pigg's Grave crossroads, a mile from Melton Constable, he ran out of petrol. He walked to Melton station with the flowers in his hand, bought a ticket for Cromer, waited for the 12.27 southbound from Holt and threw himself in front of it. The money he'd drawn from the bank was still in his wallet.'

Lubbock paused. He reached out to the table beside him and switched on a lamp.

'He was a farmer named Alfred Jacques. He lived at Coston Green, two miles east of Bradenham, and about the same distance from the Rodway woman's cottage at Bridgham. They're both within what I call the Bradenham Triangle.'

He took his pipe, scraped it out and refilled it, tamping down the tobacco with his thumb.

'You said of young Jagger that he must have been mad. He probably was. So was Alfred Jacques. Such men don't need motives. Their instincts are feral. Instead of asking why they did this or did that, you should be asking yourself a very different question. You should be asking what it was that drove them mad. Or perhaps, to be more accurate, who drove them mad. Go and ask my friend the shopkeeper in Bradenham High Street. He'll give you an answer. Maybe it won't be the one you want to hear, but who's to swear it isn't true? Didn't someone once say there was more in heaven and earth than men in their frailty could possibly comprehend? Wasn't it that sage that you're always quoting, good old Will Shakespeare? Or could I be wrong?'

Tench looked down his nose.

'Put the coffee on,' he said.